The Legend of Lady MacLaoch

THE CLAN MACLAOCH CURSE SERIES
BOOK ONE

BECKY BANKS

Ha'ikū
Press

Published by:

Maui, Hawai'i | Portland, Oregon
haiku-press.com

Cover design by James T. Egan of Bookfly Design.

beckybanksbooks.com

3rd edition

Paperback ISBNs: 978-0-9882614-9-5, 978-0-5780756-6-2

ebook ISBN: 978-1-4524-7218-8

ASIN: B0052FXQAE

This book is dedicated to you, dear reader.
Yes, you.

Prologue

Castle Laoch, Glentree, Skye, Scotland
The Year of Our Lord 1211

P ain gripped her abdomen in convulsive ripples, telling her she would not survive to see the morning. Her last breath would be soon—with it, she would accomplish her last wakeful deed in this world.

She looked up at the man who possessively held her newborn child, the man she called father and enemy. She spoke the words that reverberated through her soul, as if they were pulled from the very earth, full of power and purpose.

I curse ye, Father. I curse the ground beneath yer feet, the air ye breathe, the blood within yer veins, and the seed ye spill upon this earth. May ye die having felt my pain and if ye havenae, may no MacLaoch chief ever know love. Only when they have walked the lonely halls of despair will I bestow upon them a peace I once held long ago, and then only for a moment. I will feast upon yer pain and drink the anguish of this curse until the one who calls himself chief of the MacLaochs has shared in my anguish. Until then, I will haunt ye and yers every eve and every dawn and all time in between, forever.

One

Middle East
Two Years Ago

T he desert heat rolled away from them in waves of sound as they tore through the atmosphere. The Royal Air Force fighter jet seemed molded around them, an extension of their own bodies—metallic, fierce—traveling just a few hundred feet above the knobby desert valley floor and just a few feet under detectable radar. Fingers of desert sandstone, etched away by wind and time, spread down from the high sides of the valley walls, bending and twisting, making the way challenging and dangerous.

"This is not a strictly sanctioned NATO op." The thick Oxfordshire accent of his captain's voice rang in his memory. Rowan and his flight navigator, Victor (also known as the Victorious or just simply Vick), had been handpicked for this not-strictly-sanctioned war zone task. It was easy enough: fly over a small insurgent's village in the eastern region of enemy territory; flip the switch; drop the goods; get the fuck out. Simple. Yet the sweat dripping down his brow—and the rolling chills, like a premonition fever—had him on high alert. Nothing was out of place, yet this time felt different.

Winding and twisting through the caverns, the jet rocketed them over the beige blur of desert floor.

The queasy feeling got worse, suffocating him in his mask.

"Status," he said, trying to distract himself.

"Closing in on the party." Vick's response crackled through the earpiece in Rowan's flight helmet.

"Roger that."

The sandstone formations blurred as the seconds counted down.

Easy.

"We are a go in three—"

With a gloved finger Rowan flipped the switch cover on his instrument panel. Up ahead the valley widened into an expanse of dunes and flat valley floor.

The last two seconds rolled by like tumbleweed toward its final destination. "One" finally came, and Rowan felt his finger hit the switch. As he did, he caught sight of something on the desert floor. It was a puff of smoke—not below him nor behind him, but in front—the kind of puff of smoke that follows the expulsion of a rocket that is set to fly high and fast, the rocket on a surface-to-air missile.

Out here, in this lonely dump of land, Rowan thought as he watched the luckiest shot on Earth rise like a middle finger from the insurgents below. He heard Vick's voice confirm the missile in the air. Rowan's mind told him to evade. He felt his hand shift on the joystick and felt the fighter respond. He heard the cursing in his headset, the confirmation that it would be close. His other hand grabbed the throttle and yanked, sending them up into orbit.

Only it was too late.

The missile exploded off the left side of the aircraft, tearing metal in a fiery torrent. The explosion rocked the cockpit; pieces of metal broke through the cabin, and heat slapped at Rowan and Vick as the blast slashed the wing to shreds. Rowan's hand was already on the lever; he pulled, ejecting himself and his navigator out into the desert air.

Suspended for just a moment before gravity took its turn with him, Rowan experienced a single moment of complete silence. He watched the tortured wreckage of their flight craft spiral out below him, billowing smoke and fire. Above him, his chute snapped open; Rowan watched Vick drift soundlessly in the distance. The village below, once so small and inconsequential, became alive and swarmed like a disrupted ant nest.

Fuck, Rowan said silently, like a prayer, up into the billowing fabric of his chute.

The ground came much too quickly. He tumbled forward and unhooked himself from his chute. Squinting against the light reflecting off the smattering of sand on his helmet's visor, Rowan searched the horizon for his navigator. He spotted Vick moving swiftly toward him, his chute billowing in the wind and yanking him along the desert floor. Rowan made his way toward Vick, the sickness in his stomach getting worse. This unsanctioned mission would not receive any help before the enemy got to them.

When Rowan caught up to him, Vick was half conscious, his flight suit shredded at the knees, the contact points where his body had been dragged across the sandpaper ground.

"Vick!" He shook his partner's shoulder with one hand and released his parachute with the other. "Vick!" he shouted again. The chute detached with a snap of the lines, rolling and billowing away from them.

Diesel-motored trucks sounded in the distance. Rowan's heartbeat ratcheted up as his body prepared for the fight that was to come. The wide valley floor spread out around them, lending no shelter except for a few large rocks. Putting an arm around Vick, Rowan lifted his struggling navigator and began making painful progress to the closest boulder.

Enemy fire erupted, spraying dust and rocks into the air around them.

He heard the enemies call to him in their native tongue, telling him to get to his knees with his hands on his head. Vick cried out as a bullet tore through his leg.

Reluctantly they fell to their knees. The enemy's leader came to them, a pistol in one hand, an automatic rifle slung over his shoulder. Spittle had accumulated at the corners of his mouth from his shouting.

The leader was making demands, and Rowan knew that he had no leverage. His pistol was at his calf, his sgian-dubh in his boot, yet his Scottish blood pounded in his ears demanding that he defend himself and his navigator.

Rowan heard Vick groan and utter, "God save the Quee—"

It happened then.

Rowan's world moved in slow motion. He had been watching the enemy leader as he made his demands. Then, registered too late as the man's mind in a millisecond made the decision to shoot, his gun sending a single bullet into Vick's forehead and through the back of him.

Now, said a voice to Rowan, and he leaped forward as the gun went off again, this time with its black eye upon him.

In that moment, metal fire rained down from the heavens and the entire event burned into Rowan's memory, vivid and uncompromising in its brutality.

Two

South Carolina
Present Day

It was Christmas, and I was surrounded at the wooden table that had been in the Baker family for generations by, well, generations of Bakers. My family. Dinner had been delayed again by a cousin coming late with the mashed potatoes, and the talk buzzed around who TJ had been playing tonsil hockey with this weekend.

That topic was started, of course, by TJ. Though older than me by several years, my brother rarely acted like it. Mother and Daddy were seated at our end of the table, the aunts and uncles and older cousins at the other—all of us anchored by the man at the table's head, my father's father, the Baker family patriarch, Grandpappy. My little cousins, too young to be at the main table, were in the other room of Grandpappy and Grandmama's old farmhouse, watching a Disney movie with their dinner. Soon Mother, ticked off to no end by hearing about TJ's escapades, tried to steer the conversation, calling across the table: "Janie is out with her new man. Did you see him, Linda?" Father and Grandpappy were deep in their own discussion: "The university contacted me this week on testing a new pesticide for that damn twig borer . . . " If talk didn't turn to peaches or pecans or the woes of Mother Nature's wrath on the orchards, I wasn't at a Baker family dinner.

That night, however, turned different. For once during the middle of dinner—Christmas dinner, no less—the entire table became quiet.

One of my cousins, who was arguably too young to be at the adult table, had somehow wiggled his way into a seat between Grandmama and Grandpappy. I hadn't heard his question, but in the space between chews and intakes of breath it was quiet enough to hear Grandpappy switch subjects from orchard woes to give his answer.

"Well, we're not Bakers."

The only sound then was the soft scraping of Grandpappy's fork as he scooped more potatoes and maneuvered for a stray piece of roast on his plate.

I sat with my entire family silently watching him, our mouths agape and eyes wide as if we all were silently shouting, *What?*

"Mmmph, by blood, that is," he said as he swallowed. "The way I was told of it, we're all, by blood, Minarys. M-I-N-A-R-Y," he spelled, not taking his eyes off his gravy-filled plate. Grandpappy chewed slowly as we all chewed with him, mentally, on what he had just said. Even my mother, who normally wouldn't let a moment like this go silent for so long, just sat with a wide-mouthed stare. Cousins, aunts, uncles, Grandmama, Daddy—all simply gaped.

He had just told a table full of Bakers—stalwart, hardheaded, proud, he-must-be-a-Baker Bakers—that we were some other name, the devoid-of-meaning, faceless name of Minary.

Grandpappy finally looked up. "What? I thought y'all knew that."

The table exploded into questions. Grandpappy quieted everyone down and explained that his biological father, a Minary, was "a drunk who found himself on the bottom of a riverbed." His suddenly widowed mother had married a very nice Englishman named Mr. Baker and, for that, we should be proud to be Bakers.

We didn't get much more in the way of details since Grandpappy didn't really much care about them, and he was sure he'd mentioned it a time or two over the years. He did say that all the information had come to him secondhand from his siblings, since he was just an infant when his mother had remarried.

This reality-shattering news was a lot for all of the generations of Bakers to digest. I watched Grandpappy through new eyes for the rest of my Christmas break from grad school at home. It was obvious that he came from a place that gave him his tall frame, light, wavy hair, freckled skin, and a knack for sweet-talking his way into just about anything. I think Grandmama always worried that he might go to the bank or the store one day and come home with more than just a deposit receipt or a carton of milk.

I was a version of Grandpappy—tall, green eyes instead of blue, and light-colored copper curls rioting around my head. We were the spitting image of some ancestor straight from . . . Well, straight from where, now?

It was only a few months later that Grandpappy went to the big orchard in the sky.

I flew home from school to attend the funeral at our small community church. The reception room was long, filled with tables of food and people old and young. Older generations reminisced to the younger ones, some who listened and some who didn't.

I was eating a piece of pecan pie and emptying my mind of everything but the blissful nutty, sugary-salty, caramel-y pastry when my mother interrupted.

"Cole, why is it that you can't dress like a lady? Are you trying to embarrass me?" My mother, too, was holding a piece of pie in one hand and a fork in the other. I knew she would carry that piece around for a while, pretending to eat it, and then give it to my brother later, claiming it was her second piece.

I looked at her—perfectly pressed white slacks (risky business for her, since it was before Memorial Day) and a navy-blue, short-sleeved sweater with matching slip-ons, her short blond hair coiffed just so.

"What are you really learning up there in Portland?" she persisted. "I can tell you it's not how to be a lady."

I looked down at my outfit. My jeans were very nice, a spendy brand (though bought for a steal from the thrift store), and paired with a silk, expensive, slouchy tank in bronze that I'd borrowed from a friend, knowing full well that I'd need something to bring the jeans up to par. My hair was a manageable mass of coppery curls that had taken me hours to perfect and could all be undone if there was even the slightest change in humidity; I'd even done my makeup just right.

"Gee, thanks, Mother. Love you too."

"Cole, I'm worried about you so far away. You know, I've been talking with your aunt Ruth, and she says . . . "

Oh god, I thought, tuning her words out. *Here it comes.*

Portland, Oregon, was the "tree-hugger, Democrat capitol of the nation," according to my mother. She worried about what that setting —known for earth, dog, and gay-and-lesbian friendliness—was doing to me.

"Wearing jeans, Cole? To Grandpappy's funeral? You might as well just say that you are a—well, you know. I'm just worried about you up there. You have no drive for these things."

I cocked an eyebrow at her. "Drive for what, Mother? You're beating around the bush. Just be out with it."

TJ sauntered up, a hilarity dancing in his eyes as he chewed boisterously—manners obviously forgotten or purposefully absent. "You know," he said, around pie and whipped cream, "that she's talking about your M-R-S degree."

My mother looked knowingly across the crowded room, and I followed her gaze to Roger Bronson, all-star quarterback during our high school years and current-day oil-rig repairman.

"Mother, Roger is an ex-boyfriend from *high school*; one that was very sweet but incredibly unmotivated in life except for the pursuit of ass. Remember? That's why I dumped him. He slept with Candice and Bernice while we were dating?"

"I think that's a noble cause. Pursuit of ass," TJ said, sealing my mother's lips into a grim line of dissatisfaction with both of us.

TJ and I exchanged the look, a mental high five.

"Cole, he is the epitome of male, and you would have beautiful children," she said, digging back at me.

"Yes, Mother, the epitome of male, and yet I still do not find him attractive enough to spread my legs and have him screw me out of a happy and successful future."

TJ choked on his pie as my response had the desired effect on our mother. Her eyes narrowed to slits. Immediately I felt guilty. At nearly thirty I should not allow my mother to get a rise out of me. Though, in retrospect, I'd gotten very good at being an uncontrollable and willful child, and that gave my mother a perpetual rise.

"Fine," she said, as my brother gave his empty plate to a little cousin and told him to throw it away. "If you want to live in Portland and become a lesbian, that's fine, Cole, but don't whine to me when you're old and wish you'd had kids! Yes, which reminds me, TJ," my mother said, volleying to him, "that if you have two cents, you'll stay away from MaryJo while you are back at home. She's a good girl. Whatever happened to Cindy?" At least she was an equal-opportunity meddler, not giving special treatment to her daughter over her son.

I tuned them both out. Looking down at my plate of half-eaten pie, I knew I didn't have the stomach to finish it.

Grandpappy was gone. The thought fell like a lead weight in my stomach. And there I was arguing at his funeral. That was the way of it in our family, I supposed. I thought of my life if I were to do all of the things that my mother wanted me to do. I glanced over at Roger. He was nodding at something Dorothea was saying to him. My elderly aunt thought she had his full attention, yet his eyes scanned the room, looking for his next pursuit. I thought about what it would be like if he and I got married—all the mistresses he'd have; me pregnant and waddling around with a toddler.

No, I thought. I was being called elsewhere. I had no idea where that was or what I was supposed to do once I got there, but I would follow it until I felt right.

"Mother," I said, interrupting her, "TJ's way too old to be scolded." She turned her gaze on me, and I turned the conversation. "Did you learn anything more about our true lineage before Grandpappy passed away?"

My brother gave me a thumbs-up behind her back and made his escape. "True lineage?" she repeated, her voice taking on an edge. "You know, Cole, if you spent half the energy you put into silly topics like that into finding a husband, you'd be happily married with kids by now, so don't start. Not here."

"I'm just asking—"

"Not now, Cole. For Christ's sake! Your grandfather isn't even cold in our memories and you want to drag this out now?"

"Mother, it's not like I demanded to know if Grandpappy left me anything in his will. I just asked—"

The room suddenly had ears for our conversation.

"What'd you ask?" my father turned from some friends he'd been chatting with.

Hand on her hip, my mother gave me a look. It said, *Now you've done it.*

"I was asking Mother," I said, giving her an equal look back, "if we had learned anything more about our family lineage."

My father shrugged. "We're Bakers."

"No. The whole Minary thing from Christmas," I said, exasperated. Was I the only one who still cared?

"Nicole Ransome Baker, that's enough. I told you, not here," my mother cut in.

"Why? I don't see why I can't ask about our history—*my* history—now." I punctuated my point by stabbing my fork into what was left of my pie. "Grandpappy was the one who told us!"

Exhausted by my family, I spent the rest of the evening walking the dusky rows of the orchards, all the while thinking that my flight back to Portland couldn't come soon enough.

Three

T he week after my graduation I made the decision to research my family history in full. When you spend two years researching and studying, the need to do it doesn't just stop the day you graduate. Plus, the truth was, even through the final revision of my master's thesis and its defense, I couldn't stop thinking about Grandpappy's revelation.

A search online for the Minary name's home base returned a few possibilities, but the most reliable data seemed to point to a place called Glentree, which was on an island called Skye, off the western coast of Scotland. With zero returned calls from jobs I'd applied for, I decided to follow a wild hair of an idea and conduct my own family research, in person. With a maxed-out credit card and a plane ticket to Scotland in my pocket I made one last try for information from my parents.

My father would no doubt still be in the fields, leaving my mother to answer the phone. My timing was excellent—it was Wednesday, and Wednesday was bridge day. By this hour, my mother, an avid player with the local ladies of society, would be sauced up to her eyeballs.

"Minary. That's right," she said after the initial lecture on going alone to a foreign country. "You don't like being a Baker? You know,

Cole, when I married your daddy, I was proud to take his name. We are a respectable family, and if you spent more than a moment thinking about it, you'd see the same. Chasing some foreign name isn't what I think your grandpappy would want you spending all your time doing, either. You should be proud of your Baker heritage." She was relaxing into what I had long ago understood as her soapbox performance, one of her heart-to-heart moments wrapped in a guilt trip, the multiple cocktails no doubt helping.

"Mother, I am proud to be a Baker, but it's not our heritage. Our heritage is this Minary name," I said and waited. All I heard was paper rustling. "You understand that, right? That by blood I am no longer a Baker but a Minary?"

"You know, Ruby says that I ought to tell you this," she said, ignoring me. I thought I heard the distinct sounds of ice tinkling against the sides of a crystal tumbler. "Ah yes, Minary. This is a copy of your cousin's report that he gave to us. I was going to send it to you but just couldn't do it. You always take things too far. Anyway, Minary is from the British Isles, probably Scottish . . . Your cousin found a name, lessee" —she slurred her attempt at "let's see"—"his name is—"

"A name!" I shouted in a fit of frustration and excitement. "You have a name?"

"Yes, yes, dear. I've had it for months. And don't get so excited," she said, taking another swallow of her drink, the tinkle echoing through the phone. "It's unladylike."

"Mother," I said, before she could get any further with her favorite line of reprimand. "The name?"

"Oh yes. It says here that the name your cousin found actually came off of the back of a photograph. Did you know that that was what started this all? He thought he found a picture of his daddy as a boy in a box full of old photos, so he showed Grandpappy. Turns out, that was what he was asking him down there at the end of the table—who this man was, and how they'd gotten the picture to look so old! Well, it turns out that they aren't teachin' cursive in schools anymore 'cause his name was right there on the back! Ha! Can you believe it?" Her drink gave strength to her Carolina accent.

I took a deep breath. "That's nice, Mother. So what was that name on the back of the photograph?"

She took a sip of her drink, smacked her lips, and said, "Iain Eliphlet Minary."

Four

S cotland is like my university town of Portland—it rains. A lot. And based on the breakfast that sat before me on my first day in the little town of Glentree, Scotland, food and drink were the staples for keeping the dreariness at bay. I stared at the food—a bowl of porridge (offered with or without whisky, but definitely without the *e* in *whisky*), eggs, sausage, toast, bacon, grilled tomato, and potatoes —and it stared back at me in challenge.

Carol, my host and owner of the stone, three-story Victorian-era townhome where I was staying, moved about the breakfast room tidying up after the other guests, who had already left. The room was small and quaint, with old wooden tables polished to a shine and vases of flowers filling the space with their own brand of cheery sunshine.

Carol had wild auburn hair and a warm, motherly attitude that I knew could change at a moment's notice, should something or someone get out of line. She was married to Will, whom I hadn't met yet because he did the cooking. They had bought the townhome to turn into a bed-and-breakfast as a fun retirement project. I had gotten all that by the time I took my first sip of tea.

"Carol," I asked as I mopped up the remnants of my egg yolk and sausage with a piece of toast, "is there a historical society in Glentree?"

Carol paused a moment. "Historical society? Like the history of Glentree?"

"Well, not exactly. I'm doing genealogy research." Thinking about it, I amended, "Yes, I suppose the history of Glentree would be a good place to start."

"Your family started on Skye? Well isnae that lovely. Let me see. I'm not really sure but ye should probably want tae visit the library first. 'Tis a good place tae do research, aye. Oh! And truly each castle on the island has deep history as well and might be a great source of knowledge."

"Excellent." *Castles,* I thought dreamily, and pictured myself sitting at an ancient desk, thumbing through volumes of antiquated texts, surrounded by the intoxicating musk of old books. "Thank you, Carol. Do you have the names of the castles I shouldn't miss?"

"Aye, well, I would ask the research librarian at the library, Deloris. The ones I can think of are Castle Laoch, Dunvegan, Eilean Donan, and Clan Donald has Castle Armdale and a very prolific history as well." Carol tapped her chin thoughtfully. "Come now, what is your ancestor's name? Maybe with a stroke o' luck, I'll have heard o' him, aye?" she said and winked at me.

I smiled back at her. "That would be some luck. His name is Iain Eliphlet Minary," I said, careful to roll the *r*, as they did here.

Carol's hand dropped. "Who?"

"Oh, uh. Iain Eliphlet Minary," I said again, wary of her reaction and thinking that I'd just sworn in Gaelic.

She relaxed a little. "Oh, I though ye said Minory, spelt with an *o*." She shook her head and gazed out the window, her face taking on an unusual look of profound regret and stern curiosity. "No, I havenae heard o' them."

"Oh," I said. I'd been hoping for something more. Minory was almost identical to Minary and a possible lead in my research.

She smiled down at me, her usual demeanor returned. "Take a look at the library. That and the castles will have historical documents ye can look through. More tea?" she asked.

I nodded. "I'll do that. Thanks for your help, Carol." It still felt like there was something she was avoiding, though. "Is everything OK?"

"Oh, 'tis nothing dear." She smiled nervously. "Only, the library is located just outside o' town on Viewfield Road. I'd hate for ye tae get lost, bein' that ye are my guest and all." She stopped, then added hastily, "But if I were ye, I would not say I was daein' research on Minory to anyone who's a MacLaoch. And whatever ye do, don't go to Castle Laoch and mention it either. Castle Laoch is owned by the MacLaochs, ye see?"

Whoa, I thought. "OK, Carol, I won't, but how will I know if they're a Mac—"

"Now there's a good girl!" She interrupted me by giving my hand a pat. "Ye enjoy the rest o' your breakfast and give me a shout if ye need anything more." With that, she bustled from the room, leaving me to stare at the empty space where she had been standing.

Five

⤜

The brisk walk to the library was just that, brisk. It was a standard Scottish day, according to Carol—overcast with the threat of rain and a high of 12 degrees Celsius (54 degrees Fahrenheit). I felt the two cups of tea I'd had with my breakfast, their caffeine as well as their warmth. My heart seemed to be fluttering in my chest by the time I walked down the stairs to the basement of the library, where the historical document room was located.

A long, oak reception counter stood in front of the rows and rows of files and books that took up the entirety of the library basement. A man was talking to an older woman in a cardigan and glasses behind the counter. I gazed about as I waited my turn. To my right was a study table and beyond that, against the wall, an antiquated computer and microfiche machine. The air was cool and filled with the distinctive smell of old paper I had imagined. I knew that within the shelves behind the woman at the counter there would be something, at least one thing, even a tiny clue, that would tell me about my ancestry. My excitement peaked, making my insides jittery—or was it still just the full effect of Carol's tea? When I looked back at the counter, it was my turn.

The woman turned out to be *the* Deloris, and we connected right away. I learned she had been with the library since she was old enough to pick up a book, her mother having been the librarian before. Eventually we came around to the subject of why I was there.

She didn't even blink an eye. "Ye know, that name sounds just like Minory. Are ye quite certain that it isnae Minory?"

"Not 100 percent, no. Do you know anything about the Minory lineage?"

"Oh aye, big legend around that one. Best ye go have a look-see for yourself tomorrow at Clan MacLaoch's castle and visitor center when it's open. The MacLaochs have a long history that includes the Minorys. Castle Laoch has been in that family for over eight hundred years. Matter of fact, the clan is still together. On its thirty-fourth chief now," Deloris said, clearly impressed. "Castle Laoch is not but a couple kilometers. Ye could walk there if the weather is fair. This time in May 'tis hit and miss, aye? Oh!" she said, as if just remembering, and nodded toward the door. "The man who was just in 'ere is the MacLaoch clan chief, and he could tell ye a thing or two about the Minorys, I'll tell ye that."

"Clan chief?" I asked, thinking the modern term meant a club president of some kind.

"We only have documentation that starts in the 1850s," Deloris continued, not hearing my question, "and the castles will have more information than we do. Castle Laoch would be the place to ask."

I paused for a moment, thinking. I wasn't sure that I should explicitly go against Carol's warning. "Do you know any reason why I might not want to mention my Minory research to a MacLaoch?"

"Och!" she said dismissively. "Some like to get upset by it, but 'tis nothing but an old fairy tale or curse, depending on what side yer standin'. I personally dinnae put much stock in fairy tales. I know just the two who could give ye firsthand knowledge of it, though. Old birds, they are. Down at the harbor they run MacDonagh and MacDonagh Tours—it's a boat tour that will take ye out the harbor and past the point, through the small fishing isles, over to Castle Laoch and back. From what I've heard, they'll tell ye more than ye need to know about the fairy tale, but I'll let ye figure that out for yourself." She gave me a knowing nod.

After giving Deloris information on where she could reach me if she came across anything useful in the stacks, I headed down to the docks.

Six

The Glentree harbor at midday was sparsely populated with boats, most of the fishing vessels at sea. The rocky shore held a lone flat-bottomed boat at its edge and two old, craggy men standing on either side of it hollering at each other.

"No, I didnae! Ye did, and if ye cannae remember where, I'll no' be the one tae tell ye. Ye blithering bawbag!"

"Nae tell me? *Me?* I was the one who asked ye tae put the fishin' knife awa' in the first place, and now ye won't tell me where ye put it? Ye are the bawbag, ye bawbag!"

"Bluddy bastard."

"Arsehole."

"Fu—"

"Lady!" one shushed the other as I approached.

"How can we help ye?" The other addressed me with a full smile of semistraight and semiwhite teeth and gave me an elegant bow.

"I'm looking for MacDonagh and MacDonagh Tours. Something tells me I've found it?" I smiled back.

Both men wore green fishing slickers with rubber boots and rain caps in the same drab color. The old men themselves were identical, too —both white haired and blue eyed—with the exception that one had a crooked nose that must not have been properly set after being broken, while the other's was straight.

"Ye sure have! This is my brother, Angus, and I am Bernie," said the one with the straight nose.

"Pleased tae meet ye," Angus said, giving me a nod.

"Ye can remember our names," Bernie said, "by remembering that I'm the handsome one and that Angus is like his name, full o' bull." He slapped his leg and guffawed loudly.

It took only a few moments to get out of the harbor and onto the placid waters, most of the delay due to the brothers arguing about which of them should help me into the boat and which was to push us out into the water.

We bobbed along, taking in the majestic, gray basalt cliffs rising like iron gates to our right, the rich green of pasture grass softening their edges. Opposite the cliffs, the ocean beckoned, small, grassy mounds indicating a smattering of isles between us and the open Atlantic.

Angus and Bernie seemed made for the water. They may have looked as if they were closing in on one hundred years of age with their dark, weather-beaten skin and the deep crinkles around their eyes—probably as much from smiling as from squinting against the sun and rain—but they were as nimble and agile as teenagers when it came to the boat. They moved instinctively as the boat skimmed lightly over the coastal waters' low ripple.

"Before we get started on our tour, we'd like tae know about our guest. Where ye're from and what ye're most interested in?" Bernie asked, affecting the composure and manner of a professor beginning his first day of class.

Angus was seated behind me, manning the outboard motor. "Aye," he agreed. "Bernie here used tae lecture at the local college, so if I know what ye're interested in, I can tell Bernie when tae shut that trap o' his if he's prattling on about some nonsense!'" Angus wheezed a reedy laugh and gave my ribs a conspiratorial jab with his elbow.

"What are ye telling her back there?"

"Just telling her nae tae be shy, brother!" He gave me a wink.

Bernie harrumphed. "All right." Then, smiling at me: "Now go ahead, dear, what brings ye out tae Glentree?"

"I'm doing family research," I said.

"Ah, aye. Come to discover which clan ye belong tae, aye?"

"Well not rea—"

Bernie interrupted and leaned around me to Angus. "Donald or Fraser, this one?" he asked his brother, nodding toward me.

"Fraser? Ye daft? Look at her. Nae, she's Irish, no' Scots."

"Irish? Nae. She's Scots—a Stewart, maybe?"

"Stewart." Angus eyed me as though I were a boat he was appraising. "Aye, maybe," he finally said, with a shrug.

"Aye." Bernie nodded. "Lass, we're ready. What's the name that ye think is yer family name? We think it's Stewart—that is, if ye are Scots."

I laughed. "Maybe I'm all of the above. The surname I think I know for certain is Minary."

"Ho!" both men exclaimed, and the boat nearly upended.

Angus straightened us out as I clung to the side, having slid to the floor with the upset.

Bernie exclaimed, "Angus! Get hold of yourself!" Then he looked at me. "Say that name again, lass?"

"Min-a-rrry," I said, enunciating the *a* and rolling the *r*.

"Ah," they both said.

"Thought ye said Minory," Angus said.

Still on the floor of the boat and still startled, I gingerly got up and resumed my place on the wood plank that was my seat. "It could be Minory. Unfortunately, my grandfather—the one who informed my family that we were Minarys by bloodline—died, and no one in the family knows for sure . . . " I trailed off. On one hand, I hoped I was a Minory, since there seemed to be plenty of information about that family. On the other hand, who *were* these people that their name would evoke such a response, that they would have created a legend so strong that people in the present day still got upset at the mere mention of the name?

"I spoke to Deloris at the library, and she said that you both might know more?"

"Ah! Deloris!" Bernie said. "Yes, well, Minory. I'll tell ye that that name has a history, 'ere it does."

"Aye, right it does," Angus added from behind me.

"I dinnae know about Minary, but I'll tell ye about the Minorys."

Angus decreased the engine power, slowing us down. It felt like the signal to the real beginning of our tour. We motored between the shore and the green humps of the islands. The towering cliffs still to our right were broken up by wide-open coves; I could see freshwater from mountain streams emptying into the ocean.

"The Minorys, a long, long time ago, owned quite a bit o' land in this area—outer isles and a significant part o' the Isle of Skye, too."

"Back in the days of the Vikings, ye see," Angus piped up.

"And they were a fearsome sort. Depending on who ye talk tae, they were raping and pillaging, but I'll tell ye, I'm no' a historian. What Angus and I know has been passed down tae us through our father and his father and so on, Angus will agree, aye, Angus?"

"Aye," he said, sounding slightly noncommittal.

"What we were told was that one of the most fearsome of the Minorys owned land on one o' the outer isles, and he wanted tae take a wife o' one o' the Scots clans in the early times tae bring peace between them. Well, the Scots were none too happy about tha', as they had wanted the Minory lands and were no' so keen on keeping peace with him, so they said nae. Turns out the Minory was just making a formality of it because he swooped in and took himself a bride anyway. Well he'd no' had her long and no' married her before the clan moved across the water and killed him and brought back their clanswoman—as it turns out, against her will."

We drifted along, motor still low, the breeze off the ocean giving me the chills. I felt a strange sensation under the goose bumps. It was the same hum from my tea buzz earlier, only it now seemed to start from lower in my belly and tingle out along my skin. I took a deep breath as the boat rocked.

"It was said," continued Bernie, in a low voice, "the Scots woman, Lady MacLaoch—"

Just then the motor quit all together and plunged us fully into the quiet of the water lapping at the bow.

Bernie leaned to the side and nodded at Angus, who shrugged and pulled the starter cord. The motor chugged and died, again and again.

"A'richt, Angus. We dinnae want tae be stranded out here. Ye keep daein' that, and ye will flood it."

"Aye, well if ye know so much, why dinnae ye come back 'ere and fix it yerself?"

Bernie glared at his brother before continuing with me. "Now, where was I? Ah yes, Lady MacLaoch. Now, lass, there is something ye need tae know about Lady MacLaoch." The tone of Bernie's voice had become stern, as if he were speaking of a woman he knew personally. "She was a fearsome lady, and she and the Minory were wild with love. She had planned her elopement with him, and she stole down tae the docks that day tae meet him and went willingly ontae his ship tae marry him. She loved him but knew that her father had intended her tae marry elsewhere. She had been promised tae another. Do ye see now? She had no other choice, and she could no' live by that decision, so she fled with the man she loved."

"Nowadays," Bernie continued, "ye can marry who ye like! But in those days, nae. Women like ye were property tae be sold and bartered with as such. Lady MacLaoch had been arranged tae marry a clansman in trade for more lands—more lands meant more power, aye?

"Aye. Well, that day came when she went tae the harbor and pretended tae trade for goods for the castle and instead stowed away with the Minory. And she might have gone far, but her handmaid spied her and rushed back tae the castle tae tattle on her. Lady MacLaoch might have made it tae Minory lands where she couldn't be touched, but the ship didnae make it. The MacLaochs slaughtered them all here in these waters." Bernie finished somberly, the story seeming to catch up to him, even though he must have recited it a million times.

Bernie turned his head back to me, his watery blue eyes looking at me as though to look within me. "It was at that isle to yer left, lass, that the Minory was laid over a boulder, arms tied tae the rock, and Lady MacLaoch made tae watch as they took his life. 'Tis said that he was so powerful that the ropes cut into the rock as he strained against them, full of rage at her having tae be made tae watch, and that those cuts are still there taeday."

I could see what Bernie meant me to understand. If the Minory was indeed my ancestor, I had a right to know what was done to him by the

MacLaochs and what the MacLaochs had done to their own. I felt downright queasy.

"Aye. Brutal. But time passed, and Lady MacLaoch lived tae marry the man to whom she was betrothed and bore him a child. It was in childbirth that she could see her life ending. Ye see, she never forgot what her father had done, and with her dying breath she cursed him.

"She said, 'I curse ye, Father, the ground under yer feet, the air ye breathe, the blood within yer veins, and the children ye put upon this earth. Ye will die having felt my pain, and only when a MacLaoch chief has felt my pain and shared in my anguish will they know peace. Until then, I will haunt ye and yers every eve and every dawn and all time in between, *forever*.'"

Bernie fell silent, and we all sat quietly—not looking at each other, but at the low mound of the island where Bernie said the Minory had been tied and Lady MacLaoch made to watch. There seemed to be a presence in the boat, around us, and the humming within me seemed to settle, as if there were something to the story meant just for me.

"But ye said yer family name was Minary, right?"

"Right," I answered Angus, feeling his voice pull me from a mental fog.

Bernie cleared his throat. Angus tugged on the starter cord, and the engine sputtered back to life.

"Well now. As we're having a bit o' trouble with the motor, we'd best turn back. Hate to be stuck out 'ere, aye?" Angus said, relatively jovial, but I got the feeling that he was worried.

"That was just a bit o' the tour," he continued. "The only part ye didnae see was Castle Laoch. Right shame that is, but ye can have a close-up look at it from land. I'll tell ye, though, that ye should be careful of the MacLaochs and asking questions. That lot is still a fearsome sort."

"Aye, that they are," Angus agreed.

"And it depends on who ye talk tae about the Lady MacLaoch curse. Some will wave ye off and tell ye tae never mind with such fairy tales. Believe me, it is a true curse. The MacLaochs have had nothing but bad luck as chiefs. They are either cheating or lying, and there isnae a one of them loving like they should, aye, Angus?"

"Aye, none of them ha' gone tae their deadbed with a wife at his side—"

"Och! Wha' about Old Dooney? He went tae his death with a wife at his side."

"Aye, that he did, his wife was holding the knife and his mistress the poison!"

Bernie and Angus guffawed loudly at this, only to subside in eye wiping and snorting.

"But ye see what we're getting at, lass? There's a darkness on the chief's seat that befalls its owner."

"Including the one they have now. Thirty-fourth, is it?" Angus asked Bernie.

"Aye," Bernie responded, "that one has had the worst of it yet. Father abandoned him and his mother—mind ye, his mum was a MacLaoch, and she drank herself so deep she couldnae take care of the wee boy. His uncle, the thirty-third chief, scooped him up off his drunken mother and took care of him as his own." He nodded at me to emphasize his point. "Now before ye go on and think highly of the thirty-third chief, understand that he couldnae keep a woman around long enough to make her his wife and have a son and an heir of his own. Seeing his opportunity with his drunken sister's son, he took it upon himself and claimed his sister unfit and took the boy for his own self."

"Aye," Angus agreed again. "Had her committed, too. She died right after the cell door shut behind her, is what we heard."

Bernie nodded solemnly. "God rest her soul," he said, and crossed himself. "Three years ago, the thirty-third chief died from a cancer in his bones, and his nephew took up the thirty-fourth title. Doing no' a bad job and no' a good job, if ye ask me."

"But we didn't ask ye, did we Bernie? Stick tae the facts, would ye?" Angus hollered forward, and then said in a low voice to me, "He's just broken up over the legend, takes it seriously, ye see. He takes it as a personal offense that the clan MacLaoch did such wrong by the lady. He has an overprotective sense for women." He winked.

"Oh, stow it, will ye?" Bernie hollered back. "I was saying, the thirty-fourth chief is a dark man, plagued, I think, with the worst of the curse."

"Aye," Angus agreed solemnly.

"We've heard many a thing about him, though we can say that with our own four eyes we have seen what a troubled man he is. He spent time in the Royal Air Force. The clan pulled him from duty when his uncle died. Rumor has it that he served on one of those special schemes while in the military, and it messed with him, they say." Bernie tapped the side of his head.

"Aye," Angus agreed. "When ye see him, he's nice enough, but ye can see the distance in his eyes, like he's carrying a burden he cannae unload. Does quite a lot for the community, giving money tae the pipe band and sharing the history the clan has. Castle Laoch is considered home for all MacLaochs, and tours are free for clansmen who wants tae have a look inside," he said and paused before continuing. "Though I'll tell ye, I'd not want tae be on the other side of a battle from him. He's got the look of a man who's seen hell and come back to tell about it."

Seven

"Face it, Rowan," Eryka said, lounging on the settee behind the library desk. With the sunny window behind her she looked like an Icelandic lizard on a hot rock. "You need me." Her voice purred, her *r*'s rolling deeply out the back of her throat.

Rowan gathered the list of book requests that the librarian had given him earlier that day. His annoyance ratcheted up at the husky, accented voice of his lazy administrative assistant. At least the vibrations in his blood had subsided. Earlier at the library, the sensation had been intense.

It was the stress of the Gathering and all associated with it, he told himself. Only it wasn't debilitating, the way his nightmares were. The vibration had shaken him to his core, ringing like a bell he'd heard before, soft and comforting in its familiarity.

"You need me," Eryka said again. "Eventually you'll need to get married, Rowan. You'll need to produce an heir, and with your history, no one will have you. I'm the only one who understands you and can look past your faults. No one will ever love you like I can."

Rowan picked the last of the books up off the shelf, wanting nothing more than to push Eryka gently out the window.

Eryka sauntered over to him. Her movements made her filmy shirt shimmy. "Rowan," she pouted, letting her thin, cold hand slide down his back.

Rowan stiffened at once. "Get your hand off me," he said coolly.

She leaned against him, the length of her body pressing against his, and whispered, "Or what, Rowan? You'll kill me, too?"

It was a power game to her—to find his most vulnerable point and dig, to try and break him into small, manageable pieces.

Rowan went ahead and gave her a small push. A wicked smile played across her face as she staggered backward and fell onto the settee.

"Face it, Rowan, you need me to be there with you at the gala. You know I can help you."

"Help me, Eryka? Ye would rather suck the blood from me and this clan than help me. As I said before, I'll no' be taking a date, least of all ye," he growled back at her.

"Rowan, if not me, there will be no one. You will be alone for the rest of your life!" She bit back at him, her sultry nature gone and replaced with the ugliness that Rowan had seen before in her.

"So be it," he said, and walked out.

At the cliff's edge, Rowan picked up stone after stone, each one larger than the last. He whipped them out over the ocean, feeling the satisfying release of energy, and watched as their inevitable destiny took hold, dictated by gravity, plunging them into the ocean far below.

Eryka's words, *You will be alone for the rest of your life,* rang through his head. Every day he knew this, knew the effect the family history of the curse had upon him, and most days he was comfortable with this destiny. But today—today it was different.

Rowan growled in frustration and picked up another rock and whipped it with all of his might.

Eight

Having said our good-byes, I left the MacDonagh brothers in the harbor and headed toward Castle Laoch on foot. Even though I'd been warned away, it was the closest clue I had so far. Not long into the journey, though, I stopped thinking about the MacLaoch and Minory legend. I was breathless from the mythical beauty of the coastline from land. Emerald cliffs rose massive and graceful from the frothing sea. Watery sunlight peeked out and hid again behind clouds, making the land and sea appear to move and shift like living things.

I had already hiked several miles before I was forced to slide down a particularly steep section of the pebbly trail into a wide shoreline cove. Dusting off, I looked back up the narrow path and just couldn't imagine Carol, much less Deloris, taking this path to Castle Laoch, and yet they'd both recommended the trek earlier that day, and this route was in the book of walks I'd found in my room at the B&B.

Sheep relaxed on the large stone outcroppings that interrupted the grassy slopes. Deeper into the cove, water shimmered from its start in the cloud-wrapped mountains, cascading all the way down into a four-foot-wide stream, which surged on to meet the ocean before me. For just a moment I stood and breathed in the cool beauty surrounding me. I ached for once, to have someone to share this moment with, someone with whom I could reminisce with later—they'd know just the moment and place, the fresh sea air. Instead, I was sharing the peace and beauty with bored, grass-chewing sheep.

The wind picked up suddenly off the ocean, blowing my hair back —out on the water, beyond the outer isles, an iron-gray sheet of angry rain was moving toward land. It would be a race—if I moved fast, I might be able to make it to the castle before the storm caught me

Up the opposite hill of the cove, I fought the slip and slide of pebbly rocks on one turn and at the next, soggy mud. All the while it felt like I was climbing straight up Everest; the wind competed with the blood pumping in my ears for the title of the loudest howl. A gentle shiver moved down my spine.

I looked down into the jagged cove below, decided up was still better than down, and kept going.

Finally, grasping a rock at the cliff's crest like a handle, I stepped precariously up onto two muck-covered boulders. With one more pull, I crested the ridge—and squeaked in surprise.

I was not alone.

A man, tall and lean, in a wool sweater and jeans, stood at the top of the cliff. He spun at the sound of my shriek. At the same time, my feet slipped out from under me.

My belly dropped as it does when an elevator sinks suddenly, and I could see out of the corner of my eye the rocks, like open jaws, below. The wind rose in my ears, deafening all sound and matching the fever pitch of my own voice. I reached out for anything, but grasped only air.

A hand—firm and strong, wrapping around my wrist—was the last thing I saw before the lights went out.

Nine

My eyes flew open. I registered three things immediately: the feel of soft grass beneath my body, the smell of salt air, and the sense that I wanted to get up and fight.

"There ye are." The man who had been standing at the cliff was kneeling next to me.

The brightness of the light behind him made my eyes hurt, and I squinted up at him. "Yeah, here I am. Now, don't touch me again or you'll lose that hand." My cheek stung, and I just knew he had slapped me. I sat up quickly and regretted it instantly.

Nausea hit me like a ton of bricks and a noise involuntarily came out the back of my throat. That firm hand came down again, this time to the back of my neck, and shoved my head between my knees. The nausea vanished, replaced by a humming under my skin, and black spots danced behind my eyelids.

"Let go of me!" I hollered.

The instant his skin left mine, my symptoms lessened. I took in a long and deep breath, letting the nausea and mood work themselves out of my system. My fingers gripped my knees. I still wasn't sure what exactly was happening, but I did remember that just a few minutes ago,

I had been perched to take a fatal tumble off the cliff. The least I could do was be grateful to this man, despite his rough tactics.

"Thank you," I said.

But instead of offering something gracious, something normal, in return, I heard him say, "Once ye get your wits about you, lass, I suggest ye explain to me how it is ye got to be 'ere."

Head still between my knees, I just breathed, ignoring the man hovering over me until I could capture my wits and restore them.

"I'm waiting," he said. His tone grated against my jangling nerves and before I knew what I was doing, I stood to give him a piece of my mind, my intentions no doubt clear on my face.

Face-to-face with this man, I was a little more than a bit concerned that he didn't even blink at me.

His eyes—almond shaped, gunmetal blue and framed by dark lashes and brows—rested unwavering on mine. The rest of his face—high cheekbones, fair skin with a black five o'clock shadow—wore an expression that said he had stared down more wild and crazy things than me.

"Well, for starters, I walked here," I said, being purposefully smart-alecky, but I couldn't maintain it. "And if you'll excuse me, I'll be on my way." Why was I feeling flustered? I had lost most of my vehemence.

"Ye're going the wrong way," the rolling Scots voice called. "Ye are on clan lands and unless ye have an invitation, I suggest ye stop now and go back the way ye came."

Jerk, I thought, but I stopped. Resting my hands on my hips, I glared into the distance, my mind running on a reel. It wasn't making sense—I was on a public trail.

"I don't think you understand." I turned to face him. He looked disarmingly sane and yet all he was saying wasn't; one of us was confused. I pointed behind me and tried not to sound as frustrated as I was. The squall was still coming, and there was no way I was going back down that hill when the information on my ancestor I was looking for was around the bend. "The castle is right there, and that is where I'm going. Be it on clan lands or not, this *is* a public trail," I added, "and I promise I'm just hiking here, not going to poach any"—I paused to look around at the rock and grass pasture—"any of the sheep."

He continued his death stare as he said, "Ye're trespassing. I suggest ye take to the trail."

"No," I said, glaring at him. "I'm not going back down that cliff, and you're insane for suggesting it. And how can you say I'm trespassing —this trail is in the guidebook I have. Who are you to say I can't be here?" I said, hearing my voice rise.

"Tha' public trail? It's about a mile tha' way." He stabbed a finger uphill.

Now I got worried. I could be making a really gigantic ass out of myself. Which in general is no big deal, but as it is said, entire nations are judged by the people from them. So there I was, the stereotypically arrogant and self-righteous American.

"Hold on." I pulled the book from Carol's place out of my pocket. It confirmed the trail followed the cliff side, just as I had.

"It says so right here." I held the book out to him.

He was out of arm's reach and for a moment he just looked at it, then to me, then back to it. Finally he strode forward and took it from me. He turned it to the front. "Mmmph," he said. "Bloody bastards."

"What?" I said.

He handed me the book back and strode past me.

"I take it I'm right," I said and started walking swiftly behind him, tucking the book back in my pocket. I glanced again out at the ocean and the dark squall.

He stopped and turned around. "Ye do know the castle is closed today, aye?"

"Well, yes. But, I'm sure they have informational placards outside. I was also hoping that the legend was printed somewhere out there." The excitement of conducting research returned to me, bowling over any other feelings or concerns in its way.

"Legend?"

"The Minory legend," I said.

"Aye, right. Tha' one. You can look it up on the Internet." He made a point of looking at me and then to the trail behind me.

"What?" I asked disbelievingly, "You really want me to go back down that nasty cliff face and nearly kill myself all over again? And with the castle this close?" I gestured to it. "And again, who do you think you are to tell me to leave a public trail?"

"Why would a woman walk all the way here, alone, to a castle tha' is closed just to read about a legend? What are *ye* really doing out here?"

I fumed more because I was asking myself the same question than because he was. "For starters, I'm Nicole Baker, and I'm trying to find more about my ancestors—who once *owned* this land." *Liar, liar pants on fire,* I thought, a little disgusted with myself. But I really felt the need to get a leg up on this guy.

This got an eyebrow lift. He stood there looking at me like I was a puzzle and the pieces weren't fitting.

"Baker? No sassenach has ever owned this land," he said with flat truth.

Sassenach, I thought. That one was a new word for me, but I would bet my plane ticket home that it didn't mean "awesome person" or "lovely tourist." Pronounced aloud, it was similar to what a snake emits before it bites—sass-en-ock, an extra something from the back of the throat at the end. It was like a big red button, and somehow I knew that this guy was pushing it on purpose—he was calling me out.

My eyebrows crammed together. "Listen, buddy, I'm not sure what you just said to me but I can tell that it wasn't nice, so don't flip me that sassen-crap just because I have an American accent. And furthermore, the reason I came all the way out here, even though the castle is closed, to read a legend that I could read online with the nonexistent Wi-Fi in this town is because I have an ancestor who very well could be the descendant of the man in that legend!"

He turned on his heel and began walking back toward the castle, tossing over his shoulder, "Everyone feels tha' way, Ms. Baker."

"Everyone?" I had to jog to keep up with him. "Everyone has an ancestor named Iain Eliphlet Minory?" I said, pronouncing the last name to my gain, with an *o*.

He stopped suddenly and I slammed into the back of him. The man was like a wall.

"Oof!"

"What did ye say tha' man's name was?" He'd turned around and was looking intently into my eyes, pinning me to the earth with his glare as if he were about to bore a hole into my core in search of any truth in what I had just said. Which apparently was of some extraordinary importance to him. I was very aware of how close he was and that we were two people alone on a carpet of green pasture in the middle of nowhere.

"Iain Eliphlet Minory was *my* relative's name." I stood a bit straighter, tossing back at him, "And *you* are?"

His jaw muscle clenched. "I'm a MacLaoch, and tha' castle ye are going to is my home."

My belly flip-flopped. He turned and strode toward the castle. I stood still for a few minutes, processing that nugget of information, and then with mild reluctance, I followed. He might be my best lead of the day.

I assumed that most castles were in a state of disrepair, with administrative offices off-site to manage estate matters. Did he really mean that the castle was his home? Who lived in a run-down castle that was over eight hundred years old and part of a public tour? And probably haunted, to boot. My mind decided that for this guy to be living at a castle, he most certainly was a groundskeeper or site manager. It was nice that the clan employed family members. Maybe he lived there for free?

The next hill put things in perspective.

The castle of clan MacLaoch, Castle Laoch, rose up before me in all its great glory. Walls, gardens, everything intact, probably looking better than it had the day it was built. Its boxy shape broke at the corners into Renaissance turrets and Victorian spires. It was a work of multiple ages, complete with breathtaking stonework.

My resident jerk was already at the base of the hill and striding to the gate at an alarming pace. I realized at that point that he most likely would keep me on the outside, if I weren't there to shove my way in along with him.

I made it down the hill in record time. I liked to think the sheep were impressed with my agility. Lucky for me, the gate was rusty, and I got to it just before it slowly latched shut and locked.

My resident jerk was a true gem.

Up a set of stone stairs, out into an open courtyard. The perfectly mowed grass was the only living thing there: cannons lined the walls, their snouts still pushed through holes in the stone; stone benches and sculptures dotted the grounds. A single door led into the castle—apparently this was where my faux tour guide had gone, as he was nowhere to be seen. Fine by me, as the walls were loaded with plaques of stories I wanted to read. Diligently, I started with the plaque closest to the door and worked my way around to the ones on the balcony. Halfway through, my heart leapt with excitement: The Legendary Lady MacLaoch. The plaque read:

In the days of old, it was in the loch below that the Lady MacLaoch of Castle Laoch was taken. Legend says that she had come down from the sea gate and was in the midst of bartering with traders for food for the castle when she was taken. The seafarer of the name Minory grasped her from the docks and made haste by the sea toward his trading port on the isle across the loch that is still here today. The small island directly across from this point was where the Minory kept her captive, despite the pleas from her clan to return her home. Her strong hand and wild spirit were feared to be broken if she was not rescued from the Minory tyrant. An army of MacLaoch clansmen rowed across the ocean and rescued the Lady MacLaoch from her fearsome captor. The river that runs through the MacLaoch estate was said to have flowed with the tears of joy she shed upon her return.

I read it again to myself. And again.

This version was very different from the one that the MacDonagh brothers had told, and the part where Lady MacLaoch shed tears of joy over her rescue ran sour in my mind. I knew joy, and I knew grief. Tears of joy are fast and fleeting, even in the midst of the deepest belly laugh. Nothing to make a river. But grief? Those were the tears that could go on for days.

As I snapped pictures of the placard and of the castle, I felt a few large drops of rain hit my head. Tucking the camera back into my jacket pocket, I found the squall I'd forgotten all about right on top of me. In seconds, all things uncovered, including me, went from bone-dry to soaked. I ran for the door that led into the castle and prayed it was open. The knob turned, and I pushed—only to feel it stick at a quarter of the way open. Rain running down my back, I rammed my shoulder into the door and stumbled into the hall when it gave. I showed it no mercy when I closed it with a slam that echoed loudly in the stone hallway.

The peace and quiet of ancient stone is quite eerie. I stood in a lower hallway of the castle; pictures lined the far walls, and windows behind me ran the length of the hall and looked back out into the courtyard. Two doors off to my right had signs for Gift Shop and Restrooms. To my left was a wide set of stairs that led up to the next floor. I shook the rainwater off my jacket and squeezed out my hair indelicately on the stone floor, then slowly made my way up the stairs.

The next floor up was right out of a more modern world. One moment I was in an eleventh-century castle, and the next, I was standing on hardwood floors and staring at wallpapered walls. It was as if the money for refurbishing the interior of the castle had run out before the lower floors could be modernized.

The cherry and mahogany furniture with gracefully curved Queen Anne legs were tastefully arranged, and farther down the hall I could see offices and sitting rooms, all open and airy.

"Hello? Anyone here?" I called, softly, rubbing my arms against the wet chill that had settled on me from the rain, but the soaring ceilings amplified my voice. An odd resonance to the left drew my attention to an open door leading into a stone chamber.

I read the sign on the door: Dungeons.

That in itself should have had me walking in the other direction. I suffer from a small thing called claustrophobia. But I suffer more from being a tad too curious for my own good.

I took a peek into the void. It was a very small room that was still the original stone of the castle. There was no way that that little chamber was a dungeon. Either the people of yesteryear Scotland were miniature or the MacLaochs didn't have very many enemies. Neither seemed likely.

I could see a plaque on the far wall, and could make out part of the first sentence: "In this room, Lady MacLaoch . . . "

I was joyous at finding another lead so soon. This place would be packed with visitors the next day. I wouldn't have to go in very far. Just a few steps.

The stone made the closet-dungeon—there was maybe room for

five or six people to stand shoulder to shoulder—cooler than the hallway I stepped from. The plaque said:

In this room Lady MacLaoch's power prevailed. Lady Abby MacLaoch, an astute historian of the nineteenth century, felt that to refurbish this room in the styling of her modern era would diffuse its historical significance. Thus this room has not changed since the day it was created and still stands as the entrance to the dungeons, which are through the hole below the iron grate in the floor. When the grate was placed over the thirteen-foot drop to the dungeon below, prisoners were forgotten. Forever.

Oh, I thought, *wrong Lady MacLaoch.* And then: *Hole?* I looked down.

I was standing on the lid to the dungeons. I stood frozen, looking into the dark pit below me, the first trickles of vertigo unbalancing the world and the walls suddenly feeling suffocatingly close.

I should leave, I thought, only my feet didn't move. Phobia took the driver's seat while my rational mind took the back. The walls pushed in on my mind, shoving the oxygen out, along with my ability to reason. Then—before I could crawl, claw, walk, or jump—the light from the doorway went out, plunging me into darkness.

The thrum of blood in my ears mimicked the sound of skin against stone, and I dove into the murky depths of my claustrophobia. The claustrophobia combined with the effects of hiking for miles, nearly falling from a cliff to my death, then getting soaked and chilled to the bone with torrential rain. It grabbed ahold of me and I succumbed to it as I never had before.

I barely recognized the din of a human voice. Blackness surrounded me and I felt a hum of energy within me before I felt the pressure on my shoulder. Then I felt nothing more.

Ten

I lay disoriented on a green velvet settee—surrounding me were books, loads of ancient books. It was obvious I was in some sort of library, but I couldn't figure how on earth how I had gotten there.

I made myself sit up, my body feeling used up and weak from the claustrophobia attack. Some of the books were tooled leather, others gilded with gold. None, though, had the glossy covers of the twenty-first-century books that line the shelves at modern-day bookstores. In the center of the room, a large reading table held a glowing lamp, despite the brightness of the late-afternoon sun through the window behind me.

I rubbed my arms, hoping to get rid of some of the fatigue that was clawing at them, and it was then I saw him. My resident jerk was leaning against the doorjamb, slightly out of view next to a massive wooden bookshelf, observing me.

"Diabetic or claustrophobic?" he said in greeting.

I was too tired to banter with him. I managed, "Claustrophobic."

He nodded. "Did you just discover this?"

"No," I said softly, hoping that there was an exit other than the one he was currently taking up.

The MacLaoch nodded again. "So ye say ye have had attacks before, and yet I found ye in the smallest, darkest room in the castle. Did someone push ye in there?"

I could see where this was going and it wasn't a warm washcloth across my head and a stiff drink in my hand, which were what I really needed. I said, "No, but I am persistent," and stood, hoping my legs could and would carry me from the place.

"Aye, I can see tha'. I'm just wondering why a woman who boldly claims herself to be a Minory descendant would willingly persist her way into a MacLaoch castle and pass out in our dungeon. Did ye no' think tha' maybe we'd just push ye into the hole and leave ye? We've done worse to your lot."

I narrowed my eyes. "I suppose you should have thought about that when you saved me earlier on that cliff—though I'll give you the benefit of the doubt, as you didn't know then what family I belong to. But really? Leave me in the dungeon? Over a fairy tale?"

MacLaoch raised his eyebrow at me. "Ye think it's a fairy tale? It's more like a curse, Ms. Baker."

"I suppose it matters what side you're standing on. Though either way, it's the twenty-first century, and this castle is open for tours—I doubt people would still come if my body were rotting in the dungeon."

"The fairy tale," he said. "Is tha' why ye are so persistent to find a MacLaoch? To cure what ails him?"

I leveled my gaze on him for a moment, really taking him in. I was surprised that he was getting worked up over my being there, so I tried again to explain myself.

"Look," I said, "I'm here to do family research. I was raised in South Carolina, as were four generations before me, and I just discovered this last Christmas that, by blood, my father's line is this Minory character." I stuck to the *o* pronunciation.

"South Carolina."

"Yes, South Carolina, since the mid-eighteen hundreds."

He just squinted at me as if trying to solve a mathematical equation he wasn't so sure he knew all the variables of. I noticed the way his jaw muscle flexed and relaxed, as if it were helping him digest the information.

Exhausted, I pointed toward him and asked, "Is that the exit?"

He took a moment to look at the doorframe he was standing in. "Aye, it is." Then he looked back at me.

I raised an eyebrow at him. "Unless you are going to offer me a moist towel and a stiff drink, I have no reason to stay." Then I added (because sometimes I remember that I do have manners and I should use them), "And I don't want to take up any more of your time—my apologies for the intrusion."

Instead of moving as I approached him, he stood still and his gaze intensified. "Why are ye here? Why now?" His voice was low and barely audible. "And how in god's name did he get to America?"

It was as if I had stepped into a separate conversation, which he was having with himself—one so intense that he had completely disregarded that I was real and still present.

I looked at him, exhausted, and simply answered with nonsense: "Dunno, fate?" I pointed at his chest. "Move?"

MacLaoch stood back from the doorway, allowing me a narrow path to pass by him. My shoulder brushed his chest and for just that instant my insides quivered as if he were made of electricity. I paused in the next room.

It appeared to be a formal dining room and looked out from the second story onto the castle gardens below. There were four doors on the opposite side of the long dining hall and no exit sign. My gut instinct told me to take the first door, but I was also highly aware of a set of eyes on my back waiting, and a charged silence that I was having a difficult time making sense of.

I pointed to the first door and looked back at him. "That one?"

"Aye," he simply said. I noted the darkness in his demeanor had returned, but something else lingered. Something that seemed to have awakened since I first met him out on the cliff. Curiosity? Wonder? I suspected a third option, something I didn't understand because it didn't make sense: hope.

I strode to the door, opened it, and felt a small surge of elation as I stepped into the hallway I had seen before. From my vantage point, I could see the grand staircase and the large front doors marked Exit.

"Ms. Baker," the MacLaoch said from behind me.

I turned back to him. He stood watching me, his eyes dark and glittering.

"Yes?" I asked.

"Come back tomorrow—when the castle is officially open—and I'll *personally* give ye a tour of Castle Laoch and the legend tha' haunts us."

"I don't think so," I said, and I moved quickly down the stairs and out the front doors, back to Will and Carol's along the main road.

FRESHLY SHOWERED, I CURLED UP ON THE WINDOW SEAT IN my room, which looked over the road below and Glentree harbor in the near distance. I picked up my pen and wrote in my journal, logging the day's events as I had planned to do in order to remember the trip and keep track of clues for my research. But by the time I got to the boat tour in my narrative, my hands were shaking so badly that I had to put my pen down.

Not only had I nearly gotten killed once and passed out twice, I had also learned about an ancestor who may or may not have been mine. It was true that the difference between the two names was just a single letter, but it was also a fact that the difference between *kilter* and *killer* was a single letter. A single letter was not anything to be dismissed, especially if I intended to be 100 percent certain where my bloodline had originated from, and that one letter would be a sticking point when I went asking for historical information about the Minarys. There would be at least one person at Castle Laoch who would not believe me should I go there to use the expansive library for research. Unfortunately, that was where I felt I would have the most luck finding information about Iain. But if the man I had met was part of the castle management, as I suspected, I probably could avoid him by going straight to the clan historian.

I just hoped he wasn't as superstitious as the rest of this island appeared to be.

Eleven

The next morning I quietly made my way through breakfast as Carol rushed busily about, attending to the other guests, a whole troop of German tourists loudly and boisterously enjoying their breakfast. This allowed me to avoid Carol—not that I was ashamed of not taking her advice but rather, because I didn't need the extra comments, especially the way the day had turned out.

I was halfway down the stairs when Carol's voice pulled me back. "Oh, Cole! Wha' are your plans today?" she asked, wiping her hands on her apron as she came down to me.

"Uh, I hadn't really—"

"If ye're going tae be about tonight around nine," she interjected, obviously not caring what I did have planned, "there's a spot of live music in the hotel next door. Good Gaelic music, not that contemporary crap. I have a nephew, Fletcher, who's playing in the band." She squeezed my shoulder. "You'll be up then?"

I had been prepared for some sort of rebuke for my excursions yesterday, thinking that Glentree was a small town, so it would only be a matter of time before she found out. I wasn't ready for this.

"Um, sure, I'll be up. Are you and Will going?"

She laughed at that. "Och no! We're tucked in by eight. Thought ye might like tae meet my nephew and see some local music, ye know, have fun."

I laughed to myself, once I understood. When you're single, you can smell these setups coming a mile away. "What does he play in the band?" I asked.

"Och, I'm no' sure wha' it's called in English, I think the fiddle."

After trying not to commit more than my just a toenail to the evening festivities, I made my way back to the documents room at the Glentree library.

It was a beautiful, overcast Scottish day, and the curls in my hair did their unruly thing and bounced on the breeze. I hoped that the clan chief went to the library often enough that Deloris could act as a liaison of sorts for me. The MacDonagh brothers also seemed to think that the chief was open enough to sharing information with the locals, so the Deloris avenue seemed like a good way to go.

"Ah! You're back," Deloris called as I stepped into her domain. She popped out from the shelves to meet me at the counter. "I hear ye went out with the MacDonagh brothers on a tour yesterday—I met up with them early this morn' and they ha' nothing but thanks for sending ye their way."

"I did, they are quite the pair, those two. They nearly upset the boat when I mentioned why I was here in Glentree."

"Aye, those two would get excited about a close reference to the Minory name. Sorry about that, aye. Hopefully they behaved themselves?"

I smiled, remembering their bows and formalities. "Yes, they were nothing but gentleman. They did mention something that made me come to see you again. They mentioned the chief of Clan MacLaoch is open to sharing the history of Castle Laoch with local people. Do you think you could request some materials for me?"

"Oh, aye. I suppose I could—what materials are ye thinking of?"

"I think I want to know more about this Minory family—it is so close to Minary that I just want to be able to cross it off the list of possibilities. Do you think you could ask for any historical references they might have on that last name? Or if they have boxes of historical material, I'd be happy to sort through it and save you the trouble."

"Sure. Though I have tae ask, have yae no' thought about going tae Castle Laoch yerself and asking? Ye could tell them that I sent ye, they should be obliging enough."

"I. Well," I blundered, "The truth is, I'm not sure that all of the MacLaochs hold your sentiments toward the Minory-MacLaoch legend. I would hate to ruin the chance to look at those documents just because I'm looking for an ancestor who shares a strikingly familiar last name."

"Oh all right, but I hope it wasn't the MacDonagh brothers who've gotten you scared tae talk with the MacLaochs? They're a nice lot, they are." Then she seemed to think better of what she said. "Well, except for that Eryka woman. Truthfully, she's not a MacLaoch, no matter how desperately she wants to be."

"Who?" I asked.

Deloris waved her hand. "Never mind. I'll make a request for you on those documents and let you know when I get them."

JUST AS I WAS FINISHING LUNCH IN MY ROOM BACK AT THE bed-and-breakfast, the phone rang. I answered ready to tell the person on the phone they had the wrong number, especially if it was my mother.

"Good afternoon to you!" Deloris said, and before I could respond, she excitedly continued. "After ye left this morning, I called up tae the MacLaoch castle tae see if I couldn't arrange tae have some documents sent down. Well, we got tae talking, the Castle Laoch historian and I, and I explained who ye are and what ye are looking for, paying mind that it's spelled with an *a*. Though I'll tell ye, he pushed that notion right out the window. He said to me, 'Minary with an *a*? Tosh! It's nae spelled with an *a*; it's an *o*, and I'll tell her myself if I have to.' Well, that's his opinion, and since he spends the majority of his time secluded away with his ancestry books and such, I'm not surprised that he's so convinced of it—knows nothing else, aye? The long and the short of it is that he said he'll see what he can find and, if we should be so inclined, we could go by this afternoon to pick up what he's found. Would ye like tae accompany me? Would be no bother tae pick ye up."

"Well, good news, it is," I said then, though a bit leery. "Is it at the castle?"

"Oh no, we would go tae the administrative offices—they are a ways down the road from the castle. It's only but a short walk from the offices, though, if ye wanted to see it. Weather looks like it'll hold today —though spring, it's hit and miss, aye?"

I signed off with Deloris, telling her I was happy to see the administrative offices. The weather was, as she said, hit and miss, though I wondered as I waited at the curb for her if it wasn't more "rain and mist."

From the moment Deloris and I entered the front room of the two-story converted stone house, our world chattered and bustled like a chimpanzee cage. Boxes lined the walls, cluttering the reception area—piled in front of the receiving counter and behind it as well—and filling what little walking space there had once been around the room's few desks. The one private office, off to our right, was partially filled with boxes as well. From the noise, it seemed like the place was packed with people, but there were only three women. All three were talking at once, to each other and on the phones.

"Oh my," Deloris said for us both.

"Maybe we should come back later," I said.

"Aye, I would, but I'm afraid that one of these boxes is from the historian, and if we don't get it today, we might never see it again."

In that light, I quite agreed. If we didn't rescue that box, wherever it was, it might get unpacked or shipped or have done to it whatever was happening to the rest of the mess that surrounded us. I noticed that the boxes weren't all filled with books and other documents, as I'd assumed. They were labeled in curly script: napkins, stationery, glassware, candles. Deloris seemed to be reading the labels at the same time.

"Oh! The gala!" she cried, as if in an epiphany. Right then one of the women finally hung up her phone and made her way toward us.

"Deloris!" the woman exclaimed as she picked her way through the room and around the counter to greet us. "What brings ye down here?" She sounded as though she had just run a long distance.

"I've come to meet Clive for some old clan documents," Deloris said cheerfully, then seemed to remember I was standing next to her. "Rather, she's come for the documents. This is Cole Baker from America. She's doing a spot of history searching. That's why we are here. Though it looks like the gala must be coming up, aye? We don't mean tae bother ye."

"Och, aye. The gala will be here in just a few days and that rotten woman—" The clerk interrupted herself to call back to one of her two colleagues still on the phone. "Mary, have ye gotten ahold of Eryka?"

Mary shook her head in response.

"Och!" our host said, stamping her foot. "Damn woman had the delivery driver unload all this here and no' down at the castle where it should have been. And she has the gall tae no' show up taeday. That's all she had tae do, arrange for delivery, and look, look at all this!"

Deloris and I looked around again at the boxes. I thought of what Deloris had said the day before. A woman named Eryka who wanted to be a part of the MacLaoch clan. Personally, I felt she wasn't trying hard enough if she had anything to do with the mess around us.

"We'll not take up much of yer time, but do ye know which one of these boxes is for us?" Deloris asked and then added, "Or if any of them are?"

"Which one is for ye? I dinnae understand."

"Oh, yer historian gave me a call this morning about clan documentation that he would be bringing down here tae the administrative offices. Did he no' tell ye?"

"Och, Deloris, I've spoken tae a number of people this morn. It would be possible that I talked with Clive, but I'll tell ye I've no' see him unless he did bring them in when we were filling up the lorry tae take another load down to the castle. In that case we'd ha' missed him, and it'd be in the office behind ye." She looked at the room behind us but didn't stop her breathless ramble. "And, in with all this, we started moving things tae the chief's flat at the castle, so now we have more boxes than we know what tae do with. I just hope we dinnae give him champagne glasses and hand out at the gala his personal affects!" she said, giving a short humorless laugh.

But then the phone rang, and our host cursed her way back to her desk. She glanced back to us, but we waved her off.

Surely it would be easy to distinguish between a box of party items and one filled with historical documents.

Just as we lifted the lid on the first of the many boxes, our host popped her head in—the phone call was for Deloris.

"I leave the library for just a few minutes . . . " she muttered. "Somehow, they can find me anywhere."

Deloris made her way from the room as I replaced the lid on the box. I'd wait for her to return. It seemed that it would be rude, almost mean, to look for the historical documents without her, since she seemed so excited (almost more than I was) to find a clue to my ancestry.

I leaned back against one of the boxes in the office and looked around, fine with having a moment to check out this MacLaoch property, too. Newer than a lot of the town, this stone building definitely still hearkened back to the eighteen hundreds—the heavy wood of the bookshelves and desk solidified the feel.

It wasn't that big of a room, and most of it was obscured by cardboard. The need to be useful became overwhelming, and I decided to start in on the boxes without Deloris. They'd either be historical documents or not, and I wouldn't mess with the stuff that was not. I opened the lid on the box we'd been about to go through before Deloris had been pulled away by her phone call. On first appearance it was what we were looking for: file folders piled together. I pulled out the first folder and opened it to what started like a very personal letter to the current MacLaoch clan chief. I was about to slap it shut and move on to the next box—ready, as a guest already nervous about stepping on toes, to assume that this indicated that the box's entire contents was too recent for my needs—but then the name Minory caught me like an anchor. Before I could stop, I'd read it in full.

DEAREST SON AND NEPHEW (FOR THOUGH YOU ARE MY *nephew by blood, you have always been as close to me as would be a son),*

It is with grievous heart that I write to you. I know that it is not long now until I die—the doctors, despite all their knowledge, do not know how to cure me. They can, however, with all their knowledge, tell me that my foe—this so-called incurable cancer—will kill me in a few months' time.

Right now you are no doubt deep in the wilderness of some foreign country bringing honor and pride to your family name, though I fear I will not last long enough to see your triumphant return. Thus, the reason for this letter. Over the years, I have imparted to you a working under-standing of your duties once I leave this earth, but all that I have taught you wanes sadly when compared with the most difficult and arduous responsibilities of this job.

No doubt you have scoffed at the curse on the MacLaoch chiefs—as a boy, I played them off as well—though I will tell you from experience that it is real. And while I have just a breath left, I will tell you the history of what I know of it.

Several generations of MacLaoch chiefs ago, there began a movement. A movement to discover the full depth of the curse and alleviate our suffering by meeting its demands. It was first done by the twentieth clan chief—it is documented that he spent countless hours researching the Minory lineage as well as local folklore on the curse. The one thing that remained constant in all versions of the curse he heard is that the pain and suffering of the MacLaoch chief must be as great as that felt by Lady MacLaoch, and only a Minory could lift the curse, and then only volun-tarily. With this, he began cataloging each and every ancient Minory throughout history, slowly and painstakingly finding the descendants to discover a modern-day Minory. Sadly, his life ended before his work could be completed. It was only to be taken up again by our twenty-ninth clan chief—you will, I hope, excuse me for not using their full names as it pains me to write even the amount that I have already—who began where the twentieth left off. It is through his work that I give you this grievous news about the MacLaoch curse. It will be with us through the rest of time.

The twenty-ninth chief poured through documents upon documents—it is said in his journals that he felt pure elation as he narrowed upon two lines of the Minory family that quite possibly could still be alive. More research, and he discovered that one of those lineages had died out during the late 1700s. He cast it aside and focused his energies on the last remaining line of Minorys. In his research of that lineage, he discovered that, right then, a Minory was residing in Glasgow. Of course, before he could contact the Minory, he discovered the death certificate of this man — as though the curse was just one step ahead of him. The Minory had died in the short time between when our chief learned of his existence and tried to contact him! While the Minory had been married, he had produced no children, and it is with a hard heart that I must tell you what has been passed down. The last of the Minorys died in 1850. His name was Iain Eliphlet Minory, and his death has sealed our fate for eternity. It seems that Lady MacLaoch has gotten her wish: we shall forever know her pain and suffering and never know the sweet balm of love and peace—that damnable woman!

My son and nephew, as I lie dying of this dreadful disease, I can only tell you that the curse is real. And had I heeded the curse, I would have done much differently in my life. Thus, I will impress upon you: do not succumb to the fickle nature of your heart and look for love. It is not your fate while sitting upon the chief's chair. Keep your distance and harden your heart; instead of a wife, devote your life to that of your clan—make sure that, as I have, they are not want for anything; provide as you can and give back whenever it is possible. In doing this, in taking nothing for yourself, Lady MacLaoch cannot take from you that which you do not have.

Again, it is with a sad heart that I say my good-byes to you upon paper and not in the flesh. Know that I am proud of you in all that you have done and will accomplish.

Good-bye, my son and nephew, and God bless you.

My eyes swam with the tears from the heavy burden of history. The sound of footsteps approaching kept me from thinking too long—I shook my head and replaced the box lid as Deloris popped her head in the door.

"Just been on the phone with the historian from Castle Laoch— now he says the documents that I requested don't exist! I just had it out with him on the phone, because it sounds like he's hiding something. I don't know what on earth it would be but I can feel it. Like a mother can sense when her babe puts his hand in the cookie jar when she's not looking, aye?" Her look changed from one of suspicious indignation to concern. "Are ye all right? Ha' ye been crying? What happened?" She rushed into the room.

I just shook my head. "Oh no, I just got a bit of allergies, all these old buildings . . . " I rubbed my nose aggressively to demonstrate my point.

"Oh, all right . . . " She sounded unconvinced but, politely accepted my excuse. "Come then, I'll drop ye back off at Will and Carol's. I'll tell ye, the clan chief will hear about this! Documents don't exist, hmph!"

I let her chatter wash over me as I reread the letter over and over in my mind. That name, acknowledged by the former clan chief as the last of the Minory lineage, was nearly identical to the one that had brought me to Scotland.

Twelve

I spent the rest of the day puttering around town, buying knickknacks from the local shops and enjoying the day in general. It was closing in on over twenty-four hours since I'd nearly fallen off a cliff and been scared to death with a claustrophobia attack and dealt with an angry MacLaoch, so this day was going well. So well that the thought of going out socially for the first time I'd gotten to Scotland was sounding like a really good idea, even if it was a setup.

After a nap, dinner, and a shower, it was closing in on a half hour since the music had started in the hotel next door. I dressed in the one fancy outfit that I had brought with me, thoroughly surprised it hadn't wrinkled, despite my not taking it out of my suitcase until then. I added a few gold bangles and matching loops to my ears and paused in front of the mirror. The Queen of Sheba would be hard pressed to find a top that fit better than this one. The top was a deep, nearly black, green and it was cut perfectly to show off the fullness of my chest and hips; the jeans were just snug enough; and my slip-on wedges made my legs look a mile long.

I threw on some mascara, a little blush, and—because I was feeling fancy—attempted to tame my mass of curls before heading out.

The hotel next door was a set of four refurbished stone townhomes from the eighteen hundreds. The bar was packed with people dancing in the middle and sitting or mingling around the edges. The main floor was an open plan, with a restaurant to one side and the bar/music venue to the other. The bar was simply that, though with nice hardwoods and modern touches. The tables and chairs had been pushed to the sides of the room, leaving a large space open for dancing. The band, from what I could see through the crowd, was on the far end of the room.

I'm not sure what exactly I'd been expecting the band to look like, but what I saw was not it. Six seemingly random people in random states of dress sitting in chairs grouped in an awkward fashion. No electric guitars, no drums; just two fiddle players, a cellist, two bagpipes, and a guy on drums—hand drums. And the music wasn't what I knew as bar music, screechy amateurish stuff or jukebox golden oldies; no, this was the most incredibly synced, melodic, emotionally moving music I had ever heard.

The rapid tempo grabbed me right as I walked in, the drum keeping time in my soul and the bagpipes adding a subtle Celtic current underneath the strings. I noticed as I made my way to the bar that some of the people dancing were really *dancing*. The lightness of their feet as they moved seemed completely natural with the music.

I made my way to the bar and ordered a pint of a Scottish lager. Sipping, I put my back to the bar and peered through the crowd at the band, looking for the nephew of Carol. There were only two fiddle players and one was female. The other looked to be just over twelve.

I downed my beer as if it were my last saving grace and asked for another just as the music stopped. I was halfway through the second— and I wasn't sipping—when he ambled over. Carol's nephew was an inch shorter than me in my heels and had the gangly features of a boy who could grow impressively into that body if he tried. From just looking at him, I determined that he wasn't trying. His large, owl-like, watery blue eyes seemed even larger behind the small spectacles he wore, and I was pretty sure his mousy brown hair and pasty white skin hadn't been washed in a while. I knew even then that what I was thinking was harsh, but when a boy is wearing what he's thinking right on his face, and he isn't thinking about his mama, it kind of brings out the bitch in me.

"Are ye Nicole?" he asked, like I were a present he had been given for Christmas.

Oh, god.

"As a matter of fact, I am, and call me Cole. You would be Carol's nephew, right?" I stuck my hand out to shake and also to make sure he kept his distance. "Pleased to meet you." I put a smile on my face.

He grasped my hand in his clammy one.

"My aunt said ye were pretty, but she didnae say ye were *hot*." He scrunched his nose up in exclamation on that last word.

Ugh, again. I thought. Now I was at a loss for words, not because I didn't have anything to say but because I had too many things to say, none of them nice.

"What's your name, Carol's nephew?"

"Argyle, Fletcher Argyle," he said, bumping the person behind him out of the way to lean on the bar with his elbow next to mine. His hand brushed my arm like a boy desperate to touch woman flesh.

I raised an eyebrow at him, not impressed and losing patience. "Thank you, James Bond. Oh, your people are calling."

His head whipped around so fast to look in the direction I pointed that I thought he must have hurt himself. The cellist made a get-over-here gesture, and he turned back to me: "Buy me a pint o' the Tennent, aye?" And he ran back to his seat.

I was floored and was going to do no such thing. I also made a mental note to talk to Carol and let her know her nephew needed a nanny, not a date.

The music started back up again as I heard a male voice say from behind me, "Please tell me that is not your date."

I downed the last sip of my second beer and turned around.

The guy behind me at the bar was straight from the pages of Scottish *GQ*. Taller than me, with thick, Scottish-red hair—not a golden copper like mine, but *red*—white freckled skin, and brown eyes. The kind of brown that had a hint of green in it. And two beautiful dimples when he smiled. And he knew it, too. He was also dressed to impress, is what you could say—expensive dark slacks matching polished shoes, a plain dark wool sweater that looked like it was made from bottle-fed cashmere goats, with what looked to be a starched, not just ironed, shirt underneath. I wanted to assume he was there alone, though from the looks the Scandinavian-looking woman—the one across the bar who had a nice leather jacket on the chair opposite her—was flinging at me, I wasn't so sure.

"Blind date," I said, then added, "Nix that, an extremely blind blinded date."

He laughed—long, deep, and excessively throaty. To make someone laugh, what an intoxicating addiction that is. I had a girlfriend in undergrad who would laugh at nearly everything I said—not in a sarcastic way but in a genuine fashion, and I went out of my way to be her lab partner, study partner, and BFF. To this day, I loved her deeply—selfishly, but deeply.

The man turned to the bartender. "Johnny, send a pint over to Fletcher on me, will ye?" he said and turned back to me. I watched as Johnny shook his head and began filling the pint of Tennent. "Another pint of Tennent, or would ye like something a *bit stronger*?" I did not miss that he was suggesting both liquor and himself.

"What'd you have in mind?" I asked.

"Whisky."

I raised an eyebrow, but was rewarded when I conceded. I learned that night that whisky, in certain regions of Scotland, is a lot like bourbon is in the South, tending to be sweeter and excellent quality. I also discovered that my palate preferred the speyside, or sweet whiskies —and by *discovered*, I mean I sampled about six until we found the one I liked. Getting tipsy fast, I still noticed that Johnny pulled each bottle from the top shelves only.

The music stopped again and I glanced toward Fletcher, but he didn't move. It was just a short break.

"I'm sorry, you probably overheard my name, but I don't seem to know yours." And again I noted the woman at the back table glowering.

"Kelly Browning MacLaoch Gregoire, Clan MacLaoch, next heir to the seat as MacLaoch chief. But call me Kelly." He winked.

"You people are everywhere," I said drunkenly. I was sure I should have responded in a more impressed manner, but he seemed impressed enough for the both of us. I was about to ask him his thoughts on the

MacLaoch curse when I decided I couldn't put up with Empress of Icy Stares any longer.

"Do you know the blond woman at the back table?" I asked him, staring her down. Just like that, the woman got up and worked her way through the room toward us.

"The only woman here worth knowing is you, love," he said softly, leaning toward me to make his point.

"Uh, thanks," I said warily, "but I don't think that *she* feels the same way."

"Kelly, let's go," she snapped. Her brows, dark against her fair skin, seemed to be permanently arched in anger, and her face, though beautiful, was pinched tight from the upset she was working on.

Kelly rolled his eyes heavenward just as the music, this time jumpy and lively, started back up.

"Good," he said and snatched my hand. "Let's dance."

"But—" was all I managed before I was dragged from the bar to the dance floor, the whiskies rolling like a heavy hand through my body. Before we disappeared completely into the crowd, I caught a glimpse of Ice Empress talking to someone on her cell phone.

Kelly pulled me in against him as he danced to the music, a hop and a twist here, then some move that I suspected was completely Kelly-only. I wasn't sure what to do, so I tried to emulate him. After a moment I felt foolish. It was as if I were a fumbling newborn trying to walk, and Kelly was everywhere and right in front of me all at once.

Bodies elbowed and jarred me as they moved in sync with the jumpy fiddle, and I thought of the mosh pits I'd been in at concerts in undergrad. The crowd jostled me farther and farther from Kelly. Taking a moment from his one-man party, he saw the gap opening between us and moved to close it.

Kelly reached forward and, planting both hands on my ass, wrenched me in against him. My head bounced off his chest and, before I got my wits about me, I realized he had also licked my ear.

"Yeah, baby. Mmmm," he said, his voice barely heard over the high pitch of Fletcher's and his counterpart's strings.

"Whoa, buddy," I said, trying to put some distance between us again. I was thinking drunkenly he'd obviously missed a step in How to Woo a Woman.

"I'm sorry, love, you are just too beautiful for me not to sample," he said into my ear, then licked it again and began ministrations that went beyond ear licking. They were far too personal, with his body against mine.

"Kelly. Yuck, don't lick my ear." I wiped the spit off with my shoulder, thinking this is what Fletcher might be like in several years, if he ever moved out of his mother's house. "And get your paws off of me." I slapped his hands off my ass.

He looked down at me without pausing in his dancing and rolled his eyes. "Stop being such an American prude. Just relax." He grabbed at me again.

"Excuse me?" I raised my voice to be sure he heard me. This dance was definitely over.

"I said, stop being such an *effing* American prude."

I sneered. "I wasn't asking because I'm deaf, but in case you are dense, I meant: your girlfriend is at the bar and I don't want to knock boots with you, so let go!" I gave him a shove, but it was like shoving a stack of bricks.

Instead of moving away from me, he leaned back again so we made eye contact. "She's not my girlfriend, and ye can't be serious about not wanting to fuck." He said slithering his eyes over my outfit. "Not dressed like that."

The room jerked to a standstill as I stared at him, hard. My mind replayed the words he'd just said to me, trying to find another set of words that he could have meant. Though I tried, for his benefit—this stranger in whose country I was a guest—I knew that's exactly what I had heard him say.

Twisting out of his mauling grip, I squeezed around a nearby couple. Kelly's hand wrapped around my arm and yanked me back to him. I stumbled backward and fell into him, and he grabbed at me again.

"Get your damn hands off me," I hissed in Kelly's face.

He tried on a look that was an attempt, I could only assume, at dark and dangerous but looked more like the California Valley girl sneer of *whatever*. His words were dark, however. "Ye don't leave until I say ye do."

It was now undeniably clear that Kelly wasn't used to hearing the word no and that in order to have him respect my wishes, I'd have to teach him sign language. With my knee.

Just as I shifted to the side for his first lesson, a shoulder moved in between us. A man pushed Kelly backward, forcing him through the crowded dance floor. Despite my unsuccessful tries earlier to make room, it seemed this man could move bodies without effort. I watched as Kelly's face went from attempted seduction to outright pouting. It was disgusting.

When I got a better look at the man who had a grip on Kelly—who I was starting to feel wasn't calling Kelly out on my behalf but for some deeper, longer standing reason—I groaned inwardly. Would I never see the last of my resident jerk? Clad in clothes similar to what he'd worn the day before, he nodded in my direction as if to emphasize a point to Kelly. His grip on Kelly's shoulder tightened, and Kelly made a pained expression at him.

Slowly the MacLaoch turned and met my stare. His expression was dark and dangerous, and it growled, *You*. He looked back at Kelly for a few final words, and I made my escape to the bar to close my tab and leave. Sure, he'd just helped me out, but I wasn't sure I wanted to be anywhere near someone like him if he was close with someone like Kelly.

Of course, the only open place at the bar was next to Ice Empress— who was wearing an expression, I guessed, that was as close as she would ever get to a smile. She was extremely smug. And I wasn't so slow as to not realize that the MacLaoch had been on the other end of the phone call she had just made. I'd thank her later.

I was just signing the check when I saw him approach from the corner of my eye and heard him say under his breath to her, "Eryka, go wait in the car." When she didn't immediately move, he punctuated it with, "Now."

Oh jeez.

He moved in beside me and very gently took the credit card receipt from my hand, read my name, and handed it to Johnny the barkeep.

"Johnny, put this on our tab, aye? And I'll have a dram of the

Talisker twenty-five year." His voice was smooth, no hint of the anger he'd just demonstrated.

I watched as my receipt got shredded and Johnny reversed the credit on the little machine he'd used to run my card. Johnny moved with silent obedience to this man, and I watched all this as the MacLaoch watched me.

"Dinnae know ye'd be meeting my cousin later," he said. "Ye get around."

"Excuse me?" I met his glacial blue eyes, hoping he could feel the daggers in my glare. "Thanks for covering my tab, buddy. It was unnecessary, but I'll take it because if that guy is your cousin, we're even now."

His whisky arrived and he swirled it around in its glass and took a sip before saying, "And how does one small bar check make us even? I'm sorry, lass, but if ye remember, I pulled ye from a cliff and didn't toss ye in the dungeon for trespass. I'd say the scales are still tilted heavily in my favor. Unless ye mean I actually ruined yer night with my cousin?"

The room became warm as I felt my blood pressure rising. "You think I came here to get cozy with your cousin?" I hissed at the MacLaoch, "Your cousin is a dirty cock-sucking pig. And had you been a second later, you would have seen him with a bloody nose and the inability to screw anything, much less take a piss without wincing, for a month."

At that moment the music stopped, and I noticed the bartender was hovering in front of us, drying an already dry pint glass with his towel.

It was still loud in the bar, with everyone talking all at once, but the MacLaoch leaned in and breathed, "Keep your voice down, and I would be very grateful."

Just as I was making up my mind to get the hell out of there, things got worse.

Fletcher saddled up to us. "He's not bothering ye, is he?" he said with as much false concern as bravado.

I was punchy—all the liquor had seemingly evaporated from my system and been replaced with adrenaline from wanting to drop-kick Kelly.

"Yes, Fletcher, he is. What are you going to do about it?" I said aggressively and stared him down. Waiting.

"Oh. I uh, uh," was all he could muster, looking from me to the MacLaoch and back.

"It's all right, Fletcher," the MacLaoch said and clasped him on the shoulder. "She's messing with ye. How's your mother?" He asked, nonplussed by the whole situation and smoothly shifting subjects.

"Och, she's good." Fletcher replied without a hitch, as if it were natural that everyone was interested in Fletcher's pathetic life. "Bitches too much, says how I have to go get me a real job. What she thinks I do 'ere, I don' know."

"Mmmph," MacLaoch said.

"She's such a pain in my arse, ye know?"

"Well, she's yer mother, and ye'd do well to mind her, aye?" MacLaoch said, leaning against the bar, cradling his whisky in the palm of his hand, regarding Fletcher as a teacher might a wayward, but ultimately harmless, student. He seemed so at ease offering advice and taking in Fletcher's ridiculous concerns.

"I *do*. It's just that she does it all the time." Fletcher shook his head in exasperation. "Psh! *Women*."

MacLaoch closed his eyes as if praying for mercy. "Och, Fletcher. Mind." He nodded his head in my direction, his brows drawn together in disgust.

"Oh, sorry, aye," Fletcher said to me, not really meaning it.

"Screw you, Fletcher," I said without emotion, but really I felt it toward both of them, so I plucked MacLaoch's expensive whisky from his hand and polished it off. It slid down smooth and blossomed like a smoky sea with an afterkiss of vanilla and honey.

I slammed down the glass. "Well it's been fun, boys, but I'll be seeing y'all."

MacLaoch had an expression that could only be recognized as humor: a light lift at the corner of his mouth and eyes.

"Aye, a screw ye to us both," he said under his breath as he eyed the empty glass. "Fletcher. Know how to play the one about the seafarer?" he said, standing and putting his hand out gently to stop me from going.

Fletcher made a noncommittal sound.

"Good. Play it for me, aye?"

He brightened at this. "Aye! Anything for the chief."

I watched Fletcher go back to his crew and pass along the request and begin to play before it fully sunk in that Fletcher had just called this MacLaoch Chief. *As in, Chief of the Jerky people,* I thought snidely in my whisky haze.

I turned back toward MacLaoch to find him looking down at me, "Come," he said, giving me his hand.

I looked at it, then back to him. It seemed as if the jovial feel of the pub had actually caught up with this man.

"I promise I won' bite."

"Fine," I heard myself say, and I let my hand slide into his. It was rough and firm and very warm.

I felt the music catch me up into its rhythm as we moved into the dance area—the song was so hauntingly beautiful that the urge to move with it was undeniably strong. I felt the Celtic echoes of the Scottish pipes meld into one with the slow pace of the strings, and beneath it all the rhythmic pounding of the drums adding an exciting anxiety I couldn't place. It was as if the sound of the drums was awakening a memory that was beginning to hum into life.

"Have you danced to Gaelic music before?" he asked. "Except with my cousin, of course."

"No, and I wouldn't consider being mauled by Kelly as dancing either." I leaned back and looked up at him so that he could see that I was serious.

"Well, this will be new for ye then," he said. "Just relax an' I'll show ye how it's done."

Before I could respond, he put one hand firmly at my lower back and the other kept its grasp around my hand and then he moved me. Really *moved* me, with the gentle strength and confidence of a man who knew exactly what he was doing. I closed my eyes, giving in, and moved with him. *This,* I thought, *is how it should be.*

The MacLaoch was a different man than the one I'd interacted with the day before, as if he'd begun to believe that I was who I said I was, and in my reason for being there in Glentree.

As the last notes of his whisky hummed in my system, I noticed small things about the MacLaoch—the faint smell of ocean and the blustery pastures of his skin. The look and feel of the soft wool of his sweater and the strength of his hands. He was a solid width and the perfect height, such that if I wanted to, I could rest my head just under his chin. This clansman had a compelling force of nature to him. Something in that thought made me think of what Fletcher had said earlier.

I leaned back to look up at him again. "Why did Fletcher call you the chief?"

He shrugged. "I suppose it's because I am the chief."

"The chief of what?" I said as the obvious explanation hit me.

He tipped his head back to look at me, as if to make sure I wasn't having a laugh. I was so busy trying to make him a groundskeeper, Kelly's caretaker/bodyguard, castle caretaker, and even clan historian that not once did I think of anything else, much less a chief—which I had assumed was a regally dressed person with a starched, affected attitude.

"I see . . . You are the thirty-fourth clan chief of Clan MacLaoch." I spoke softly, feeling my embarrassed blush start at my neck and cruise up to my hairline.

"That I am," was all he said, watching my reaction.

All the things that transpired between us began to replay in my mind's eye: My yelling at him, my physically threatening him, my trespassing. My busting into his castle, and later, my reading the letter from his uncle. And he'd paid my bar tab. Sure, his cousin was an ass, but . . .

I could feel my skin getting hotter and my stomach getting queasier and looking him in the eye was getting harder and harder to do. I had to go, and right then was the time.

"Whoa," he said and firmed his grip on me, reading my expression exactly. "What are ye running from, lass?"

I twisted my hand from his grip. "Please just let me go," I mumbled, the queasiness getting stronger.

He stopped dancing and released me.

I turned from him and walked out the front door without a backward glance.

Thirteen

I didn't sleep well that night. I kept waking up thinking of all the things I had said and done to the man who was head of Clan MacLaoch.

When I did sleep, it was a sleep filled with lucid dreams.

One in particular stood out from the rest. I was standing at the water's edge across from Castle Laoch, on the ill-fated Isle of Lady MacLaoch. I could see the castle in the distance, the steel gray of the still ocean water reflecting the light of the overcast sky. My feet were bare—the round, hard stone of the shore's tumbled black rocks were beneath my feet—and the frigid water lapped at me gently.

While I knew in my dream that it was my body I was in, in the same breath I knew I was not in it alone. Our hair was down and curling about us, alight on the on-shore breeze blowing gently about our face. We pushed it back and looked into the wind, the gauzy white of our ancient dress floating on the soft, moist ocean air.

The woman within me was happy: someone had arrived. She could rest in peace now. I could feel the ease in her heart as if a great project, one that had consumed her in life and in spirit, was coming to an end. The door to her chapter was closing, while mine was just beginning.

Her happiness caught me up—giddiness bubbling through us, we couldn't wait any longer. Around the bend at the end of the rocky beach, he strode, and our body lit like a torch. Warmth and a soulful love bloomed within us at the sight of him, and we ran to him.

I yearned with each stride to hold him once more to me, to feel his embrace. It felt as though I had waited centuries for his return, yet I knew in that place between reality and dreaming that it was I who was returning; he had been there all along.

I started to recognize him, but before my sluggish, dream-addled mind could place him, a glint on my ring finger stopped me. I staggered in my dream, caught by the light reflected off the gold. The ring was a fine engraving of a thistle, and I felt I knew the clan crest; I looked closer, curiosity distracting me. I felt rather than knew that the ring upon my finger was mine, destined always for me.

Yet, I had no one in my life that I felt so drawn to. Never had I felt this connection to another, and I hungered for it.

In that moment, the woman who shared my dream left me. I was me, it was now.

All the powerful feelings within me manifested into life the instant the arms of the man wrapped around me. He slid one hand into my hair and the other around my waist, pulling me close. I embraced him in return; it felt like the sharing of souls, each of us pouring a piece of ourselves into the other.

I woke suddenly, my heart pounding.

The man in the dream hovered on the edge of my consciousness, turning to vapor when I reached for him again.

Fourteen

T he next morning I woke as the first trickles of defused light
came over the horizon. I'd slept little after the dream and, lying
in bed, I stared at the ceiling, my mind on a racetrack. *What
had that dream been all about? I can't believe the man I met yesterday
was the MacLaoch chief. Oh lord, did I really shout at him and slam his
whisky?*

I groaned and rolled over, stuffing my face and all my problems into
the pillow.

Worse than just being embarrassed, I was going to have to rectify the
situation. My stomach churned, due in part to being slightly hung over
but mainly to the thought of admitting to all the things that had transpired between us.

Restless, my mind fully awake then and yammering away on my
problems and how to fix them, I decided to get some fresh air.

I tossed on clothes and jotted down a note for Carol, letting her
know I was skipping breakfast, and shoved it under the door of the
breakfast room. Outside, I felt a tad clearer in the head, with the crisp,
foggy morning air filling my senses. I turned toward the downtown area,
hoping there was a café open with Internet access. I needed to know

more about this MacLaoch, and what it meant to be a clan chief in the twenty-first century.

There was only one coffee shop in Glentree—a place that prized its tea—but it was open. Moments later, with a frothing cup of coffee, a scone (still warm from the oven), and a slow Internet connection on the café's lone public computer all before me, I searched online for the thirty-fourth clan chief and came up with one Rowan MacLaoch. Links showed his name everywhere: parliamentary documents, witness testimony over escaped sheep, an old article mentioning him as the newest clan chief—and the youngest. The last link I clicked on was an article naming him as the benefactor of the Victor Ivandale Memorial Garden in Lassiemouth; Ivandale had been a fighter pilot who had died in action.

The clan's crest dotted many of the web pages I looked at, matching in complete detail the one on the ring in my dream. A medieval shield with a massive sword bisecting it, an abundant thistle bouquet to one corner, and encircling the entire thing, what looked like a decorative belt. The clan's motto was inscribed in bold letters on the belt: A warrior unto death.

Fitting, I thought, given what I knew of the clan's history of fighting. It seemed, from my few interactions with him, that this chief still carried that fearsome trait in his blood.

By far the most impressive report was from a *Scottish Living* article that pegged MacLaoch as the number-one richest clan in Scotland. Not only did it still have political sway, it was worth a fortune, due to its ownership of a large number of highly collectable and historically rich artifacts. Due, most likely, I thought, to the clan members' pillaging habits in earlier centuries. No one had tried to take anything back, apparently, because the MacLaochs were a miserable lot with a curse on their heads.

Despite that, I was the one feeling cursed—there was an underlying theme to all the things that I had read: the MacLaochs were a large group and governed by one man. He was a leader, protector, and land overlord, mentor and skirmish queller. He was the clan's chief and his name was Rowan James Douglas MacLaoch. The list of indignant things I'd done to him ran through my mind yet again—all the way back to the first moment I laid eyes on him, threatening his person for having slapped me awake.

Feeling queasy again and thoroughly stuffed full of information, I wrapped up my search and headed outdoors. Remembering signs on my way into town to a rare coral beach, Tràigh a' Chorail, I headed back the way I came and then down the well-marked trail.

The day was turning out overcast again and the short trail was sparsely populated, following the steely ocean's edge, winding through cow pastures and over small hills.

I made my way up the tall hill that jutted over the beach, which offered a 360-degree view of the shore below and the low-sloping, foggy mountains behind. The last little hill peaked and the white of the sand gleamed. If it weren't so chilly, it would be just like an overcast day in some tropical paradise. The emerald-green of the pastures rolled down to meet the cream-colored sand, which spilled from the grass's edge and into the ocean, revealing its true color—turquoise. Throw out a couple beach umbrellas and take its picture you'd be hard-pressed to find someone who would guess this was Scotland.

But in person, it was all Scotland. The weather was a mirror of my mood, storm clouds threatening on the horizon and the wind blowing my curls around my face.

I remembered the MacLaoch chief's words as I'd danced with him the night before. "That I am," he had said when I'd finally understood his true role in the clan. Those three words confirming that I had treated a Scottish dignitary about as well as I had an incoming college freshman. If I ever wanted to learn anything more about an Iain Eliphlet Minory, I was going to have to kiss and make up with this clan and its chief, no matter how brutal their ancestors may have been.

Sitting in a protected rock outcropping overlooking the beach, I began mentally drafting an apology letter—I'd tell him in writing about myself, come clean on the true spelling of my ancestor's last name, my research, and why I was doing it. Explain to him that it was just pure coincidence—that there was no relation that I knew of between the Minorys and my family name, Minary. I'd offer the possibility that they were brothers separated at birth, or cousins who were never invited to the same family reunions, or that this was just one of those freak coincidences, a strikingly similar name that differs by a single letter. I would elaborately and painstakingly explain the importance of a single letter difference.

Being in the open was soothing, and the tedious activity of mentally drafting and editing my letter distracted me long enough that exhaustion snuck in.

I hadn't realized how tired I'd been until I jolted awake—no doubt my mind being alarmed that it'd allowed me to nap cradled in a rock outcropping, in a foreign country. Despite the stiffness that had settled in from my snoozing on rock and in the gentle drizzle, I felt better. Standing, I scrubbed my face to clear the remnants of fatigue.

Back along the trail, I decided that I would head to the B&B, write my letter, and mail it. I was not sure I'd be able to face the chief in person and speak my words of apology aloud—a detailed letter would be the best way.

I made it all the way back to the trailhead parking lot with my clear plan before it was sabotaged.

I returned to find Ice Empress Eryka and her black Car of Doom waiting for me.

Eryka's face emerged over the frame of the open back door of an idling, tinted-window luxury car. She stepped one heeled shoe out of the car and looked me up and down. She was dressed as if she were headed off to work at a New York fashion magazine: second-skin pants, see-through white shirt (with lacy bra), and leather bomber jacket. Her hair was pulled back so tight I was surprised her lips didn't blink every time her eyes did.

Instinctively I thought of Kelly and looked around. Eryka didn't seem like she was dressed for a kidnapping, but I was taking no chances.

"A word with you," she said, pink lips highly glossed so that they looked like plumped pastries. "What are you doing here?" The *w*s in her speech sounded like *v*s and, to my untrained ear, she spoke her words like she had a mouth full of marbles.

She held a cream-colored envelope in one hand. She stepped her other foot out of the car and slowly walked a circle around me in her four-inch pumps, somehow avoiding the multitude of potholes.

Feeling like that question was typical of the people associated with the MacLaochs, I spit out, a little more harshly than needed, "Why? Is this MacLaoch land too?"

"Ooh, tut-tut," she said, coming to a stop in front of me and tapping my shoulder with the corner of the envelope. "No need to get upset. I was just asking vhy you are here, in this place, in Glentree." She looked around us, gesturing with the envelope.

There was something about this Eryka woman that set my teeth on edge, something about the way she spoke to me. As if I were a dolt or a small child and she were someone I should look up to and respect—all I wanted to do was knock her off her teeter-totter shoes into the muddy pothole behind her. She and Kelly were of one mind, it seemed—they both wanted the same thing. What it was, I couldn't put my finger on, but I knew for sure that anyone associated with Kelly was someone I wanted nothing to do with.

"Doing research." I said, exercising some patience.

"Mmmm," she said and dragged the envelope down my arm. "What kind of research?"

"Stop that." I batted the envelope away, sending it fluttering onto the soggy ground.

Eryka looked at it, then back to me. "What kind of research?"

"Family research. And if you'll excuse me, I need to get back to it." Patience thoroughly exercised, I walked off through the parking lot toward town.

The woman had me fired up for no apparent reason, other than her attitude and her association with Kelly. With everything that had happened yesterday, the day before that, and particularly last night, I was already nursing a sore mood and in no way ready to deal with her.

I heard Eryka's car; it pulled up next to me. I watched my reflection disappear as the glossy window rolled down.

Eryka looked me up and down, again. "I don't know what they see in you," she said disdainfully.

I held my hands up, frustrated. "What? What do you want from me?"

She shrugged. "Nothing." Then she nodded back toward the parking lot. "That letter? It's for you."

I stopped walking and watched as her car pulled away, the window rolling back up. I kept watching as the car picked up speed and disappeared around a corner before I went back to the parking lot and picked up the letter.

The envelope flap was embossed with the MacLaoch crest; the paper had gotten soggy from sitting on the ground and the adhesive gave no resistance as I lifted the flap and gingerly withdrew the wet contents.

While the ink had bled, making the once-black letters a purply-blue, the words were completely legible and their owner's signature unmistakable.

Ms. Nicole Baker ~
I formally request your presence at Castle Laoch,
at your earliest convenience.
Sincerely yours,
RJD MacLaoch

My stomach did an acrobatic flip and I felt a mild case of anxiety come over me. This was regarding the night before, no doubt. It seemed that I would be hand delivering my apology letter after all.

Fifteen

I arrived at the castle in the late afternoon with my letter in hand.

The front entrance to the castle was much more open, welcoming, and grand than the back door I'd barged through the other day. The front entry hall opened directly onto the carpeted staircase and I immediately recognized the airy second floor from my prior, hasty departure. I made my way to the massive oak reception counter and the two women behind it.

"Hi," I said, and paused, realizing I hadn't thought about what I was going to say. If I told them, "Your clan chief asked me to stop by before I leave town," they might think I was crazy. I assumed it would be like walking into the White House and saying the president had asked to see me.

"Hallo, 'ere to do a tour?" one of the two women said. She was an elderly woman in a cardigan with a Castle Laoch logo and a tartan skirt. Her partner at the desk was nearly identical.

"Not really, no," I said. "This might be an odd request, but your clan chief, Mr. Rowan MacLaoch, asked me to stop by."

Rather than the rebuff I expected, the taller woman said, "Oh, you must be the Ms. Baker he spoke of this morning. Yes, he is expecting you, though today he is at the administrative office down the road. I'll ring him and let him know you're here."

"Would you like to tour the castle whilst you wait?" the second woman asked while the other used the phone in the small room behind them. "We're closing in a bit, but you'd be welcome to roam. It could be a while before he gets home."

"Ah. Thanks, I'll do that," I said, thinking it was odd that she referred to the castle as the chief's home, as it seemed in a permanent state of being on display, and nowhere had I seen closed doors or personal affects.

I made a donation—larger than requested, hoping that a bit of that goodwill would come back to me—and set off toward the main floor.

The upper floor was divided in half by the grand staircase—to my right was the large, open sitting room the size of my apartment, and beyond it, the dark dungeon. My body gave an involuntarily shudder at the memory of the place, and I turned in the opposite direction.

I meandered through the rooms, reading the plaques and taking note of the history. The place had seen every generation of MacLaoch since they had arrived in town over eight hundred years before.

The last room was a large, circular one, its long, slatted windows letting in what light there was from the overcast day. In spite of the soft lighting, the room felt heavy. I was surrounded by artifacts, each one passed down through the clan and stored lovingly under glass. The ones I passed by the door dated from the early eleventh century. Ceremonial pewter quaiches, ram's-horn brushes, and goblets were identified with neatly typed cards set in black velvet. Some cards described the history of the piece in detail, others simply said, "brush, 1500 AD," or "silver tea set, 1650 AD."

There was something about the room that drew me in. It felt as if another person were in the empty room with me—as if I were back in my dream, the woman in it gently guiding me toward something. I made my way slowly to the back of the room, scanning the glass cases, reading each card, seeing if I remembered anything.

I tried to rationalize my thoughts—I must simply be having déjà vu.

I reached the final case, and found what I had been subconsciously looking for under glass and perched on the top shelf—small and placed between two larger artifacts, a simple gold ring. The *exact* gold ring from my dream, its Celtic twists on the band interlacing the clan crests and Scottish thistle.

My breath caught in my chest and I just stared. And stared.

Oh my, oh my god. The nicks and dings in the ring were where I remembered them. I put my hand to the glass, as if that simple action would cause the glass to give way, allowing me to hold the ring again. To place it on my finger and have it warm that place again.

Again? No. It would be for the first time.

And the last, I felt someone else say, yet I was completely alone.

The description style of the ring was different than those of the other artifacts in the room. I could see it in my mind's eye, even as I read the words:

With this ring, I thee wed . . .

One (1) gold—solid—ring; imprinted/engraved with MacLaoch Clan Crest, interspersed .15mm with thistle over wedding knot; 4.5mm diameter; 2mm band width. This ring is assumed to be the wedding band of the fabled Lady MacLaoch of Castle Laoch of the early 13th century. According to the legend, Lady MacLaoch became betrothed against the wish of her clan to that of a sea-going man by the name Minory. It is assumed that after her return to Castle Laoch, following the death of her betrothed, Lady MacLaoch placed the ring in a copper box and interred it in the lower sea wall. It was discovered during the 19th-century refurbishment of the decrepit wall . . .

The sun sank deeper in the sky while I stood entranced by the ring. I didn't hear the footsteps behind me, but I did feel the slow hum wake in my blood, telling me the current MacLaoch chief was standing right behind me. I looked up into the reflection of him watching me.

Without turning, I said softly, "This ring . . . " That was all that I could manage. As if saying the words out loud would render something important impossible.

"Aye. What is it about the ring?" the chief said from behind me, his voice barely audible, the two of us still like ancient statues, both having trouble finding our words.

I continued to stare at him, and he at me. The soft hum dissipated into a feeling of warmth and familiarity—had we done this before? No, but he had come unbidden into my dream the night before. The man on the beach who had clasped me so lovingly—I knew who he was. He was standing directly behind me, and if the reflection on the glass did not deceive me, he knew it too. But how, I could not fathom.

"The ring," I said, finding my voice again, though this time it was shaky. "Did this really once belong to Lady MacLaoch? The one the legend is about?"

"Aye, it did," he said, matching my tone. "But," he added, sounding, it seemed, incredulous, "how'd ye know tha'?"

I turned finally to look at him, no glass between us.

I'd say this for the MacLaoch chief—the way he was dressed then, I would not have mistaken him for anyone but the clan's chief. He was a man of impressive bearing, hands relaxed in the pockets of his tailored black slacks; the black sport coat he wore pulled snugly across his shoulders, flattening his light-blue, collared shirt.

I gave him a small smile in greeting. "I know that because I can read."

MacLaoch squinted at me. "Explain," he said, the mood shifting away from the metaphysical and back to the present.

I pointed into the glass case. "It says right here . . . " Again I lost my train of thought as I looked into the case. The card next to the ring just said Antique Ring. That was it. Nothing else.

I scoured the case. Perhaps the simple act of looking away had caused the card to fall into a nonexistent crack, or to spontaneously combust.

MacLaoch came up close behind me and looked over my shoulder into the case. "Ye were saying?" he said quietly.

"It was . . . there just a second ago . . . I'm pretty sure," I mumbled, baffled that I could have seen that text on my own.

MacLaoch leaned against the case next to me, close enough that I could feel the warmth of his body. "No. We have never put the true description of that ring anywhere, except with the insurance company."

Insurance company. The description I saw earlier had been detailed down to the millimeter, just like an insurance description.

And yet, there I was, shoulder to shoulder in another awkward situation with the MacLaoch chief. How would I explain that with any semblance of normalcy?

"I must have been mistaken, or remembered it from something similar, and made the connection." I gave a small wave, dismissing the whole thing. "You asked me to stop by? If it is in regards to the research I'm doing, or last night . . . " I trailed off as MacLaoch just watched me—as if he had a thousand questions for me as well.

"Come," he said, and strode from the room.

I took a deep breath. I was not excited about what I felt was coming next.

Sixteen

I followed the chief out of the artifacts room a short distance, then stopped as he opened a narrow door that he had to turn sideways to get through. The stairs leading upward were merely notches in the stone wall and only a bit wider than the door. MacLaoch seemed to simply disappear up into the stairwell and, after a moment's hesitation, I followed.

By no small feat, I was able to close the door behind me and nearly scaled the dark staircase as though I were climbing a rock wall. The room at the top was surprisingly open and bright; the floors were made of a rich hardwood and the walls were solid stone, though tapestries and large rugs covered most of the surfaces. A handsome wood desk with a computer workstation filled the center of the room; bookshelves anchored the far wall and the wall under the windows. The windows took up the entire wall to my left and, from where I stood, I could see out over the castle gardens. The space felt very much like it was MacLaoch's personal office. If I wasn't mistaken, behind the far door would be a kitchen—it was a push door, no knob—and the smaller of the two rooms to my left would be a bathroom and the other a master bedroom. This was the den of the MacLaoch chief, his home.

MacLaoch was pulling together papers on his desk and gestured me into a chair in front of him. I sunk into the plush leather chair as he handed me what looked to be some sort of official report.

The report was moderately thick, about half the size of my master's thesis. I automatically started skimming the report, thinking more about the note in my jacket pocket I had yet to give him. Then some text stopped me, refocused my attention fully on the report. I read back through the pages of the report, flipped again to the beginning. I read the title page thoroughly one more time for good measure. I was looking at the history of a man named Iain Eliphlet Minory.

"How?" I asked. "Is this from my records request through Deloris?" I heard the volume of my voice rise. I remembered distinctly that Deloris had received a phone call from the historian saying that the documentation that I held in my hands did *not* exist.

"Aye, our historian sends all requests tae do with the Minory and MacLaoch lineage though me. And since ye and I are well *acquainted*," he said, with more inflection than necessary, "there's no need tae have tae go through Deloris. Go on, read about your great-great-granddad." He sat on the edge of his desk.

My great-great-granddad. My mind repeated his words, each one landing like a lead weight in my lap. I read the title page yet again, and felt warming in my cheeks. I'd led the MacLaoch chief to believe that my family's spelling was exactly like that of the man in my hands and the one I'd read about in the letter from his uncle. No doubt the clan had the full history of this Iain; they probably even knew if he sat to pee. But, technically, he was *not* my ancestor—one little letter made sure of that, and all of this I had explained in the note I wrote to the chief. The one still in my pocket.

"This," I said, not knowing the best way to start, "isn't my great-great-granddaddy. You see, I had learned before I hiked over here the other day about the Minory and MacLaoch tale, and when you and I met, I was a little flustered with everything that had happened. I really didn't think I'd see you again, nor even fathomed that you were the chief of this clan, so I pronounced his name to my gain." I finished quickly and painfully.

MacLaoch became like stone. "Aye? And what is your great-great-granddad's name, if it's not Iain Eliphlet Minory?"

I had not thought that the chief's demeanor before had been warm and welcoming; in fact, I had felt the opposite. However, I was suddenly aware that there was a level of subzero possible from the man. I was suddenly out of favor—in the few moments of being together with the ring, we had brokered some trust and now, just as quickly, every ounce of it had been revoked.

I tried to speak, yet no words came out. I snapped my mouth shut but still felt foolish. I could see my research and all the goodwill of the clan and their historical documents getting closed off to me. Swallowing, I found a croak of a voice. "Iain Eliphlet Minary," I coughed, my voice scratchy with anxiety. "It's with an *a* not an *o*."

With each second that ticked by, I watched my research source closing up before my eyes. I realized I'd been clutching the document in my lap, and I forced myself to place it on the coffee table. Hands purposefully loose in my lap, I found when I looked back at MacLaoch something had happened with him. I couldn't be sure, but it seemed that the hard lines of his face and the stiffness in his posture had softened ever so slightly.

"Minary," he said, trying out the name as I had pronounced it. "With an *a*?" he asked.

"Yes."

He thought on this before saying, "This Iain Eliphlet spells his last name with the common spelling of an *o*, and I'll tell ye that this clan knows of each and every Minory that ever lived. If there was another Iain Eliphlet and he lived on this scrap of land, even if his was spelled with an *a*, I'd know of it. Before ye dismiss him as not being your great-great-granddad, have a look."

Hesitantly, I picked the report back up and started reading again. By the end of the report, I was glad this character possibly wasn't my ancestor. The history of this man was less of the quiet hero that I was hoping my Iain Eliphlet Minary would be and more of a rap sheet.

This Iain Eliphlet Minory was a brawler, a drunk, and a gambler. He lived in Merchant City within Glasgow for a bit—maybe under the guise of working to send money home to his wife, Marion Anne Campbell Minory, and her children, five to be exact, from her first marriage (she was a moderately wealthy widow when he married her). More likely he spent his paychecks down to the last cent. The report ended with the equivalent of a modern-day arrest warrant and then documents saying the authorities assumed that he had died.

"He was a busy man," I said under my breath, thinking that "busy" didn't quite cover it.

"Aye."

Despite the lack of great accomplishments by this Iain Eliphlet, there were a few dates and places in this man's history that were notable, and they didn't line up with that of what I knew of my Iain Eliphlet, his death being the biggest one.

"Well," I began, "there's a problem. This man died about twenty-five years before, and an Atlantic Ocean away from, the known death of the Iain Eliphlet I'm researching. So this is probably a strange coincidence of similar names, or possibly the first case of identity theft. This man might have taken the name of my ancestor to avoid his gambling debts, for example . . . " My words hung empty in the room.

"Ms. Baker, have ye done research before? I mean, before ye started with your family search."

I eyed him questioningly. "I have—quite a bit actually, for my graduate program and master's thesis. What are you implying?"

"I'm implying nothing, though I'm trying to understand why ye have just dismissed important research documentation as irrelevant due to dates of death—"

"Mr. MacLaoch—"

"Rowan."

"Mr. MacLaoch," I said, refusing to use his informal name—I was not feeling informal at the moment—"I have spent hundreds, thousands even, of research hours for my master's thesis, which was scientific research. Science tells me, and this is *basic*, that if a man is dead, he cannot take a wife and produce offspring. This applies to the entire animal kingdom, in fact."

"Aye, if he was dead," he said, folding his arms across his chest.

I just looked at him. "What do you mean *if*?" I asked.

"I can see tha' you are fact based and take written documentation to be true—I suspect this is from your schooling—but with historical documentation, Ms. Baker, ye have to expect tha' there will be some anomalies. Sometimes people will write what they *think* is the truth, but yet it is far from it."

"There are anomalies in science, I am not unfamiliar with them," I rebuked. "But what are you implying? That the man here in this report faked his death? What documentation do you have to prove that?"

"Ms. Baker, for a moment, pretend tha' ye are in nineteenth-century Scotland, Glasgow, no less—a bit of a rough-and-tumble place at the time—and then think about tha' man. Ye ha' no coin, ye are dead thirsty for drink, ye dinnae or cannae go home, and the law and every other knee-breaker ye owe money to is looking for ye. Now, imagine ye are hearing about a place called America where every man can own land and be free. What do ye think happened then?"

"I don't buy it. He faked his own death and slipped onto a boat headed to the Americas? He'd have to be on a ship manifest and if that was the case I would have found that in my research. I specifically searched ships' manifests before coming here."

"Aye, he would have had to come out of hiding at some point during his trip, I'll give ye tha', but, Ms. Baker, ye cannae assume tha' you have looked through *every* ship's manifest."

"No, I haven't, but I didn't need to, because someone else has done that research. There are dozens and dozens of archives that have all been painstakingly transcribed and put into electronic format for research purposes. If there was written documentation that existed, I would have found it. The only things I was able to uncover were his wedding certificate, birth certificate of his son—my great-grandfather—a property deed, and his death certificate. I will add, his marriage certificate is dated just a month after this Iain Eliphlet in your report *died*. It's not him."

"Weddings were performed regularly on ships heading to the Americas then."

"You are trying to stretch the truth for your gain. This man is not my ancestor."

"Ms. Baker, the similarity in the name is not without cause. It is the same man—he got married on the ship and got off in America a new man."

I just shook my head. "The dates are all off, and unless several of these clerks were having a bad day and forgot what date it was, there is no explanation for these two to be the same. They are not."

"The dates are off? Explain." He squinted as if trying to puzzle out why I was daft—which was annoying.

"Well, for one, if he didn't die in Glasgow, as you say, but rather took off as a stowaway in the cargo hold of some ship going to the Americas, the next date is the marriage. And no, I don't believe that he somehow miraculously fell in love with some woman and married her on the ship. *But* giving you the benefit of the doubt, if he didn't die, if he did fall in love and got married—"

"Love isn't necessary for marriage, Ms. Baker, but yes, please continue."

"Whatever," I said, dismissing his comment. "If he did get married just a couple weeks into his trip, it still doesn't line up with the birth of his first son. My great-grandfather would have to have been born almost three months premature at just six months after they landed."

"Or?" was all MacLaoch said.

"Or what? There is no or."

"Yes, there is an or, and ye are just not wanting to see it. For a moment, just one moment, do not think of all the numbers in a perfect world. Think of the numbers in the world tha' this Iain Eliphlet Minory lived in." He stressed that irritating point again, as if I weren't.

"He was still living in the real world, there are just simple facts about—"

"Ms. Baker," he said, interrupting me, "just *think*."

I was quiet and stared at him, hoping he could feel some of my contempt.

After a moment I said, "Still thinking. Though I'm thinking now about why you want these two ancestors to line up. Why is it you so desperately want them, want me, to be that descendant?"

"Ms. Baker, before ye embarrass yourself by assuming I want ye to be anyone other then who you are, let me lay it all out for ye: yer great-great-granddad, Iain Eliphlet Minory—so deep in his debts, with no love for his wife or her children—he fled to America. While on the ship, he met a woman and got her pregnant, then married her, most likely at the end of a gun barrel. Your great-granddad was born a nice healthy nine months later and the rest ye can map for yerself."

I sat there trying like mad to formulate an argument, something to prove him wrong. And yet I came up with nothing. It was simply another theory—one that I wanted so badly to be wrong because of his attitude, but not because of his argument alone.

"I think we'll have to agree to disagree on this point," I said to the impassive MacLaoch.

"Which point? Your great-great-granddad being the philanderer I present to you, rather than the saint ye envisioned?"

I clenched my jaw not be baited by him. Calmly, after swallowing my first retort, I said, "I think I'm done here." I stood, still holding the documents.

MacLaoch stood as well, but he turned and walked to the sideboard under the window and poured himself a whisky.

"Whisky?" he asked over his shoulder at me.

"No," I said, then remembered the letter in my pocket and quietly placed it on his desk, hoping he would see it after I had left. Left the country.

"There is just one more thing," he said turning from the window. "We need to discuss last night."

I really had no idea which part of the evening he wanted to discuss, but the low roll of anxiety in my belly said this was going to be even less fun.

"The charges ye laid against Kelly," he began, "I take them seriously. If someone from my clan or from outside of it lays a judgment against a clansmen, I meet it. And since ye did not stay so tha' I could talk with ye about them, I had to find out for myself." He took a sip of whisky, watching me over the rim of the tumbler.

"And?" I said, not feeling the love toward anyone right then.

"The pub has surveillance, and it's obvious that Kelly was extremely out of line. And because he was out of line, I'll ask if ye plan to press charges against him," he said flatly.

I closed my eyes and prayed for calm, not because of his question but because of what he had done to be able to ask it. "You watched surveillance video?" I opened my eyes and met his stare. "Was that to make sure I was telling the truth?"

"Ms. Baker." He paused, then continued, "I spoke to Kelly after ye left the pub and his take of the event was quite the opposite of yours. I had Johnny pull the feed to see for myself."

"What did the heir to the clan MacLaoch throne have to say?" I said bitterly as the last dregs of my self-imposed calm began to evaporate. "Did he mention anything about the discussion we were having?"

"Aye, if I remember, he said a few things—"

"So he told you that right before you showed up, I said to him, 'Kelly, your girlfriend is at the bar, and I don't want to fuck you.' Pardon my language, but that's what I said. And his response? 'That's not my girlfriend at the bar, and you can't be serious about not wanting to fuck me, not dressed like that.'" I felt the heat of that moment, the warmth of anger at being taken advantage of coloring my tone. "But you know all this, don't you? Because you watched the surveillance video, you saw what he did when I walked away. You saw him yank me back to him, you saw him grab my ass, and you saw him say something to me, which was, by the way, 'You don't leave until I say you do.'"

MacLaoch was silent. His knuckles went white as he gripped his tumbler. He set the glass down.

"What?" he asked.

I stared back at him and said softly, trying not to shout, "Oh, you heard me. Did you get your jollies, too, watching the video?" I was pissed, feeling like everything up until then had been the carrot to get me into his den and corner me about last night.

His eyes narrowed, and the hard edge of his jaw clenched and unclenched. "I turned off the video when ye walked away. I dinnae—" he said and stopped, his eyes blazing. "I dinnae see Kelly pull ye back, I am sorry. The question still stands: do ye wish tae press charges?" He spoke in a near hiss, his accent becoming stronger.

For sure, I wanted Kelly to pay, but I wanted him to pay in a little bit more of an old-fashioned way. Pressing charges, while a very American thing to do, wasn't really what we Bakers were brought up doing. You solved your issues one-on-one, and if you couldn't, you would have someone close to you do it for you. Say, for example, an older brother, or a father, an uncle, or a savage mother—take your pick.

"I'd really like for Kelly to learn that he can't treat women the way he treated me, and if he could learn that lesson soon and forcefully, I would be grateful. Should he ever see me again, he should know to keep his distance because if he ever touches me again, I will break his nose with my fist and his balls with my knee. This I promise. As for the charges," I said, thinking about how to phrase it, "right now, I won't press any."

MacLaoch had turned back to the windows, hands in his pockets. His reflection in the glass showed me he was still working up to a quiet fury. "Kelly will be *dealt* with."

The way he said it—that Kelly would be dealt with—made some small part of my being feel scared for Kelly. Kelly would no doubt be moved by whatever this MacLaoch chief had in mind for him. He would be punished.

Feeling like we were done, I looked down at the report in my hand on Iain Eliphlet, thinking I should say something, like "thank you," when MacLaoch spoke again.

"Ms. Baker," he said, turning to look at me, his flinty-blue eyes back to being impassive, belying nothing of what was on his mind. "One last thing." He went to his desk, pulled a file, and handed me a check.

I looked down at it, puzzled. It had his signature on it, made out to me, Nicole Baker, for an amount that made my head spin.

"Wha—?" I said, confused. "Why are you giving me money?" Before he could answer, I connected the two.

This was buyout money. It was keep-quiet money. It was we're-done-here money. "Oh-ho-ho. Oh no, you don't," I said and flicked the check back on his desk. "Keep your goddamn money." I tore the air open with my words, losing all fancy-pants pretense. His status no longer meant anything to me and any last bit of cordiality was lost, gone, burned.

I turned on my heel, dropped the documents—oh, precious history —onto the low table, and strode to the stairwell.

"Ms. Baker, stop, please."

I turned at the top of the stairs. "Why? So you can insult me some more? No, I think I'll head to the constable's station—or whatever you people call the police here in your bass-ackwards little town—and file a report against your bastard of a cousin." I stabbed the air with my finger. "From there, I'll press charges so fast it'll make your prestigious head spin. And if you have the town constable in your pocket, I'll go a little route called freedom of the press and see how you like the world knowing how your clan does things up here."

MacLaoch's jaw was working overtime as I yelled, but in a very controlled voice he said, "Keep your voice down, please."

"Why? Oh right, the reputation of one large clan is everything compared to that of one lowly tourist?"

His eyes narrowed and he took two strides toward me before I added hastily, "I closed the downstairs door."

"Good." He stopped. Then he gestured to the chairs. "Please sit, Ms. Baker, so we can discuss this. I am not paying ye off—"

"Explain," I said.

"Please. Sit. Down."

I wanted to say no and march my righteous ass down those stairs while flipping him the bird, but I refrained. I glared at him as I made my way back to the chairs and sat across from him. He took up his position again, leaning back against his desk, arms folded, staring me down.

"It's no' a payoff. Ye said ye would not be pressing charges against Kelly and yet ye have been used unkindly by him. I'm no' so daft as to think tha' ye will walk away from Scotland, from MacLaoch lands, with a pleasurable mind right now. I have no other way to ease the discomfort Kelly has done tae ye other than monetarily."

I scoffed at him. "These documents would have been more than enough, and don't tell me that you aren't paying me off. You've written me a check for thousands of dollars! How'd you even come up with that number? The average cost of what I'd get going to the tabloids with this information?"

"No. It's—" he managed before I cut him off.

"Oh my god," I said. I'm not the fastest person on the planet with numerical puzzles, but I'm no slouch. The day I flew into Scotland, the exchange rate was point-six-something to the British pound, so with that rough estimate, I calculated the check amount into dollars. Nearly ten thousand US dollars. That was a lot of money, which made me think of the last time I said that phrase. I was sitting in my apartment checking the limit on my credit card before I bought my plane ticket and room at Will and Carol's. The limit, which was ten thousand exactly.

"Not a payoff? Not a payoff?" I stood again—I couldn't argue sitting down. "This check covers all my debt! How the hell did you get that information?" I nearly screamed.

"Ms. Baker, please be calm. I am doing no such thing," he said, his voice straining for control.

"Oh, really? So if it's not a payoff, it's more like insurance, isn't it?" I growled, "It's insurance that I won't press charges on the clan's golden child after he molested me in a bar."

That struck a nerve in the chief.

He came off the desk and got within an inch of my face, his Scots accent thick. "No," he said forcefully, "I have told ye it's no'. Either ye take tha' check or ye don't, Ms. Baker, but dinnae trifle with me."

We stood glaring at each other. I could feel the fire in my veins at the fight that was rolling between us. Then, as might happen when a song-bird flutters, singing, through the battlefield, the mood suddenly changed. Something happened, something else entirely. It was as if we had not been screaming at each other—all the tension, raised tempers, and hot-blooded fight turned into something carnal. MacLaoch and I stood face-to-face, and I watched as the emotion slipped suddenly from undeniable anger to an attraction that would cause screaming of another kind.

My breath caught in my throat as his gaze traveled from my eyes, slowly down my face, and back up, his intent crystal clear.

Only then did I take a step back.

"I come from a proud family, and in no way would any of us ever take money for something like this. Ever." I walked over to his desk, took the check, and tore it into tiny pieces and dropped them like rain out of the palm of my hand onto his desk. "Instead, we call these favors. And now you owe me one."

Seventeen

I got to the top of the stairs before he spoke.

"I'm sorry," he said quietly from behind me. "For giving ye the money."

If he had asked me to stop, I wouldn't have. Even if he had begged, I would not have stopped, but that statement stopped me dead in my tracks.

I turned around slowly, deliberately. "What?" I asked.

"I dinnae mean to insult ye." He watched me, then said, "Here," and pulled an envelope from his inner jacket pocket and held it out to me.

The envelope was a crimson, blue, green, and black plaid that shimmered. Half of me wanted to walk over just to flick it to the floor and proceed on the path I had been hell-bent on not a moment before. Yet, the other half wanted to know what it was.

Reluctantly, I walked over to him and took the envelope. "What is this?" I asked, as MacLaoch walked back to his desk.

He shed his sport coat and laid it over the back of his office chair. He looked tired, weary even. As if what I held in my hand was going to take all of his remaining energy. Picking up his whisky, he sat heavily into one of the leather chairs and began rolling up his sleeves as he spoke. "Every four years the entire clan assembles for a gathering and week-long fundraiser. This is taking place next week. In light of your research, ye might like to attend. If so, ye may, as my guest of honor."

I wasn't sure that round three of our fight, or round one of something else, wouldn't happen, but my curiosity was winning over the heat between us.

I slid open the envelope and pulled out its matching invitation. It was an invitation to attend the entire week's worth of festivities, which they referred to as the Gathering—from an opening gala Monday evening to a closing gala on Friday evening. A list of activities was available upon my request—I was to RSVP.

"Who will be there?" I asked, thinking about my research once again.

"Members of the MacLaoch clan from all over the world. Some have spent a good lot of their spare time researching family documents and clan history. They will want tae hear of your research—as well ye might learn something from them—even on Minary," he said, knowing exactly what I had been thinking.

I nodded in response and looked down at the invitation. I realized that it had been signed R. MacLaoch.

"Who else are you inviting?" I asked.

He thought about it for a moment. "We've invited all the clan members and some others, but I expect only two hundred will come."

"That's quite a few people, but not what I was asking. Who else have you personally invited? I'm assuming we'll be grouped together, sit at the same table or something."

MacLaoch watched the amber liquid in his glass as he slowly turned it back and forth. It slid like oil around the inside, making wide legs that slithered back down to pool at the base.

"No one. And it's a yes or no question, Ms. Baker—yes, ye will attend, or no, ye will not." His gaze traveled from his glass to meet my eyes.

While his look was fierce and unwavering, I could feel how guarded he was. This was a man who did not trust easily and in general seemed to be a lone wolf, yet here I was, with a personal invitation to attend an event that only happened once every four years. And if I wasn't mistaken, he was asking me to be his date, and feared my answer.

The thought of being his date after all that had just transpired between us hit me strangely and I had the undeniable urge to laugh.

I couldn't help but ask directly, "Are you asking me to be your date?"

"Ms. Baker, yes or no. And why do ye have a look as if ye are to burst out laughing?" he asked, his expression darkening.

"Honestly? You have to be kidding me. After all that just happened, you are asking me to be your date?"

It seemed from his look that it was this moment that he had been dreading. "Yes."

I just kept looking at him, calmness restored, my mood sobered by his honesty. He wanted me to go with him.

"Is this so that you can keep an eye on me? The whole 'keep your friends close but your enemies closer' thing?"

"Ms. Baker," he said, standing and closing the distance between us. "Is this something ye are interested in? Do you want to go?" he asked softly.

I looked back down at the invite—ignoring the closeness of his body—the scrolled writing, the elegant invite, his personal signature on the bottom all said I'd never get a chance like this again.

"Yeah, I do, I'm just trying to figure out if I should be on my guard waiting for you to push me off a cliff."

MacLaoch grinned, and it lit up his face with an emotion I was sure was rare for him. I felt an odd, lovely sensation in the pit of my stomach.

"I promise no' to do tha' until after the final gala," he said softly.

Eighteen

We moved the conversation back to the comfort of the plush leather chairs, discussing the details for the next week. He would pick me up at seven in the evening on Monday, unless I wanted to attend the clan meeting prior—to which I said no. I liked him, but not enough to pledge my soul to the clan; he conceded that this was fair. I learned that there would be a hunt, lawn games, and other happenings, and if I was interested, he could get me a sign-up list. Everything was costume optional, and not being one to reenact or play make-believe on such a grand scale, I declined the offer—though the hunt sounded interesting, even if it was labeled a male-only activity.

The afternoon faded outside the windows. Through the discussion, one thing kept bugging me. I decided, after a long pause, that I had to clarify at least one part of our brief history together.

"There is one thing that I'm not sure I understand—and it doesn't have to do with the Gathering next week," I plunged in. "Why did you really offer me that money? Were you serious?"

"Aye, tha'," he said. He considered his response for a while, then answered, "I'll repeat what I said earlier, it was no' a payoff. The fact tha' ye dinnae take it tells me something of ye. Ye are a prideful woman, Ms.

Baker, and I'll no' fault ye for it." He said it seriously, as if he were commending me.

"Why that amount? That cannot be a coincidence—it is the same amount as my, well, of what I owe to various places."

MacLaoch raised is eyebrows at me. "Ms. Baker, I assure ye it isnae based on anything other than what I assumed ye paid for your plane ticket here, the cost of your rented car, and how much your stay with Will and Carol is costing ye. No more than tha'."

I looked at him with my own questioning brow lift. "You obviously pay too much for things—it didn't cost me nearly that much. Do you do that for everyone Kelly manhandles?"

"Ms. Baker, as I have said before, if someone raises an issue with one of my clansmen, I rise to meet it. I dinnae hand out money to everyone who has a complaint, but would I do it for a woman whose ancestor is Iain Eliphlet Minory? The descendant of the man my ancestor loved? Who cursed me—and all the chiefs before me—because of what we'd done tae him? Oh aye, I'd do everything I could to make sure she's happy."

Nineteen

MacLaoch smiled, a little curve at one corner of his mouth, and stood. "We still have some light left, Ms. Baker—will ye permit me to show ye the castle gardens?"

I looked out the window then back to him. "Ah, yes. That'd be nice," I said, feeling the formality of his request.

I followed the MacLaoch chief, who still carried his whisky in one hand, out to the many gardens that took up the rear of the estate. Lush forestland blended into the symmetry of the gardens, the distinction between them made soft and subtle in the profusion of flowers and the rigid structure of bordering hedges. We entered the first garden by walking along a low stone bridge over a narrow river.

The river reminded me of the placard that I'd read the day I'd met him. "Where is the river that Lady MacLaoch supposedly filled with her tears of joy?" I asked.

MacLaoch smirked, pointing down with his whisky hand. "This one." He leaned against the railing.

"All this water from one person, huh?" I asked, my sarcasm meeting his smirk.

"Aye, well, it was carved by her tears but is fed now by the rains."

"Yes, but I think the question is not how it was formed but rather by what kind of tears."

"And what are your thoughts on it?" he asked and took a small sip of whisky, watching me closely.

I was quiet for a moment. Had he been anyone else, I would have simply let him know the plaque was full of bull. But instead I employed my manners. "Well, for starters, I'm curious to know who wrote the story on that plaque you display here, in your *home*."

MacLaoch watched me for a moment longer and then said, "No, I think ye should tell me yer opinion first. I can see tha' ye think one thing yet ye say something else. I'd prefer ye to be frank."

"I appreciate that, but I was raised to act like a lady, and what I was going to say was not very ladylike." I added, looking down at the running water below us, "My mother would drop in a dead faint if she heard me say that. So, who were they?"

"But your mother is no' here," he said encouragingly.

"And yet, I will not give in." I said, leaning on the rail as well.

"Would ye believe it was just a bunch of little old ladies who made tha' plaque?"

I laughed out loud. "No, I wouldn't. It seems to have too much of an ulterior motive for it to be from innocent little old ladies."

"Och, come now. I dinnae say they were innocent."

"You're serious? They were little old ladies? Who was feeding them the information? Because someone must have."

"Ye dinnae believe the story? It's from little old ladies, though, who would ne'er lie."

"You," I said and shook my head, "are trying to goad me into saying what I almost said earlier. Which was, I don't believe that the plaque was made with the full truth in mind. Rather, it was made to make the MacLaochs look good."

"Och, ye pain me," MacLaoch said, lifting his free hand to his chest in mock consternation. "Created to make us look good? As the laird of the MacLaochs, I'm deeply offended by your words, Ms. Baker. How could ye?"

"Ha ha," I said, looking over at him. "You should be offended. Mock me, but those tears Lady MacLaoch cried were in joy? Right, and my name is Queen Elizabeth."

"All right, your majesty, and why would they not be? She was extremely grateful her family came to her rescue. Joyous even."

"Keep it up," I said, "and I'll have to put on my muck boots."

I came to the first of the gardens, which was creatively named Circular Garden. Low box hedges outlined the garden's curved edges, inside a maze of brightly colored annuals. The path followed the arching perimeter.

The gravel crunched behind me as the chief caught up. "Muck boots?" he asked. "Oh aye, ye think I'm full of . . . well now, that wasn't very ladylike of ye."

"You don't believe the plaque any more than I do, admit it."

"Now, ye know I cannae confirm or deny tha'."

"But what I'm wondering is why, when it's obvious that you don't believe the version of the story that's written on it, you keep it up."

"The three old ladies that made it are still alive, and out of respect to them, I keep it up," he said sincerely.

I looked at him as we neared the exit to the garden. "Noble," I said. "So you aren't completely heartless." I smiled, thoroughly enjoying the ease that settled between us.

"No," he said, quietly looking from my smile to my eyes. "No, not completely heartless."

"Yes, well," I said to no one and about nothing; my heart squeezed as I walked out of the garden and into an open field. The path curved upward. The view was breathtaking; reddish greens meandered down to distant cliffs and the moody color of the sea beyond.

"This way, Ms. Baker," MacLaoch said, behind me.

I turned to find him a few paces up the gravel trail. "Wait, what garden is this?" I asked.

"Garden?" he said, coming to stand next to me. "What garden?"

"This area here—is this not one of the gardens?"

MacLaoch's eyes scanned the area. "This bit of land here? It's soon to be another garden, but the head gardener hasn't gotten to it yet. How'd ye know of it?"

"You mean this right here, this wilderness area? Are you saying that this isn't a managed natural area?" I asked in disbelief. "There must be hundreds of native species in here."

MacLaoch watched me. "How do ye know what are native?"

"School. I did a piece in undergrad for my botany course on the native species of the British Isles. There," I said, and pointed.

"Aye, Scots thistle, I know that one, and heather," he said. "But they are only two. They don't make an entire wilderness, Ms. Baker."

"Right, but," I said, stepping off the trail and into the open space. It was filled with many plants I could not identify, but those I could, I called out: "A type of wood sedge," I said, pointing, "and . . . *Primula veris,* cowslip . . . and yarrow. Oh! *Odezia atrata,* a chimney sweeper." I crouched down to get a better look at the charcoal colored moth motionless on a blade of sedge several paces in. The white blush on the tips of its wings confirmed my identification.

I felt the MacLaoch chief come up behind me. "If ye had this space, if this land was all yours, what would ye do with it?"

I looked up over my shoulder at him. A sea breeze had pushed its way over the land. It moved through the low-lying greenery and tossed my hair gently about.

"Hypothetically?" I asked.

"Aye. Hypothetically."

Without pause I said, "Preserve it. Study it." I looked over the land again—it seemed pristine and untouched by humans. The forest stopped in the distance, the thickly girthed, ancient trees giving way to the dense undergrowth of shrubs and low-lying bushes, deep green and ruby with lush spring growth. "It looks like this land has never been cleared for grazing, which means that the ecosystem here must be the closest thing to native. Meaning, you probably have some very rare and possibly endangered species in here. It's just amazing," I said, and stood.

"Then tha' is what I'll do with it," MacLaoch said.

"What?" I said, surprised. "I thought that was a hypothetical question you asked me."

"So ye don't think that's what should be done with this land?" he asked.

"No, it is, but . . . " I said, momentarily at a loss for words. I remembered the original plans. "What about your gardener? He has plans for this land—you can't be serious about taking my advice!"

MacLaoch simply shrugged one shoulder. "Ye have the education and have studied the natural plants of Scotland—why would I argue with ye?"

"Yes, but—"

"Ms. Baker, if my head gardener looked at a piece of land as ye just did, I'd let him do as he pleased as well. Ye have a passion for this land, so why should I deny ye? Now, there is the walled garden I think ye should see, and then my driver will escort ye back to the inn."

He surprised me with his generosity. The authoritarian way he had said it, I had no doubt that that piece of land would indeed be saved for study.

"Who will you have study it? Will you have it open to a local university?" I asked as we walked along, and then, just because I couldn't resist, I added, "Or will it be open to only those of MacLaoch bloodlines?"

"Ah, good question. I think it'll be open to everyone," he said honestly, and then added, "except for Minorys."

"That seems reasonable," I mocked.

"Aye, and *Minarys*, even though they dinnae exist."

"Ha ha," I said dryly, coming around to that line of argument once more. "Then how do you explain me?"

"Oh," he said, as a low rumble of a laugh escaped him, "that, Ms. Baker, is a loaded question."

"Oh, really?" I asked. "And how is that? And you can't use the line of argument you used earlier, about Iain Eliphlet getting on a ship and—"

"Ms. Baker," the chief interrupted. He lifted the latch on the next garden, letting us into another breathtaking place.

The garden's walls rose up, creating a private oasis. Walks covered in climbing roses anchored the central area—the outer areas were filled with splashing fountains and lush plantings.

I temporarily forgot about our conversation. "If your head gardener made this, maybe you should let him do what he wants with the wilderness area."

"Come now, Ms. Baker, are ye having second thoughts?" he said as his eyes seemed to find a not-so-secret joy in my awe.

"No. I just think that he's incredibly talented." Forgetting myself, I wondered aloud, "He's not single, is he?"

MacLaoch stopped suddenly and turned, laughing. "Ye know, he is. Shall I introduce ye to him?"

"I was just kidding," I said, catching up to him and walking past, my cheeks warm. My eyes fixated on anything but the chief's smiling face.

"Aye," he said, following. "Ye know what Freud said about jokes?"

"No," I called over my shoulder and came to rest by a man-made bubbling brook, the bench invitingly open next to it.

"I dinnae know either, but it has to do with jokes being versions of the truth." He took a seat on the bench, one arm stretched across the back. "Though I should warn ye, he's not been with a woman for some time—since his wife died. I think he's fairly lonely, so he'll not object to meetin' ye."

"Very funny," I said. "Sounds like he's over twice my age, so no thanks."

"Aye, so now ye discriminate against age?"

"Only when death is an immediate concern."

"Aye, so ye are looking for someone younger."

"I—" I caught myself. "Wow. You're good, you nearly had me distracted enough to forget that we were arguing about the Minory-Minary scenario. I still think you are wrong." I continued walking.

Entering the quiet and deep shade of a rose-entwined walkway, MacLaoch caught up to me. "Your Iain Eliphlet changed his name by a simple letter either by mistake or by purposeful intent to avoid the law."

I turned to face him as he approached, closing the distance between us, his whisky gone, in the shadowy dusk, the roses fragrant and blooming above us, dangling lazily from their perch. "Mr. MacLaoch—"

"Rowan," he said softly.

"Rowan," I said, feeling the pleasant weight of his first name, very aware of his broad warmth filling the air directly in front of me, "if it was as simple as you say it was, then why didn't your clan find him?"

"Luck or chance. A simple oversight."

"Or perhaps," I said, making my point, "that single letter makes all the difference in the world. A single letter changes things like the words *read* into *reed*, the action of understanding the written word into a plant. Or in this case, two different families."

"Let me ask ye this, how is the research on Minary going? Finding much?" he asked.

"Not yet, but—"

"Because it doesn't exist beyond Iain Eliphlet, does it?" he said, cutting me off again.

"That's not true. I haven't explored all the avenues yet," I said, not wanting to divulge that it was indeed going nowhere.

"Stubborn, aren't ye?"

"Not as stubborn as you."

"I've had a few more years of practice than ye," he said, good-naturedly.

"More like a decade more," I mumbled, thinking he sorely misinterpreted my age.

"Decade? Ye think I'm a decade older than ye?" he asked, genuinely surprised.

"Oh, sorry," I said, "is it more like two?" It had gotten so dark I could barely see the outline of his face.

"Och! Two? Now ye really ha' wounded me. Unless ye are just on the other side of eighteen."

"I'm much older than eighteen—add ten years and you have my age. Which makes you what I thought you were, thirty-eight."

"Aye, 'tis close. But no, I'm—"

"Older?" I asked.

MacLaoch just laughed, a low chuckle in the darkness that told me I was wrong, that he was indeed younger. But how much younger, I didn't know—he acted and moved like a man who had experienced the world, who had seen the underbelly of life and knew how to deal with it. He carried the responsibilities of a man twice his years, and no doubt had the stories to prove them. *The MacDonagh brothers would agree,* I thought.

"Come." I felt his hand slide down my arm until it clasped my own. As it had been the night before, the chief's hand was warm and strong, and it steered me left and right along the pitch-black path back to the castle. We barely spoke, each of us no doubt concentrating on not tripping. Really, I was mostly occupied by the skin-to-skin contact I had with the chief. My body hummed with a light energy, excitement induced by the simple touch of clasped hands.

We emerged from the darkness of the gardens and crossed the river of tears. A car idled on the road opposite us. MacLaoch released my hand, but not before his fingers trailed along my palm. At the car, he opened the back door for me. "Have a good evening, Ms. Baker. Until Monday."

"Thank you," I said and settled into the backseat.

On the drive out, I noticed the research documents that MacLaoch had given me earlier sat on the seat next to me, as did the invitation. I placed them on my lap and replayed the later portion of the evening with him, the wilderness area, and the playful banter that seemed such a contrast to the man I had first met. I thought of him holding my hand once more—to feel the heat against my skin made me light-headed. The car turned out onto the main road and sporadic street lamps cast a sulfuric orange glow against the night. Suddenly, a large wall broke the forest up to my left. A wall that looked just like that of the garden we'd last been in.

"Excuse me?" I said to the driver. "Is there more than one walled garden here?"

"Aye, no, miss. Jus' the Walled Garden there."

"Oh," I said, "and is it accessible to this road?"

"Aye, yes, miss. Tha' is how the head gardener gets supplies to an' from tha' garden."

My mind rolled over the simple fact that the garden was easily accessible to the main and well-lit road.

I smiled to myself. Of course, if the MacLaoch chief had asked his driver to meet us here, he wouldn't have had an excuse to hold my hand all the way back to the castle.

Twenty

The next day at breakfast, Carol presented me, with a squeal, with invitations from two high-end dress stores to come in and "sample" their dress collections. I wasn't quite sure what that meant, but I knew I didn't have the money for whatever it was.

"What I really need is a good secondhand store or something like that," I told her.

You'd think I had said pigs could fly by the look Carol gave me.

"Och, do ye really think he'd have you buy your own dress? For gosh sakes, child, those two stores have credit with the MacLaoch estate, I'm sure o' it. Ye will not be needing tae spend a dime." She beamed with pride. It seemed that this gala was just as big a deal as I had assumed.

Even though I needed dresses, jewels, and the lot, I couldn't—not with my gigantic pride—allow the MacLaoch to drop that kind of cash on me, someone he'd just met. But I had only one alternative.

The call, I knew, was not going to be short if my mother answered the phone. It was late in South Carolina and the gods were with me when my father answered the phone. Sighing with relief, I dove into the standard pleasantries about my trip and how things were going back home before I sprung my money question on him.

"Oh. Sure." He sounded a little confused. "Well, how much do you need? A couple hundred?" Then I heard my mother in the background.

"Is that your son on the phone? Is he asking for money again? You tell that boy—"

I could hear my father cover the mouthpiece a bit. "No, it's your daughter."

"Cole?" The other line picked up, and I was talking to my mom. "Why do you need money, Nicole Ransome? Are you hurt? Do you have a place to stay?" Then she said to my father, "Honey, boot up your computer and find your daughter a place to stay. Cole, where are you?"

"Mother, stop, I'm fine. I just need money for some dresses."

A big, fat, giant pause. I could almost see them swapping glances on the other side of the Atlantic. Their ever-casual jeans-loving daughter wanted dresses.

"Let me explain," I said, then did. In detail, so they'd understand the full ramifications if I went in any of the clothes I'd brought with me.

"How much do you need?" my mom asked.

"Well . . . the exchange rate isn't in my favor and nice things here are really spendy, so with shoes, jewelry, and two dresses, I need at least a thousand dollars."

I held my breath.

"Honey. No. How much do you *need*, n-e-e-d."

"Mother, really, I can't do with less. It won't go very far. The MacLaochs have offered to pay," I said, as if there had been more than one MacLaoch who had offered to pay. "But I think—"

"Nicole Ransome Baker," my mother admonished, "you are going as your family's representative, and you will not humiliate us. You will get the best damn dress you can find—and hell, buy three! I can't believe my Cole is going to a ball!"

"Gala," I corrected.

"Oooh, Cole! This is wonderful, I wish I could be there!" my mother squealed, obviously forgetting herself.

"We will transfer a thousand, Cole—" my father tried to say.

"If you really think that a thousand will be enough, with this exchange rate and the quality of the dress she will need, I'm divorcing you," my mother interrupted with a threat she had lobbed often at him in their thirty-year marriage.

I heard him sigh. "Well, I know when I've been out numbered. Cole, my dear, I love you, have fun, and whatever price your mother comes up with will be fine. Even if we don't actually have the money, I'm sure your mother will find it." He signed off.

"Well, so how much do you need?" my mother asked.

I ended the call a bit later, after much time spent talking my mother down—she was ready to re-mortgage the house and farm for me.

With money transferred, I set out to peruse the selections at the two shops I'd received invitations from. The invites were standard-looking, preprinted invitations—the only personal touch was my name across the top. I envisioned that everyone on the fund-raiser gala list had received one.

Downtown Glentree started a block away from Will and Carol's, continued down the hill for five more, and extended back up the hill behind the B&B for another five. I made my way, avoiding puddles, to the first shop. Its front window was well lit, and the two older women I could see through it were in what I was fast learning was the standard professional wear for Scottish women in the service industry: wool skirt, cardigan, and no-nonsense pumps. Though the one woman had a bit more flair: she was wearing a blouse.

As I walked in, they were heatedly discussing something that had just happened and seemed to involve two mannequins that were naked. Both women held garments in their hands.

"Hi there," I called when they didn't acknowledge me.

They both jumped in surprise. "Oh, for heaven's sake!" the one in the blouse said, gripping her chest.

She turned from me and spat at her associate, "Purple, Lily. Really, don't even think of putting the brown one up." She turned back to me. "I'm so sorry about that! Welcome, are ye seeking a special dress for a special occasion, dear?"

"Yes, I am, I received your invitation this morning and thought I would come by to see what you have."

At this, her eyes got big and she swallowed hard. "Not for the gala on Monday, I hope," she said with false cheerfulness and shot her cohort, who'd glanced our way, a knowing look.

"It is. Is there a problem with that?" I asked, feeling a little put out that these women, who had invited me, were less than welcoming.

"Oh, well . . . " the first woman said, and looked behind me.

Following her gaze, I realized what I had missed when I first walked in. The shop was smallish, the racks were spare, and all the mannequins were nude. The only two dresses left had shoulder pads and excessive amounts of sequins and lace.

"Oh," I said, "is this all you have?"

"Ah, yes. I'm so sorry—you are just a few moments too late. A lady just came in and bought—"

"Bought," the other woman spat. "Used store credit, is more like it!"

"Yes. Right, credit—hush, Mabel. A large purchase. Well, actually, all of our most fashionable dresses in"—she paused, looking around—"every size."

Store credit? I thought. *It must have been thousands of dollars worth of dresses if the empty space is any indication of how many were taken.*

From their reaction, it seemed that the women, too, felt that they had been robbed. They said they could order me a dress on express shipment. With another shop still to see, I let them know I'd think about it.

It was starting to drizzle as I rounded the corner and worked my way across the street and through the middle of the town square to the next shop. A farmers market was going on, and people were milling about on the cobblestones, chatting and haggling good-naturedly over produce and baked goods. It was quaint and felt so good that I wished I could walk this way every day of my life. I imagined walking to this square to buy groceries, then back to some stone house overlooking Glentree Bay, where I'd settle in after a day's work.

Work. It seemed that I had not thought about work since I started researching my ancestry. Yet my lack of finances made it obvious that I would need to be thinking of it soon. I always knew that my career would have to do with the natural world, working with my hands and teaching people about it, but now I wanted to add researching my family history to my plan, too. And then a solution, one I hadn't considered until now, came to mind: the Castle Laoch wilderness. The area that the MacLaoch chief said he would set aside for research. I mentally went through the wilderness again, and then what a day of cataloging plants in that natural area would be like—the cool breeze off the harbor, the team of research students carefully setting up plots, identifying and counting the various species.

I was deep in my daydream as I exited the square and crossed the street. As I stepped up onto the opposite sidewalk, I stopped, jarred back into reality. Directly ahead of me was the dark car of the Ice Empress of Doom, parked at the curb with its trunk open, which was full of shopping bags. As I stood there, I watched as Eryka emerged from a store with more bags loaded up on each arm; she shoved them into the trunk like they were stolen goods. She noticed me just as she slammed the trunk shut and gave me a grin that made my blood freeze. She slid into the backseat, and motored away.

Everything fell into place. I didn't need to go into the store to see that it would be devoid of any clothes that I'd like to wear to the gala. I didn't need to witness the clerks arguing to know that they had lost over half of their inventory. And I didn't need to go in there to know that she'd put it all on Clan MacLaoch credit.

Right then, as if on queue, the sky unloaded and, without an umbrella, I started the walk back to the B&B.

Twenty-One

Mood getting fouler by the moment, I splashed through puddles back up the hill. The shop was on a side street I had not walked before, and I probably wouldn't have noticed it if the blinds hadn't ratcheted open just as I walked by, startling me.

Its windows were brightly lit and filled with bolts of fabric. Reds, silken golds, creamy greens, all like gems in the gloom of my day. I stopped and stared. Just as I reached for the door, it opened. A large women grabbed me by the arm and yanked me into the shop.

"What are you doing out there with no umbrella? Come, you dry off in here. I see you like bright fabric—look from inside and stay dry."

She spoke in an accent that I tried to place. The large woman was shorter than me. She had a beautiful, youthful face but was probably closer to middle age, and had a matronly way about her. She wore a dark-green suit and an apron whose pockets overflowed with bobbins, pins, thread, and needles. She was like a walking sewing machine. I realized when she returned from the back of the shop with a towel that she had the same pure, stark features, and blond hair—with strikingly contrasting brows and lashes—as Eryka. Only this woman looked happy.

"Thank you." I took the towel from her and proceeded to dry off.

"You need dress, eh?"

"How'd you know I needed a dress?" I said, impressed.

"Well. You stop. You look. I make dresses—beautiful dresses." She pointed to the sign that was nearly buried in the bolts of colorful fabrics, threads, and embellishments that crammed the shop. The sign said: Dressmaker.

"I, ah, missed that. Your fabrics are beautiful, but unfortunately I need a dress very quickly, and while I'd love to have one in every fabric in here, I'm afraid it's not possible."

She snorted. "You need it for tonight? Because that is the only timeline I cannot meet, and even then I could create something." She looked me up and down as though I were a prized animal she was about to bid on at auction. "I can do tonight—what you need?"

"Tonight?" I said, shocked. "You're kidding, right?"

"You challenge me?"

"No, I . . . It's just . . . No, I don't need a dress for tonight. I need two, one for Monday night and the other for Friday. I just thought, the way my day has been going, that would be impossible."

A smile broke across her features, as if I'd just handed her a present. "Gute! I am Wanda. I will be your dressmaker." I would learn that *good* was the word in Wanda's English vocabulary that was most heavily accented.

We shook hands, but I was not convinced. "Yes, well, I need a gala-worthy dress," I said, eyeing her.

Her brows drew together, and she observed me shrewdly. "Gala? You go to the opening gala for the Gathering on Monday for the MacLaochs?"

"Yes, ma'am. So I need something very nice," I said, giving her an equal stare in return.

"You challenge me. I understand." She nodded her head once, turned and picked up a large binder, and plopped the massive thing in my hands. "I accept your challenge. But you look like you have been, how you Americans, say? Ah, yes. Put through ringer. Look," she said, jabbing at the binder.

In it were photos of dresses, loads of dresses. Everything from evening gowns worthy of a Hollywood red carpet to simple summer frocks.

She must have seen my favorable expression because she grabbed back the book. "Gute! We begin!" She put the book down and came back at me and yanked off my jacket. "We get look at you," she said and started pulling and tucking at my clothes, sizing me up for real. "Now, who is competition?"

"Competition? I've, I'm . . . " I stuttered. We weren't good, after all —she thought I was starring in some sort of beauty pageant.

She stopped prodding and looked at me. "Yes. You are beautiful, and well sized, for sure." She pulled out a pad of paper and started taking notes. "Hourglass, for sure." She yanked a tape measure from her apron, walked to the front of the store, pulled the blinds, and locked the door. "Take sweater off—I must know exact measurements." She stood waiting. I obliged and she said, taking the measuring tape to me, "Now, back to it. Who is our competition?"

"You mean the other dresses that will be there? Jeez, I really don't know. This is the first time I'm going, so I have no clue *who* will be there, much less what kind of dresses they'll have on."

This was unsatisfactory to Wanda and as she jotted down numbers on her pad, she tried again, "No. Let me see how to explain. Who are you looking better than? I know this, I know what direction to go with style. Your body, color skin, eyes? I put wet rag on you, you beautiful. I make you dress that will take you from beautiful to goddess. Now, what goddess are you? When you walk into that room, what people think? I want to fuck her?"

I blinked at Wanda, not really sure I'd really heard her say that. But she just plowed on.

"I want to dance with her? I want to get to know her because she is full of money? I make you dress that evoke feeling, not just look pretty. Pretty you can buy in store down the street."

I snorted. "Not anymore I can't. They've all been bought out."

"Explain." She stopped taking measurements to devote all her scrutiny to my predicament.

"Well, just this morning, a woman whom I've . . . encountered," I said, feeling that *encountered* was severely understating what my meetups with Eryka had been, "here in Glentree, for some reason bought all the clothes that I could have possibly worn from both dress stores." It sounded crazy, saying it out loud. I let that one sit.

Wanda eyed me, thinking. "No one has money like that I know. Who is she? What her name? What she look like?"

"Oh, she doesn't have the money; she put it on store credit—"

"Eryka Aase. I know her. She is from Iceland, like me." She shook her head at this as if disgusted.

Wanda continued, "She came here and demand I make her a dress. She think because we are of the same nation she can demand me to make her dress for free." I thought for a moment there that she was going to spit on the floor. "I tell her get out. Don't come back, and don't tell people she is from Iceland—she is shame to its people."

"Whoa. When was this?" I asked.

"Months ago. But, I do not care." She studied me again. "Why she hate you? She hate me because I deny her my famous dress. You. You American and you be here how long?"

"In Glentree? I saw her the second night I was here, and she's hated me ever since. Or if not hate, she's definitely having a joyous time trying to make me unhappy." Again I felt this understated what Eryka was trying to do to me.

"Why?"

I shrugged, knowing I didn't have an answer for her.

"No! This will not do! Think!"

Crap, I thought.

"Did you pay for your ticket to the fund-raiser?"

"No. I don't—"

"Who is your date?"

I rolled my eyes, because I could answer that. "Rowan MacLaoch."

"The MacLaoch chief?"

"That's the one." I sighed.

What she said next I could never have anticipated. "The MacLaoch chief has never taken a date. Not in all the years I have been here, and I was here many years before he left for Royal Air Force. Even when his uncle lived, God rest his soul." She crossed herself.

"Never?" I asked, completely shocked. "Ever?"

"Never. And if there is one thing Eryka wants most, is the MacLaoch name." She scoffed, "You are the competition! I am surprised Eryka has not driven you from town. Gute, very gute!" she said gleefully, and clapped. "The chief's date! We will make Eryka eat her hat for want to be you!"

Oh god, I thought. Wanda was going to get me killed.

"Now," she said, jotting one more thing on her pad before she tucked it into her apron, "what is your name?"

"Cole. Nicole Baker." I said.

Wanda stuck out her hand. "Well, Cole"—and we shook—"it is gute to meet you."

"Likewise. I just hope I stay alive long enough to wear one of your dresses," I said, trying humor.

"Oh! Don't worry about Eryka—she's harmless." She waved me off and stood back analyzing me again. "Monday . . . not enough time do bonings. We do slip dress. Yes, slip. We will line it, too, cut it on bias, yes. Yes. Very gute. Hug your curves and move like water over your body. Water, yes. We do," she said, looked around, and made a beeline for a wall of silks. The color she pulled was at first glance white, but when I looked at a yard of it, it was as if snow and moss had gotten together and had babies. I was drawn to it, and then touching it—it felt like oil against my skin, silken and slippery.

"*Oh my.* What is this made of?" I asked.

Wanda patted my hand. "No need to know that dear, but know that when I am done with it, it will move like water over your gold skin. Rowan MacLaoch will want to watch it fall to the floor to see if it will puddle at your feet."

Oh my, I thought, and shivered.

"And Eryka will eat her hat! Gute!"

Twenty-Two

I left a few moments later after giving all my measurements, even shoe size—Wanda ushered me out so she could get to work right away. I felt great heading back to the B&B—not only had I secured a dress but Eryka had actually helped me get a dress that had the potential to be better than one I could have bought ready-made. For the second time, Eryka had inadvertently helped me out.

Suddenly, I realized I was squinting. The sun was finally out! It was lighting rainbows on the clearing horizon, the rain moving off into the mountains.

The sun did miraculous things to the isle, reflecting off the water on the sidewalks, the plants, the streets, the roofs—everything sparkled. I carried my camera with me for such occasions and, in an instant, I was putting it to good use.

I spent the better part of the afternoon capturing the sun and the shimmering, late-spring greenery. When late afternoon came, I grabbed a sandwich lunch from the local grocer and headed to the twenty-six-mile long trail I had read about in the book of walks. The trail began at Castle Laoch, and while I had hiked that part just the other day, when I first met Rowan, I was planning to head the other way today.

I meandered along the trail, reading interpretive signs relating significant geological and historical information, taking pictures, and looking for a park bench to enjoy my late lunch. The trail was packed with the young, the old, and their dogs. It seemed forever before I found a bench.

The low afternoon sun shone brightly above the horizon, giving the sky and sea a shimmering warmth. I sat and ate with glee; I was almost alone in this perfection. I found myself curious about Rowan, what kind of a man he was underneath it all and why hadn't he ever brought a date—or a friend, even—to what seemed like a very important event. The answer came swimming up from my memory.

The letter I had read back at the administrative building—it was addressed to this man whom I was starting to see more as a person, an everyday person and not just the powerful figurehead of the MacLaoch clan. That letter had been written as Rowan's uncle lay dying and knew that he needed to impart knowledge to his heir before he passed. *Do not love*, were his uncle's words—then Lady MacLaoch can take from you nothing that you do not have.

Then there was me.

Maybe I was truly just a guest to the clan chief—it made sense, especially for my research purposes and definitely for his. He was sure that I was the descendant of the Minory line and would no doubt want to have my family line mapped. If not him, I was sure his historian wouldn't let me leave without getting that information.

But, what if—and before my mind could cut off the silly thought, I thought it—*he liked me more than as just a guest?*

And with that thought, I shoved the last of my sandwich into my mouth, sucking remnant jam off my fingers.

Movement caught my eye to the right. Someone had been leaning on a boulder in the distance below the trail, and now was moving. As the figure made his way toward me I recognized the gait and stride, sure-footed and confident.

Rowan's face was a mixture of humor and trying to be serious as he approached, as if he'd heard a great dirty joke and wanted desperately to share it, but knew he shouldn't. "I would pay a king's ransom to know what tha' last thought was tha' crossed your mind, Cole."

The use of my shortened name caught me by surprise, and in the same breath made my heart ridiculously joyous that he felt we were on first-name basis. Of course—I argued sarcastically with the feeling—how could we not be, after he bribed me with money then asked me to be his date?

Ignoring his question, because I sure wasn't going to answer that, I said, "Actually, my middle name is Ransome. As in, I am worth a king's ransom." I leaned back against the bench, folding my arms across my chest and regarding him right back. I was hoping that this would buy me some time, as I was racing to figure out how long he had been watching me, what I had been thinking, and had it really shown on my face?

"Nicole Ransome Baker," he said, trying out my middle name felt on his tongue.

I tried an aristocratic slow blink and arched brows. "And that's spelled with an *e*, as in R-a-n-s-o-m-e," I said nasally.

This got a full-wattage smile from the chief. "Then I would buy you from your kin just to know what it was tha' ye were thinking just a moment ago."

My breathing failed me. I coughed and said, "I, it, was nothing of importance." Unhelpfully, I remembered the night before, his fingers dragging along the palm of my hand.

"Aye," he said, sitting carefully at the farthest end of the bench. "And yet . . . " He watched me, his eyes begging me to say, *And yet what?*

"How long were you watching me?" I asked instead, hoping to turn the tables.

"I saw ye a little after ye sat down. Ye didn't see me?" he asked.

"No." I said, "I was a bit wrapped up in my own thoughts, I guess."

"So, ye really won't tell me about what ye were thinking?"

This was a side of the chief I found incredibly distracting. He was insanely good with mixing my mind up, muddling it with simple smiles and what I could gather was flirtation. It was such a contrast to the man he seemed to be the majority of the time.

"I don't see how it could possibly seem interesting, just from my facial expression." Then realized I left the door wide open to continue the subject. What was wrong with me?

"Ye didn't see your face," he said slyly.

"And I'm not sure how you did at that distance!" I said, exasperated, gesturing at the rock he'd been hidden on.

"I have very good eyes, and your face was most expressive at the end of your sandwich. Especially that . . . last . . . morsel . . . "

I remembered that last taste, sucking Nutella and jam from my fingers, thinking about love and what I meant to the MacLaoch chief. I felt the heat rise in my cheeks, and the chief's miss-nothing, know-all gaze on them.

The low rumble of contained laughter had me looking over at him. "What?" I demanded.

"Ye just thought it again." His eyes narrowed to slits, daring me to say no when the truth was so obvious on my pale skin.

I just shrugged. "My thoughts are my own. If you really want to know them, I'm afraid all you'll be able to do is guess at them."

I gave myself a mental kick—I'd done it again.

MacLaoch leaned in, an arm across the back of the bench. "How many guesses?"

Oh god, this was not happening.

"None." I said and changed the subject. "Isn't this weather nice?"

He was not distracted. "The last time I saw ye blush like that," he dragged out his words, "ye were thinking about asking my gardener on a date."

I cursed under my breath and closed my eyes as another flush of heat gave me away.

Heart thumping in my chest I turned to defend my pink cheeks and instantly regretted it. Rowan looked directly into my soul, and those metallic eyes saw everything, down to the most delicate portion of my inner self. He didn't hide his thoughts either, and they were telling me several things.

I laughed—I couldn't help myself, spurred by a moment of clarity. "Not only does my skin give me away, so does my face, apparently. But before you think that I was removing your clothes in my mind while I removed jam and Nutella from my fingers," I said bluntly, "I'll have you know that I was just curious as to how a man like you has stayed single for so long. Many people have said that you've never had a wife or girlfriend, and of course there are a lot of assumptions and rumors flying about with you taking me as your date. I was merely weighing them as I polished off my sandwich. My very innocent sandwich."

The smile faltered on Rowan's face as if clean, cold water had doused him. He closed up, the remnants of his smile faded, and he leaned back to face the ocean, slowly and silently retreating back into himself.

I may have won that round, but I couldn't help but feel like an ass.

"How well do ye know of the Lady MacLaoch legend, besides what we spoke of last night?" he asked me after a while, almost as if he had been debating the pros and cons of that question and where he planned to go with it.

"Well, I'd say I know the basics. I've read the version at Castle Laoch, and I think on some level we agree that's a biased version of the story. The only other version I've heard is the one the MacDonagh brothers told me. The way they tell it, Lady MacLaoch left Castle Laoch on her own with the Minory, then there was a battle of some sort where the Minory, her betrothed, was killed violently. She returned to Castle Laoch, wept a river of tears—as we discussed yesterday—cursed her father on her deathbed for killing her betrothed, and the curse continues to hang over the clan." I surmised from his face that this version was the one he believed. "Is it close?"

"Aye, close," he said. "Her pain is very well known as one of heart-break, no' disappointment in a late rescue."

"Do you believe in the curse? I mean, do you feel that *you* are cursed?"

MacLaoch weighed my question and asked one in return. "Have you ever been in love, Ms. Baker?" MacLaoch looked not at me but out at the ocean, leaning forward, elbows resting on his knees with his hands clasped.

"I've—" I started, and then stopped. "Really and truly in love with someone?" The personal nature of his question caught me by surprise, yet the way he held himself, closed up and cold, said that this was not a romantic moment.

"Aye."

"Have you?" I held my breath. Odds were one in ten that this clan chief would tell me the truth.

He quietly studied the horizon.

It was a while before he responded, so long I wasn't sure he would.

"No," he said. "Not in the way ye think, but I had a life I loved many years ago, and from the instant I inherited the seat as clan chief, I lost it all. My father, or rather the man who raised me as a son, the man whose footsteps I follow as laird and chief of the MacLaochs, died a painful and slow death. One tha' he blamed on the curse." He paused, then reluctantly continued, "I used to be a fighter pilot in the Royal Air Force and the instant my predecessor's last breath left his body—making me the thirty-fourth chief—my wings and the closest thing I've had to a brother were taken from me."

He turned, giving me a rueful smirk. "I think tha' each person makes the bed he lies in, but mine, no matter how well I make it, will always have a thorn. The eternal reminder from Lady MacLaoch tha' she has not forgotten—and tha' I cannot either. So ye ask why is it tha' I've kept single for so long? I'll be honest, it's fear. Fear tha' I will lose yet another person I love."

The sun delved deeper in the afternoon sky.

"I'm sorry," was all I could think to say.

"I don't need yer pity, Ms. Baker—I'm simply trying to tell ye tha' while ye have just run across this fairy tale, as ye may see it, we here have lived with it our whole lives."

"I didn't say sorry out of pity—"

"Does not matter. The reason I'm telling ye all this is tha' tomorrow you will meet people who believe tha' there is no reason for making their own plans for their lives because the curse will come as a death sentence once they or their children step into my shoes. They will not take lightly the news tha' ye are a Minary and possibly the descendant of Iain Eliphlet Minory—and they won't care tha' it's one letter different."

It was as if that massive brick wall had come shuddering down between us again. Rowan was a private man, and I could respect that, but I didn't want him thinking for another moment that I pitied him.

"I appreciate your warning," I said and then added, "Rowan, I don't pity you. It's more like admiration. You aren't hiding under a rock waiting to be beaten again. You've risen to the challenge and met it head on. But you can't really believe that you have no hand in your own destiny, that everything is decided by this legend."

This earned a small tug at the corner of his mouth. "I may have been raised here, spoon-fed the history of our clan, but I've spent the better parts of my life strapped into a cockpit doing twice the speed of sound over nations all over this world. I know tha' I guide my own destiny, Ms. Baker—but I'll live my life with a heavy dose of caution, if ye don't mind."

"That's fair, but easy for you to say as a MacLaoch," I said, feeling the need to lighten the mood. "From what you said earlier, I'm scared about how tomorrow will go—I'm not sure you've decided not to throw me in the dungeons after all. It sounds like you'll be feeding me to the lions."

I stood and gathered my things. Rowan stood as well, and we started the journey back. "What does the clan have in place for a plan once you do find a Minory?" I asked.

"Dinnae know, actually," he said as he kept pace with me, hands safely in his pockets. "I suppose no one has thought much beyond them knowing how to remove the curse."

"Or what if the other version of the legend is correct, that Lady MacLaoch was heartbroken over her lost love and not over her horrible ordeal? Then, isn't she supposed to remove the curse once the clan chief has walked in her shoes or some such?"

"Details." He flicked his hand. "We cannae be bothered with them." He looked over at me, amusement lighting in his eyes once more.

"Ha ha, very funny. But really, people won't be expecting me to lift curses tomorrow night, will they?"

"Well now," MacLaoch said, and stopped walking. "Have ye just admitted tha' your great-great-granddad is Iain Eliphlet Minory?"

"I. No, I . . ." I stumbled, feeling caught in my words.

"Admit it." He folded his arms across his chest, staring me down with a wolfish grin. "Ye just did, anyway."

"I didn't mean me, but everyone else seems to think the names are the same—*I* don't think I should be lifting curses tomorrow, but others might not understand the complex details of the *a* versus the *o*."

"Aye, and ye shouldn't either."

"Whatever," I said, and continued walking.

Rowan kept up with me, chuckling softly under his breath. We continued down the trail. *Was he going to walk me all the way home?*

"So," I said, "what is it that you do for work?"

"Do?" He gave me a questioning look.

"Well yeah, I'm not sure what exactly a chief does day-to-day for work, or if it's a full-time job or . . . " I said, feeling the cultural divide distinctly.

"Och, well, I suppose ye could say I'm a businessman. I run the entire MacLaoch estate."

"Oh, everything?"

"Everything, from settling small farming skirmishes, to seeking more funding for our schools and town schemes."

"Schemes?"

"Aye, ye call them programs or projects in the States."

"Oh, and apparently everything goes by you for approval?" I said, thinking of the research documents he'd given me yesterday.

"Aye, everything. Well, most everything. My staff is able to take care of the small daily bits. It's no' a luxury estate tha' I can have a staff of a couple hundred; there are less than fifty in the peak season and now, with the gala, over a hundred, the majority temporary help."

"Ah," I said, "that would explain why you were out for a walk. Trying to clear your head?"

"Aye, I walk the pastures and swim the loch when the walls get a bit stuffy, if ye know what I mean."

"I do. So, I take it the gathering and fundraising activities are getting a bit overwhelming?"

"There have been a few rough patches, but no, it's going as well as can be expected for an event we've been doing for centuries. Only this year, one of my staff purchased over £100,000 worth of dresses for it," he said simply. "On the estate's credit."

"Wow," I said, shocked anew—that number was close to twice that in US dollars. "Why'd she do that? Couldn't make up her mind on which one to get?"

"That is exactly what she said. I wish I could say she is just a silly little thing—"

"—but Eryka Aase is a nasty little thing," I finished for him.

"Aye, how did ye know?" he asked darkly.

"Ah, how do I explain this?" I felt like I was walking on eggshells. "Eryka and I have built something of a quick history since I've arrived. It started the other night at the bar. Just today I was looking for a dress for the Gathering and all I got was empty dress stores. I rounded the corner on the last one to see her stuffing her trunk full of clothes."

MacLaoch was silent, absorbing all that I had said. "Ye met her the night that ye met Kelly? The night he pawed ye at the pub?"

I made a guttural sound of disgust. "Yes, that night."

MacLaoch let out a string of words that was far from English.

"What?" I asked and then, thinking better of it, said. "Never mind. It sounds like I don't really want to know what you said."

He just shook his head. "Aye, I didn't say it before because I didn't think it mattered, but her version of tha' night was exactly like Kelly's."

"Ugh. I don't understand people like that," I said, and I really didn't. "You know what would be a great punishment for Kelly—in case you need ideas? Make him wear a sweater that says, 'My name is Kelly, stay away from me and my blond friend.'"

MacLaoch snorted, looking over at me, "Ye know, ye are funny when ye are like this."

I gave him a snarky look. "Thanks, I guess."

"You have a way about ye," he said, continuing without my encouragement, "very different from what I've seen women do, which is brood about it and get weepy. Ye, though. I dinnae know." He let his words roll, unformed, between us.

"Go on, say it. Don't forget we're well *acquainted*," I said, using the word he'd said to me the other day.

To my surprise, he did. "Aye well, ye have a way about ye, good-natured, when ye want," he said, thinking about it. "Though I have to say that despite all tha', ye are a Minory, and that lot are legendary aggressors. Come to think of it, I was in grave danger yesterday when I insulted ye—"

"Which time?" I asked innocently, knowing he probably meant when he offered me money—it was the only time I'd really been steamed with him.

"If ye dinnae remember I'll no' be reminding ye," he said, and actually looked relieved.

"The bribe, you mean?"

"Och," he said, disgusted with himself, it seemed. "Aye, tha'. And it wasn't a bribe."

"I'll not be forgetting that moment anytime soon," I said. Then added, "Because you owe me one."

"Aye, well," he said, "I'm just glad to still be alive, ye being a Minory and all. Hell hath no fury, aye?"

"Like a woman mythologized?" I finished for him and laughed. "The clan chief of MacLaoch scared? I doubt it."

MacLaoch smiled over at me "Deathly afraid."

"But we still don't understand why Eryka loathes me," I said, coming back around to the point at hand. "Are she and Kelly dating?" I asked.

"Dating? No."

The implications of what Kelly and Eryka *were* doing hung in the air between us, neither of us wanting to mention that imagery.

"Now tha' I know it's ye that she's aiming at," he continued, "I think I have some idea on why she's set her sights on ye."

"Really? Enlighten me."

"Eryka's a jealous woman—" he said and broke off the thought as if checking himself.

"And?"

He was silent for a bit and then said, "Ye have what she wants."

I thought about that. I have what she wants. What did I have?

"What do you mean I have what she wants? Being American? Not having a job, because that's certainly not perfect. Curly hair?"

MacLaoch didn't respond right away. I could feel the wall being built, once again, between us—building itself brick by brick.

"Doesn't matter anyhow. She's not in my employ anymore."

"You fired her?"

"Aye, I did."

"Oh."

We were quiet the rest of the way back to Carol and Will's, each of us immersed in internal dialogues. Mine was very much on the hamster wheel of: *He fired Eryka? What did he mean, I have what she wants, and should I be sure to look over my shoulder more often?*

He, I had no doubt, was concerned about how much he had shared with me and was admonishing himself for all that he had divulged.

Rowan spoke again as we came to a stop at the B&B's stoop. "Were ye able to get a dress for tomorrow?"

"I did. I'm actually getting one made at the dress shop down the way from here."

"Is that with Wanda?" he asked. Small towns made the guessing easy.

"Yes, it is. Have you seen anything she's done?"

"Aye, I've heard she's quite good."

"Yes," I said as I fished my key out of my pocket. "The fabrics she has there are incredible, better than anything I'd be able to get from the dress shops. In a way, Eryka helped me out there."

"Aye, I should have recommended her to ye . . . " he said.

"Don't worry about it," I said in a rush, awkwardness replacing the ease we'd had between us not so long ago. "The dress she's making me for tomorrow night is amazing. Wanda described it best—she said that you will be amazed because it'll move like water against my skin and puddle around my ankles when it comes off." I realized, too late, what I had just said. Aloud. I did not check his reaction. "Goodnight!" I rushed into the B&B, slamming the door behind me and leaping the stairs two at a time.

In my room, I threw my keys on the bed, light still off and just stood, then pinched the bridge of my nose in disbelief.

I crept to the window, staying in the shadows, and looked down to the front door. Rowan was standing there, hands in his pockets, face tilted up at the second floor. Then, slowly, a grin broke out on his face; he turned from the door and took his time walking down the sidewalk back to Castle Laoch.

Twenty-Three

Monday arrived and the butterflies in my stomach almost made me lose my breakfast on the way to Wanda's dress shop. Not only was I about to try on a dress hand made for me and that I would wear at a gala that night, but I'd realized that morning, thanks to Carol's squeals about it, that I had no shoes and no jewelry besides my simple gold bangles. And even if everything superficial somehow turned out just dandy, I was walking into some big stuff tonight: the research opportunity of a lifetime, a very public date with a very public official and, not to mention, a centuries-old curse.

"Gute! You are here! Here is your dress!" Wanda exclaimed.

I instantly forgot all the worries I'd carried into her shop with me.

"It's. It's. Whoa."

The dress hung simply on a hanger on a coatrack in the middle of the small shop, but as I closed the door behind me a faint draft caught the edge of the dress and it moved like liquid.

"Try, try!"

Wanda locked the door, pulled the drapes, and changed the door sign to say Closed. I tried on the dress and held my breath.

"Oh," I breathed out.

The dress *moved*, whispering in harmony with the creamy gold of my skin. My copper curls showed off the subtle highlights in the icy green. I'd never felt so beautiful in my life—the dress literally floated against my curves like, yes, oil against water. The straps were gauzy, so they looked like tiny wings and finished the otherworldly feeling of the dress. Wanda hadn't been kidding—I had no doubt that when I took the dress off, it would pool like water at my feet. I just hoped Rowan didn't think that when he saw me.

Wanda nodded, beaming at me. "Gute, very gute. Now, the finishing touches," she said and held out a vintage white fur stole and silver shoes.

After trying on the dress for fit, I spent the rest of the day under Wanda's watchful eye. Turned out that Wanda was the oldest of ten sisters and as much a wizard with hair and makeup as she was with cloth. At a quarter until seven, there was a rap on the door. Wanda left me to put on my shoes, and I took one last look at myself in the mirror as I did so. My red-stained lips were Wanda's final accent for my ensemble—she said that she wanted people to hear what I had to say. Or at least look like they were listening.

When I stood up and looked to the door, my butterflies fluttered back in full force.

Up until this moment, I realized, I had been walking on the outside of Scottish culture. Only there, standing at the front of the shop, was true Scotland in my world.

The MacLaoch chief stood tall in his formal clan regalia. Extra fabric from his kilt draped over his shoulder; there was a decorative knife at his calf, and at his waist, a fur pouch. The silver brooch that secured the red tartan to his black evening coat at his shoulder matched the one on the waist bag, both emblazoned with the clan crest.

"Hi," I said, realizing that I had just raked him head to toe with my eyes. His expression was one of a man trying to hold and catch his breath at the same time.

"Good evening Ms. Baker," he said quietly.

Wanda stood between us beaming—then, realizing I hadn't moved, came over to usher me to him. She propelled us both out the door with exclamations that she had work to do for my next dress.

Rowan helped me into the dark chauffeured car waiting outside the dress shop and slid in after me.

"God help me, I cannae imagine what the next one will look like. I'm not sure I can take it," he mumbled as we got under way.

"What?" I asked, not sure that I'd heard him correctly.

"Nothing. Ye look well this evening, Ms. Baker," he revised.

"Thank you," I said, still taking in the full ensemble of his attire. "You look nice, too—though I have to say it's the first time I've been out with a man in a skirt," I said and smiled, waiting for the dirty look that was sure to follow.

Rowan cut his glance over to me. "Skirt? Oh aye, you're having a laugh," he said, and looked away.

"That I am. Really though, I've never seen a full evening suit with a kilt." I touched a finger to the woolen fabric. "Seems like I should be wearing a tartan and not mink." Realizing I was touching his thigh, I snatched my hand back and instead worked my nervous fingers in the large fluff of my stole, the fur moving under my breath as I looked down at it.

"I think you will be excused. You will not disappoint for sure." Then, as if just remembering something, he said, "Though I had thought to bring you something." He lifted a black felt box that had been camouflaged on the black leather seat between us in the darkened cab and opened it.

"Those had better be on loan or cubic zirconium," I choked out. The necklace was a cascade of diamond lace dripping into a single teardrop-shaped stone the size of my thumb. The earrings were two more tears.

"Turn around."

"You're kidding," I said, but did, pulling my hair out of the way.

As soon as the weight of the stones was around my neck and safely secured, there was no doubt they were real. I touched them, and my fingers warmed.

I turned to face him. "Rowan," I said softly, "please tell me these are rented."

"Why?" he said, and placed a large drop at my ear. I was no help.

"Because, these are worth millions!" I whispered, exasperated.

Who the hell gave diamonds to a woman on their first date?

"No, Cole," he said. The single syllable of my name was infused with the weight and emotion of what he was giving me. "These are not worth a thing." And he fastened the other drop at my other ear. Rowan's fingers ran warm along my jaw, tracing, memorizing. "They are priceless." He looked at my lips, then back into my eyes. Slowly, I felt him shift, his fingers stronger against my chin, encouraging.

Just then, the back door of the car swung open and the driver announced our arrival.

Reality poured over me like ice water splashed in my face. I hadn't heard the car come to a stop, much less known we had arrived.

Twenty-Four

Rowan kept me at his elbow as he worked the grand marble ballroom, and I was one part glad for his constant presence and one part uneasy that I couldn't just escape without notice. It was comforting that he guided me through the intricacies of meeting the other clansmen, him murmuring under his breath who they were and what they did for work before we actually approached them to shake hands. What made me uneasy was that everyone seemed to know my name before I said it, and when those from the older generations addressed me, they called me Lady Minory with a bow and a kiss to my hand.

These greetings made Rowan's arm under my hand stiffen. "It's Ms. Baker," he said each time in a clipped voice before moving us along.

As we got moments to ourselves here and there, Rowan explained to me that, earlier in the day, at the initial Gathering meeting, Clive the clan historian had something fresh to share in his opening speech. A Minory had been discovered.

That Minory was me.

I felt a chill ripple through me as we moved through the room; I really was like a lamb who had been invited into a den of lions. The head of which would either protect me or feed me to them as dinner, I still wasn't sure.

After a while MacLaoch said, under his breath, "There he is. Come, Ms. Baker, there is someone I think you will be fond of meeting."

Dr. Edwin Peabody was a short man with glasses, thinning brown hair and, I'd learn quickly, an infectious attitude. He stood with his hands clasped behind him, rocking softly back and forth, observing the room at large until he saw us approaching from the other side of the dance floor, and then he smiled broadly.

"Oh-ho-ho! This is the fabled Ms. Nicole!" he said and gave my hand a vigorous shake.

"It's fabled now?" I said, smiling back at him. I glanced at Rowan; he was grimacing.

"Dr. Peabody is a professor with an American university—Vassar, is it?" Rowan asked.

"Yes, yes, but please just call me Ed."

My curiosity was certainly piqued. "What do you teach?"

I felt Rowan turn as someone grabbed his attention on his other side.

"Oh, nothing of consequence," Ed said, waving his hand. "My passion is in what I don't teach or, rather, what I wish I could be teaching: paranormal science."

"But I'm sure you could be allowed to teach paranormal sciences at Vassar," I said encouragingly.

"Oh yes, surely if I put my mind to it, though I teach microbiology and unfortunately do so quite well enough that I'm unable to do much else. But alas! My hobby, or encore career, as my wife has started calling it, is the study of the metaphysical, and most recently my research has been on my clan. This clan," he said, his eyes gleaming with excitement.

I smiled back at him, guessing at what was making him glow. "I take it that you are studying the family curse?" I noted that Rowan was still engaged.

"Why yes! And it's extremely fascinating!"

"So what part of it are you studying, exactly?"

"Energy!"

"Energy? As in, metaphysical energy?"

"Yes! First, are you familiar with the concept that energy is neither created nor destroyed?" he asked, launching immediately into a subject he was obviously passionate about.

"Yes, somewhere in my six years of postsecondary, I believe I took a physics course. Energy is merely transferred?"

"Well . . . " he said, hesitating, "yes and no, but for this purpose let's say yes. In the case of metaphysical energy, it is essentially the energy left of—oh, I suppose I should ask if you are devout in any religion?"

"As in, a devout something or other who wouldn't believe in the supernatural?"

"Ah, yes."

"No, I am not, Dr. Peabody."

"Please, call me Ed."

I smiled. "Alright Ed, please continue."

And he did.

"Every being, when it dies, leaves its mark. An energy fingerprint, if you will—one that, over time, becomes consumed by life and the tangled web of energy consumption through birth and death."

"Wait, I don't follow you. Energy consumption through birth and death? What do you mean?"

"You see, as human beings, we are full of energy, potential and kinetic; it goes down into the molecular structure of our selves, beyond the cells. We are, in some circles of opinion, just manifestations of energy."

"Oh. OK . . . "

"So when things die, since energy is neither created nor destroyed, some of that energy is left behind and some of *that* energy isn't consumed again by life."

"Consumed again by life?"

"Think of a stag that falls dead in the forest of old age. His body degrades through time as mold and fungus and bugs consume him. Those then feed the soil when they die or defecate, pardon the description. Plants then consume the nutrients in the soil, animals feed upon those plants, and so on. The energy is passed on through the cycle of life and death. But there is residual energy that cannot be consumed, and that energy is what makes the metaphysical imprint. Energy like that which makes up the waves in the mind or, as some refer to it, the soul."

"Oh. I see," I said, and more or less, I did.

"So my work in researching the legend of Lady MacLaoch and the Minory seafarer has been most fascinating," Ed said. "I did quite of bit of other metaphysical energy research in the United States before I began our clan curse research. About ten years ago, a friend of mine who led rather hokey ghost tours around town had an actual energy meter. He accompanied me on some of my early grave searches. It was then that we discovered, well, I discovered, that when people die they leave dissipated energy markers." Ed was still smiling. "My friend, to my surprise—and his too, perhaps—discovered that his energy meter actually worked. So, it is most fortunate that you are here!" Ed clapped his hands.

I couldn't help myself—I rolled my eyes. "You can't be serious." I had been hoping that a man of science wouldn't be interested in dragging me into the curse.

"I get that quite a bit! And yes, I am! You see, Rowan has been most kind to us—my family and I are his clansmen, after all—and has allowed me to meter him."

"Really? *That* Rowan?" I turned and located the chief across the room with a tumbler of whisky in his hand, in conversation with two older men.

"It was odd," Ed continued as though he hadn't heard me, "because he is carrying metaphysical energy beyond the meter range I had expected."

When he didn't explain further, I asked what he meant.

"Well, from the age of the legend, I'd calculated that the energy fingerprint would be low. Lady MacLaoch watched the violent death of her betrothed a millennium ago. But Rowan was off the meter."

"But what does that even mean?" I whispered, as people danced in front of us, swirling tartan and silk flickering our view of the chief across the ballroom floor.

"I, too, wondered if there might be some deep meaning," Ed said, rocking back on his heels, "that would be exciting. But of course, I put my serious mind to it, and it probably just means that he was in close proximity to someone who died, and died violently."

I sucked in air and turned back to Ed, expecting him to suddenly laugh and tell me he was joking. He did not. "As in, he killed someone violently?"

"No, not necessarily, but he has *seen* someone die by violence, and since he's a man who has served on clandestine missions for queen and country, I've no doubt where he has seen it."

I nodded. Of course. That made sense—perfect, logical sense—and I remembered Rowan mentioning to me that he had in fact lost a friend he considered a brother. "Did you ask him about it?" I asked.

"I did. I'm afraid I wasn't so composed about it. I was quite sure I was going to see one number, and so when I saw another, I more or less accused him of something quite violent. I'm embarrassed when I look back on it, but Rowan was quite at ease about my outburst—I suspect now that he knew what my meter was going to do before I did."

"Wow," I sighed. "I'm not sure that's what he was hoping we'd end up talking about when he said I'd be interested in meeting you."

Ed's own outward energy lowered, and I heard his sober professorial voice. "Yes, I'm sure he was thinking that I'd share my theories on what we could likely expect from the modern-day Minory . . . "

"My family name was Minary, though," I said, heading off that thought at the pass. I was sure by then that I'd never know about my Minary heritage while waist deep in Minory lore.

He waved my protest off as though it were a fly. "Yes, one-letter difference. I heard that argument—our chief lobbied hard in your defense this morning after Clive spoke." He laughed at the memory. "I dare say Clive thought that those moments when he was retelling the story of finding you and how you fit into the legend were his last. Clive said, 'With her return, our chief is truly saved,' and Rowan stood." Ed clapped his hands to indicate something speeding away. "Clive skittered like a field mouse off the podium then!"

He sobered as soon as he saw my expression. "Ah. I see you don't view things this way?"

"Not at all. I certainly feel that I'm *not* going to be lifting any curses during my stay, but beyond that, I am downright frustrated with everyone assuming that I'm a Minory!"

"I see," he said, and clasped his hands together in front of him. "You know, Nicole—"

"It's Cole," I said coolly.

"Cole," he said, continuing like a professor at the lectern, "I've done all the energy reading I can with the MacLaoch line. If you wouldn't mind, I'd like to take your energy reading."

I think my mouth literally dropped open.

"I don't think I have time. Sorry, Dr. Peabody." I looked about the room to find Rowan and take my leave from the professor.

Ed just nodded. "My wife gives me that same look," he said, looking slightly apologetic. "Cole, you mentioned you spent six years in school?"

"I did."

"What did you study?"

"Biology."

"I assume that you received your bachelor's or master's in that?"

"Master's."

"Ah. So you've done quite a bit of research yourself, for your thesis?" he asked rhetorically. "I have a theory myself about the Minory and Lady MacLaoch. I believe," he said, not waiting for me to respond or even to acknowledge that he was speaking, "that the love they had for each other, combined with the violence of their separation, would make for a very unique passed-down energy. It would create ripples if they came together again. Ripples like sine waves or sound waves."

"Sound waves? So we should hear loud humming like a humming-bird?" I snorted.

"No. More like—have you ever been near high-voltage power lines?"

I stopped looking for my exit and looked back at Dr. Peabody.

"Yes."

"So you have felt the internal humming that they create? In your own body?"

"Yes," I said simply.

"It's my theory that when the two descendants who carry the burden of the legend come together, they will create an internal hum in each other. Though how strong it would be and whether it comes to an equilibrium point, I still do not know. I would assume that the hum would be so minor that one would mistake it for just feeling off."

I just stared at him, speechless, my mind unwillingly thinking of the hum that I'd first come to think of as too much caffeine. I tried to swallow, but my throat was suddenly dry, constricted.

"My other theory is one of reciprocity. The two descendants of the curse could feel the emotional extremes of the other. For example, if one were to experience pure elation, that would send a ripple to the other. The same is true for distress—if one is in great pain or anguish, that energy is felt by the other. Of course, the closer they are to each other, physically, the less extreme the emotions would need to be to be felt by the other. For example, if the two were separated by oceans and one were in a horrendous accident, the other would feel it. Whereas if they were at the same party, say, and one heard a terribly good joke, the other would be able to feel even that little joy."

I stayed silent. No. No, no, no—I doubted it on every level.

"Of course all of these are simply theories of an aging professor," he said, as though reading my mind—reading what I was forcing my mind to believe and stick to. "So please do excuse me." He looked away across the room.

I turned in the same direction and saw that Rowan was engrossed in another conversation, this time with a man and a woman who were dressed to the nines, for the late eighteen hundreds. Then suddenly, a sharp pain pierced the back of my arm.

I gasped and reeled, catching Peabody pinching me, seemingly for all he was worth.

"Ow!" I hissed. My heart hammered in my chest with adrenaline as I rubbed my arm. Being in the middle of a gala, though, I wasn't sure this was the appropriate place to feed him my shoe.

Dr. Peabody wasn't looking at me, but beyond me, his mouth agape. "My god, it's true," he whispered. "He felt that."

"Listen Dr. Peabody, I don't appreciate you treating me like a laboratory test mouse! I, like everyone here, am just human," I said hotly, but soon realized it was all in vain.

Peabody stared. His eyes tracked something across the room and came to a rest directly over my shoulder.

"Is there a problem?" I heard the deep authoritative voice of the MacLaoch chief from over my shoulder.

Dr. Peabody's face split into an enormous grin. "Amazing . . . " he said, looking at me and then to the chief and back to me again.

I felt my face crumbling into shock, and I said—in the same moment as Peabody replied—"We are done here."

I turned and made my way through the crowd to the refreshments table as though it were a pond in the middle of the desert and I'd been traveling for months.

The heavily laden table was holding more than just glasses and a champagne fountain, which I put to immediate use—it was also holding up the wearily drunk and those wanting to immerse themselves in deep conversation away from the brightly lit dance floor.

I felt him behind me even before his fingers gently brushed the skin on the back of my arm.

I looked over my shoulder at him. "Does it look bad?"

"No, a bit red 'tis all." He was silent a while. "Cole . . . " he said softly.

I finished the drink in my hand and set it down before turning around.

"Yes?" I said tiredly, thinking he was going to ask me what had just happened.

"I am so sorry for bringing ye into this whole mess. I should no' have brought ye here—I knew some people might be trouble, but I dinnae think all of them would be. Ye'd think ye were a mystic or shaman here to work your magic for all of them to see."

I smiled a tad bitterly, it was true. I felt the same.

Rowan placed a comforting hand on my back. "If ye want to leave, I'll personally take ye home now," he said, moving us effortlessly through the crowd toward the patio doors.

I wasn't sure what his expression was, but people seemed to be steering clear of us.

"I also want to apologize. I thought Dr. Peabody a scientist and a gentleman—I cannae understand what made him attack ye. I'd have no' introduced ye to him if I'd thought he'd hurt ye."

His tone was so sincerely regretful that I felt a small piece of bitterness melt away. Somewhere in the more malicious side of my mind, I had been thinking that this was all of his design.

"Don't worry. I think if he had his energy meter, he wouldn't have felt so compelled to prove his point by pinching the back of my arm."

"Prove his point?" Rowan asked. "What point? That ye are a deity sent from god tae save us all, and he was proving tha' ye wouldn't bruise if he pinched ye?"

I smirked at his sarcasm. "No, more like you and I are descendants of the legend and if he pinched me, you'd feel it too."

Surprise crossed Rowan's features as he opened his mouth to speak. He was interrupted by a paunchy—and punchy—old man.

"MacLaoch ol' boy!" He grasped Rowan's shoulder aggressively. "Lady," he said, rolling his eyes in my direction and giving me a small bow that was more like a nod.

"I've been meaning to speak with you all evening," he said breathlessly in Rowan's face. Even standing next to him, I could smell the alcohol.

"Gregoire," MacLaoch said, greeting him in short. "Ms. Baker, this is—"

"Forget the formality, Rowan, none is needed here, aye?" he said thickly, as if his words were becoming entangled in his mouth.

I felt Rowan stiffen next to me, and as this Gregoire man continued, in Gaelic, he became taut as a bowstring beside me. I'd not known the chief long, but it seemed he was suppressing the urge to strike the words from the man's mouth. His fingers twitched against my back, in time with that regular tic of his, the clenching jaw.

Rowan broke in, suddenly, in English. "It's no' a throne, Uncle, it's a position more akin to the president of a business than a king with power and gold. Dinnae confuse the two."

But the Gregoire continued his tirade.

In the next moment, Rowan bent to my ear, "Go to the outdoor balcony. Wait for me there. Cole—do not, *do not* leave with anyone but me."

His head beside mine, I gave a small nod to indicate that I'd heard him—I'd ask him later what this was all about—and took my leave.

At the doors to the patio, I couldn't help but turn back. Gregoire was still growling in Gaelic while Rowan's gaze was off with me, as if I had taken a piece of him with me.

I pointed to the balcony where I'd be, and he gave a slight nod, sliding his eyes back to the assault in front of him.

Twenty-Five

And that's when I got pinched, hard, for the second time that night. I'd barely gotten to the stone railing of the balcony and enjoyed a few moments of cool night air when my other arm was attacked.

"Ouch!" I whirled.

Eryka. She was wearing a fiery orange number that slouched and billowed appreciatively around her thin frame; her fire-engine-red shoes matched her nails and lips. She screamed without saying a word.

I glanced around for witnesses, but found none.

Eryka's pinch turned into a sensuous nail drag up my arm, then back down. "Surprise," she said huskily, far too close for comfort.

I took a step back and came up against the stone railing.

"I bet you didn't think you would see me here tonight. I can see it all over your face," she said, and laughed, deep and throaty. "Of course you didn't—it's hard to pay attention to the competition when you have the attention of so many men to manage. Just the few seconds I spent in that horrid room, all I heard was Ms. Baker this, and Lady Minory that . . ."

If I were a man there would be no doubt that I would be hanging on her every word and enjoying the flirtatious motions she was making toward me. But I wasn't a man and had not even a single ounce of interest in her.

"You've made quick work of all this—very smart for the whore and liar that you are," she said with vicious melodrama.

I could feel my eyebrows arching as she continued.

"He'll never be yours, you know," she said, biting the air between us. "No matter how hard you try to get rid of me. You thought that little stunt of getting me fired would get rid of me? It didn't—though I have to say, that was some nice work on your part. I didn't see *that* coming."

I held up my hand. "Stop." I didn't have much left in me for more crazy-person babble. "Eryka, I have no idea what you are talking about. The only time I think of you is when you show up. So your assumption that I am working a master scheme is completely ridiculous," I said, then added, "and please take a step back."

"Oh. You are good," she purred. "I almost believe you. No, I know all about you. You think I don't know about your kind? You think you can just walk right in and ruin everything with this talk of curse breaking? I didn't invest ten years of my life to just let some arrogant American come in and valk all over me." She sneered. "You had best keep an eye out and it best be on your back."

None of her words were making sense. Especially the last piece. "I'm not sure I understand what you said to me. Did you just threaten me?"

Eryka showed me all her little white teeth in what I can only assume was her attempt at a Cheshire grin. "I'm not threatening you, love," she said. "But if you don't get on that plane in a few days and return to that filth you call a country, I promise you'll still be leaving."

"Right," I said. "As in, in a body bag? Eryka, again, let me be plain. I'm here to do research, not steal boyfriends or rock the boat of social standards. So when you threaten me, you are just making a fool of yourself. At no time am I ever a danger or threat to you. You've done that all by your little self." I had one last shred of common courtesy left, and Eryka had taken a double fisted hold on it and was trying her damnedest to snap it in half and feed it back to me. "If you'll excuse me, I have somewhere—"

"You'll go nowhere!" she shrieked and slapped me hard across the face.

Growing up with an older brother, I was no stranger to being struck —it's something of a rite of passage for older brothers to hit their younger siblings. Anytime I was with family, I knew that, at some point even still, I would receive a blow: a punch to the arm from a brother, a head slap from a mother or aunt, any number of other friendly physical interactions. This, however, was a grand gala in an ancient castle and the person doing the slapping was most decidedly not someone who loved me. In those fractions of a second after she struck me, my brain shut down and left my body to defend itself.

Out of the corner of my eye, I watched as Eryka's hand came back from the initial slap to give the other side of my face a feel for the big shiny ring she wore on her middle finger. Inches before it touched my skin, I grabbed her wrist and reciprocated with a closed fist.

Eryka went sprawling backward onto the stone terrace. I methodically slipped off my shoes and mink and strode to where she'd landed.

She sat up as I approached and everything but Eryka and I went underwater—all sounds and sights muffled except for ours. I could hear her heartbeat, smell her fear. I straddled Eryka, batted away her hand as it came up to defend herself, and raised my other fist to break her nose. I had become single-minded: I was going to be methodical about punishing her, and I wasn't going to stop until the debt was paid in full.

That was, until I was gripped around the middle and lifted backward off of her.

I twisted and nailed the person with my elbows. But the grip didn't lessen; instead, strong arms pinned me tighter, like iron bands.

I fought, and the hold on me got stronger. I doubled forward, trying to bite the arms that had me; I thrashed my legs and went pleasantly wild.

It took me a while fighting and clawing before the din in my ears stopped and the tunnel vision I had created for Eryka widened. I realized I was no longer at the castle, but at the ocean's edge, in the lower cove. I bit and scratched at the person who had me, and recognized the swearing.

"MacLaoch." I hissed, "Put me down. Now."

"Are ye calm?" he said, and swore as I wriggled and kicked at him.

"Yes! Now put me the fuck down!"

"No, ye are not," he said calmly.

It took me a millisecond to realize once he hoisted me up over his shoulder that I wouldn't be there for long. But it was too late. He strode into the ocean and tossed me in.

Twenty-Six

"No!" I shouted just before the freezing Atlantic seawater choked my voice off.

The diamonds felt like ice cubes against my ears and chest. My dress felt like it simply dissolved in the glacial water, as it no longer loaned me any warmth. I managed to kick to the surface.

"Holy shit, this water's cold!" I gasped.

In that simple instant, I was suddenly more worried about my own survival than working over Eryka. As I kicked, my dress sealed about my legs like plastic wrap and I couldn't keep above even those low, sloppy waves near shore.

I heard myself make a gurgling sound and clawed at my dress, the first fingers of panic shifting my adrenaline high into fear. I got a foothold on some rocks and pushed forward—into MacLaoch, who hoisted me out of the water by my arm.

My teeth chattered as I stumbled out of the water next to him, "Oh—my—g-god. Th—that—water—is—cold."

"Aye," he said softly, gripping my elbow and steering me toward the cliff face, away from the water's edge.

Being out of the water was even colder—the soft breeze I had enjoyed earlier was now the kiss of frosty death on my skin. My whole body took up the chatter and I stumbled—my feet had swiftly become painful from the cold. Rowan lifted me into his arms.

He was warm, but I could barely feel it, my skin numb with both cold and the aftershock of adrenaline leaving my system. I clutched my hands together to stave off the full-body shuddering.

We approached a thick, old, wooden door with iron hinges—in the cliff face. If the evening hadn't been so strange already, I would have been surprised. Stepping through the door and up several stone stairs, we entered a large, cellar-like room where soft lights flitted on, set off by our movement. The air in the room was humid and held the musk of warmth and cedar. Two stone benches carved from the walls of the room lined either side; Rowan set me down on one and grabbed a wool blanket from a stack of them at the back of the room. Wrapping my body within it, he vigorously rubbed my arms while I just observed, like a mannequin.

"I'm so c-cold," I whispered. My jaw was chattering uncontrollably, and I could think of nothing else.

Rowan sat behind me and pulled me in against him. "Shh, no' for long."

Slowly, I started to feel his warmth, his breath whispering against my cheek as he gathered my sodden hair and pulled it out from under the wool blanket.

My body gave a violent shudder, as if it were physically trying to expel the chill that had settled within my bones. I looked down at my white feet; they were tinged purple.

"H-how are you not c-cold?" I managed.

I could feel him shrug behind me. "I'm wearing a wee bit more than ye—wool socks, tartan, kilt. I've been sweating like a pig the whole night."

"Hmph," I grumbled. "You're a bastard for throwing me in there." Then I added, "Even if I deserved it."

"It wasn't about whether ye deserved it or not," he said. "I needed ye to be calm so I could ask ye what happened." Then he said, as an afterthought, "Tha', and ye bit me."

I gave him a tooth-chattering grin in response.

We were quiet for some time. I warmed up to just plain cold.

Rowan was actively quiet behind me. I had many things to review before I could speak, though it seemed that my mind wouldn't let me in just yet. I stared blankly ahead at the opposite stone bench.

"Are ye feeling better?" he asked tentatively.

"Warmer or less likely to fight?"

"Less likely to fight."

"Yes," I answered, and then cut to the chase: "You're probably wondering why in the world Eryka was on the ground defending herself."

"Actually, no." I heard him sigh and lean against the wall behind us. "I'm wondering how it felt to punch that bloody woman."

I smiled to myself. "Been wanting to do that for a while, huh?" Thinking of my fight with Eryka reminded me of how I'd come to be alone on the terrace. "Gregoire," I said. "I'll tell you what, how about you tell me in detail everything that drunken ass said to you tonight, and we can blame him for putting me in Eryka's sights."

Rowan shifted uncomfortably behind me and settled once again against the wall. "Well, there's nothing to tell. He was drunk."

I scoffed. "How is that a detailed description? You're dodging." I added, for encouragement, "He was no doubt talking about power and gold, from what you said in English to him, but why did he keep rolling his eyes at me?"

MacLaoch was silent for a while. "Ye don't speak Gaelic, aye?"

"No."

"Good, because ye shouldnae know what he said."

"Is Gregoire Kelly's father?"

"Aye, he is," MacLaoch said, offering nothing more.

"Oh," I said, feeling suddenly queasy. I sat forward with my elbows on my knees. "I hope, somewhere in your conversation, you told him to stay away from me."

"I told him as such but, Cole, he's an old man and a penchant for drink. It's hard to say what he thinks is serious, since much of the time he does not know it himself. I wouldn't worry yerself about it. He's harmless."

We were silent again as I chewed on that bit of information and then remembered, "But if that's the case, why'd you send me out to the balcony? And," I exclaimed, remembering more, "told me not to leave with anyone but yourself?" I felt like I needed to stand up and face him, but I didn't trust my cold legs to keep me upright.

Rowan sighed. "When a drunken man is discussing absconding with your date while she's standing right next to ye, a smart man will send her to a safe place to wait while he disposes of the drunken man."

A little chill ran up my body. "And I suppose Gregoire has a black eye, too?"

"Had I been given a moment alone with him on the balcony, he'd have more than a blackened eye." Rowan was quiet for a few moments, no doubt fantasizing a world where he did have Gregoire alone on a balcony.

"Aye, now I want to hear about Peabody," he said. "Tell me what ye two discussed."

I thought about all that Peabody had told me and retold it to the best of my ability. I left out the part about Peabody taking Rowan's energy reading and the horrific thing he must have seen to have a reading so high.

"Then, I assume, to prove his point, he pinched the back of my arm. A few moments later you show up, and he thinks his theory is true, but no doubt you either heard me yelp or saw him pinch me."

"He's a very smart man, Dr. Peabody," Rowan said. "Do *ye* believe his theory?"

"I don't know, Rowan, you tell me." I turned to look him in the eye.

The distance was small between the chief and me, though at any distance, it would have been easy to tell that the invisible wall that he held up in defense against the world was gone. He was just Rowan. And I was just me, sitting between his muscular thighs. He reclined, arms relaxed. His fingers ever so slightly pulled at the wool wrapped around me as if gathering me in bit by bit.

I felt my heart squeeze and my stomach flip-flop at this recognition.

Rowan was looking me straight in the eye, closing the distance between us further as he spoke. "I did not feel a pinch to my arm as he had done to ye, so nae, it was no' that which pulled me tae ye. It was your reaction to it tha' I felt like an ocean wave, Cole. Low and power-ful, plowed right through me." He paused, then continued, "The part tha' was unbelievable was tha' I knew it was ye. Clear as a bell calling my name—as if ye'd been standing right next to me and whispered it in my ear."

Rowan's hands made their way slowly up my arms, leaving the hair standing on end under my wool blanket.

"But what I cannae figure out is why when I wake in the morn, to when I lay down at night I can't stop thinking of ye. And even then," he said softly, "I think of ye when I'm asleep."

Rowan's fingers moved to my chin where they had been earlier in the night in the back of the darkened car. "We have unfinished business to settle," he said softly before brushing his lips against mine.

I closed my eyes, feeling the soft tingle in my lips pour down into my belly and light my very soul on fire.

Twenty-Seven

Rowan had me on my back on the wide stone bench, the wool blanket under me, in a single move. I made swift work of his clothing, sliding his evening jacket off, pushing in blind lust at his tartan, buttons, and tartan pins—all gave way to my demands.

Rowan looked as if he'd strode out of the pages of a historical novel, an ancient Scottish warrior who'd thrown down his sword and was having his way with me. His physique told me much of him. His musculature, lean and lithe, moving under his skin, spoke volumes about the vigorousness with which he exercised against his demons. Power and need poured into me as our skin connected. His breathing quickened and mingled with soft Gaelic oaths.

His mouth against mine once more, he slipped his tongue in, tasting, sampling, and moaning with the tightening pressure that held only one release. It was in that moment, when the mind takes a backseat to the body, that I felt that Minory legend. I felt it like a heat wave move through him and into me, reverberating to my very core. The one-letter difference I'd so doggedly stood by became a moot point in an instant. There was no Iain Eliphlet Minary—it was Iain Eliphlet Minory, and I was his great-great-great granddaughter. The final recognition of this let loose a floodgate of emotion, so overwhelming and electrifying that I groaned, knowing that I never wanted this feeling between us to end.

Rowan's hand slid down to my toes, taking in the feel of all of me, then moved up under my dress, pushing it up my thighs. The wide palm of his hand caressed my hip and then gripped it, and he groaned.

"Aye, god. Ye aren't wearing anything under this . . . " he said, breath catching in his throat.

Wrapping my legs around his waist, I arched, discovering I wasn't the only one without undergarments. As my fingers dragged along his skin, they bumped over something the size of a dime, uneven on his skin.

As quickly as I felt it, I didn't.

Rowan broke away from me. In the same instant, I realized that my hand stung. I looked to find it pinned against the wall, crushed under Rowan's.

He laid his forehead against mine and breathed in deep. "Fuck, fuck, fuck."

I licked my lips and let myself fall back down to earth, fast. Like lights flicking on in a darkened room, my mind began to piece together what had happened. I had physically touched something that had made Rowan shut down. My mind recalled the feeling under my fingers, and I suddenly knew what I had felt but not immediately recognized: a scar.

My brother had been in the National Guard and spent time abroad; he had friends who had come back from war with stories in the scars on their bodies. The scars that bullets left were distinct, especially the clean-hit ones.

"Rowan," I breathed, "I'm sorry. I didn't know."

"Bloody hell," was all he said as he pulled himself up off of me. I watched as his internal wall shuddered back down and slammed firmly in place.

"What happened?" I whispered.

Rowan couldn't even speak; he just shook his head.

My head swam with emotion, feeling sorrow for the brutality he'd seen and experienced. Peabody was right. Rowan had seen violence and, from the shape of the scar, had met it full on. My mind supplied the rest. The other bullets had hit and killed the man Rowan had served with, the man he considered a brother. I burned with curiosity to know those dark details, to pull him back to me and soften those memories.

Rowan raked his hand through his hair in frustration, went over to a cabinet, pulled out a dry fleece and jeans, and dressed. I sat up and wrapped myself in the blanket. He sat back down opposite me. He looked like he was struggling with his words, but he did speak. "I should not have let it get this far."

The anguish in his words made me stumble for some of my own. No words could erase the pain he felt or what had been done to him, and yet I needed to say *something*. I had no real experience to draw on to soothe him. Even though I simply wanted to go to him, sit beside him and wrap him in my arms, I had not known him long enough to even dream of attempting it. For all I knew, he would toss me to the floor and stalk from the room—it was cowardly, but that image kept me from going to him.

The silence became too long.

"The scar on your side . . . " I started hesitantly. "Did that hap—"

"Rowan! Ye down 'ere, ye prick!?"

Rowan stood, looking almost relieved for the diversion of his ill-mannered cousin, and stalked out the lower door. I cursed Kelly liber-ally as the door swung shut.

Twenty-Eight

I found a small Castle Laoch–logoed, fleece-lined windbreaker, and someone's forgotten yoga pants in the cabinets. With an absent-minded touch to the diamonds I was somehow still wearing and without shoes, I walked out to find Rowan.

A fog had rolled in off the ocean, moving quietly, as I had learned it does, in tall, softly materializing fingers up the rocky shore to the cliff.

Kelly's snarl hit me just a few paces from the cliff face. "Eryka is in bad shape, black eye and all, and we called the emergency services. They've taken her to hospital to be looked at—ye need to warn that woman she needs to be careful, no' the other way around, Rowan. Eryka will want punishment." Kelly turned at the sound of my approach.

"What's that around her neck?" he yelled at Rowan. "Oh! And at her ears? Bloody fucking diamonds!"

"Ms. Baker," Rowan said, detached. "Head back to the castle—I'll meet ye on the back balcony and take ye home. I need to speak to Kelly alone."

I opened my mouth to reply, but Kelly beat me to it.

"Aye, ye bet we do! Ye have some explaining tae do." He pointed dangerously at Rowan. "Ye think that ordering me awa' to some training is going to teach me respect, aye? Well, I'll teach ye some respect—"

"Kelly!" I yelled in surprise at Kelly's foolishness as he took a swipe at Rowan.

Rowan grabbed the offending fist, yanked his cousin forward, and took Kelly down. Rowan held him on his knees on the rocks, his palm shoved in his shoulder and Kelly's arm pulled backward awkwardly.

"Ow!" Kelly yelled.

"Ye done?"

"Fu—" Kelly choked as Rowan tightened up.

"I asked if ye were done," Rowan said again.

Kelly seethed; the tint of his skin had gone beet red.

"Good," Rowan said. "We *are* done 'ere." Rowan released him.

Kelly stood and rotated his shoulder, making a face, then turned and walked back up the cove. Rowan simply watched him, waiting. It felt like they'd done this before and, in those instances, Kelly had come back for more.

Kelly had gotten a few paces away when he indeed pivoted and walked back, shouting to Rowan, "Maybe in officer training school, cousin, I can become just like you! Yeah, that would be great—then I can have my war stories, too, and go crazy with my nightmares, just like ye."

I must have had a confused look on my face because Kelly threw his arms in the air and continued, "Oh! I see, ye haven't told her everything, aye? Maybe not anything? Were ye hoping that she'd never ask and ye would never have to tell? Or were ye waiting till ye woke up one morn to find that ye had strangled her in your sleep?"

Rowan took one step forward, and Kelly turned, running away for all he was worth.

After Kelly disappeared, Rowan, smoldering, turned on his heel away from both the direction his cousin had gone and the place where I stood. Hands in fists, he walked toward the far hillside—but I felt that he needed to hear from me before he sank deeper into his personal darkness.

I jogged behind him, feeling the rocks dig at my bare feet. "Rowan, stop," I said. "Please."

He stopped walking but didn't turn around to face me. The white tendrils of fog eddied and swirled around him.

"I just need space, aye?" Before I could respond he continued walking.

"Rowan," I said, catching up to him once more. "Is that what gave you that scar? The war, the same battle when your friend was killed?"

Rowan stopped again and looked up into the night sky as if praying for mercy. "What is it tha' ye want from me, Ms. Baker?" I felt the impersonal blow of him using my formal name. "Haven't I told ye enough for ye to understand tha' the bed I lay in is one of thorns?" Looking back at me, the demon knife twisting in his gut, he asked, "What will it do for ye, knowing my darkest moments?"

Reeling from his aggressiveness, I remembered back to when he had met me—his tone and countenance were just the same. The same way that blackberry thorns worked to keep the soft fruit protected behind the spines. Steeling myself against his rebuke, I responded quietly, "It will do nothing for me, Rowan, but don't you think it will help you? That's what I want. I want to help you."

The fog, it seemed, grew thicker, like a cocoon, a gentle protection from everything around us, allowing us to focus on just here, and now. Rowan simply lifted a finger to my hair, gently brushed a curl off my shoulder. He looked me in the eye. "No one can help me," he said, and simply walked away into the mist.

That time, I let him.

Twenty-Nine

E xhaustion came quickly for me that night, and just as quickly came the dream. As if it had been hovering all along, waiting for the shutdown of my conscious mind.

The Isle of Lady MacLaoch was once again beneath my feet—cool waters lapped at the cove rocks, and the dusky evening breeze played with my hair. I was just as I was in the last dream, only this time I recognized the ring upon my finger immediately, and knew that it was mine. Closing my eyes, I described the ring to myself as if it were a game, the simple act of concentration pulling me deeper into the dream.

I remembered what came next—the man in my dream, the one I could not recognize but loved with an aching heart. I looked back down at my ring and then up to the shoreline where he had been before. He wasn't that far away this time. He was standing next to me, wearing what he had the day I met him in real life.

Rowan turned as if he was just discovering that I was standing next to him as well. A slow smile spread over his lips—it was one of relief. In that very moment, the cove dissolved into a hot desert, sandstone mountains jutting up in the distance surrounding us. Rowan was dressed in a drab olive flight suit and suddenly, he hunched over in pain, grasping his side.

In the distance, there was a skirmish—to my untrained eye, I could only make out parachutes fluttering. Then gunfire riddled the air, and fear tore through me. I was in Rowan's nightmare.

I looked back at Rowan. "Cole," he whispered. "Help me." Behind him the firefight raged on.

"Rowan, what's happening? What happened?" I said, reaching for him.

Rowan pulled his hand away from his side. Blood had saturated his flight suit and still oozed from the small tear under his hand. His hand, too, dripped blood. "Help," he said again.

I thought of Dr. Peabody and what he had said about the two descendants of the curse, and about reciprocity. If Rowan could pull me into his nightmare, I could pull him into my dreams. Hugging Rowan to me, I thought of home. I thought of my family and our orchards in South Carolina, the pecan and peach fields I'd run through in late summer, filling my shirt with the last of the season's dropped fruit, and the sweet smell of ripe peach juice as it clung to my arms and dripped off my elbows. I opened my eyes within the dream—juice was indeed streaming down my arms, and the heavy, warm air was South Carolina, not the Middle East. I looked over—Rowan was with me. He held a large peach in his hand and stroked the fuzzy surface with his thumb. "Peaches?" he asked simply.

I could feel myself smile. "Yes, why do you sound surprised?"

He gave me a wicked smile. "Aye, I was thinking tha' it would be your breast. Seeing tha' ye have come to me in a dream."

In the next moment, Rowan and I were on the ground, both of us naked, and he was indeed gently cupping my breast. Then he lowered his mouth to it.

"Holy shit!" I gasped and sat straight up in bed.

I sat there in the dark, breathing deeply, looking around my chilly room at the bed-and-breakfast. "That wasn't real. It was just a dream," I said out loud to myself, and repeated it once for good measure. Then once more.

But it wasn't the last portion that had me doubting—rather, it was the vividness with which the desert battle had replayed itself for me.

Thirty

The next morning Carol hovered while I picked at my breakfast. Finally she pulled out a chair and sat across the table from me.

"Och, now," she said, rolling her eyes. "Tell me all the details! Who was there last night, and what is all this commotion about someone getting struck, and the MacLaoch chief himself saved the day??"

Oh god.

I did my best to reenact the entire night for Carol over my porridge. Omitting the pinching, the punching, the sexual lusting, and the emotional trauma. I was sure Rowan would thank me.

"Och, good! It sounds like ye had a nice time. I bet ye can't wait for Friday now, can ye?" Carol asked, beaming.

"Friday?" Then remembered before she said it.

"Och, ye are so modest, the final gala of course," she said and gave me a wink before reporting back to the kitchen for round two of the meal.

A short time later I found myself at the research section of the library's basement.

"Good morning, Deloris," I said as I dropped my bag at one of the desks.

"Aye, good morning tae ye." Deloris came to the front counter. "I suppose ye didnae find what ye were looking for last night then, eh?"

"What I was looking for?" I asked.

"Aye. Or ye wouldn't be here this mornin'."

I nodded, realizing what she meant. "I learned much last night"— she nodded; she'd heard at least some gossip—but, unfortunately, nothing that will be of help to my original search." I took a deep breath and admitted defeat aloud: "I think I need to know everything there is on the Lady MacLaoch curse."

Deloris blinked. "Oh, so ye didn't find out about the Minarys then?"

"No," I confirmed. "I'm beginning to believe that I am in fact the descendant of Iain Eliphlet Minory. I think," I paused, not sure I wanted to say this aloud, "that I am indeed meant to, somehow, fulfill an ancient destiny."

"Oh."

"I know," I said. "It's weird. But I just feel that if I could read all I can about this curse, something will pop out at me that will tell me what I need to know."

"Well, I'll round up what I can for ye."

A short while later Deloris and I settled in together to review the documents she had uncovered. The variety of curses the MacLaochs were apparently under was amazing.

"These all are dramatically different depending on the person's bias," I said. "'And she said unto him that he should never love another, though if he shall, his babes will have the heads of horses.' Heads of horses?"

"Well, it's more exciting than this one—this says the male MacLaochs will all become strong and virile. Not much of a curse if ye ask me."

"Ugh," I said, and put my chin in my hand. This was going nowhere.

Just then the door chimed open and Dr. Peabody strolled in, holding a large box.

"Ah, hello, Nicole and Deloris! Doing research?" He sounded as though the strange evening mere hours before had never happened. He placed his box on the reception counter and came over to us.

"Yes. And you?" I asked. Thinking of my bruised arm, I added, "I hope you're not here to prove any more theories."

"Wasn't it magnificent!?" he beamed, obviously missing my point.

"Which part? Your proving your theory or bruising my arm?"

"Oh yes, I am sorry about that, Ms. Baker, though what it proves is substantial," he said. "But sadly, I must conclude my business here in Glentree—my family and I are headed back to the States after a tour through Craigellachie. So," he said, looking at Deloris, "I've come to return those materials I borrowed. I didn't know which ones belonged to Castle Laoch, so I've just included everything in the box."

Dr. Peabody took a deep breath. He had the obvious look of a man who didn't want to rush away from a center of research—more specific, to leave his research subject behind.

I smiled at him knowingly. "Ed, before you leave, I bet you can help Deloris and me with our current question."

"Yes?"

Why did I want to give him a little going-away gift? I had no idea. But it *was* fun to see how giddy he got over research.

"There are as many versions of the curse as there are days of the year. How can we weed out the most credible of the bunch?"

Dr. Peabody beamed. "Ah, yes. Which one is the truest form? A very good question, and I think I can help."

"Really?"

He turned to his box, unloaded a few top files, found the one he'd been looking for, and flipped it open. "Here," he said, handing me a sheet of typewritten paper. "This is dictation taken from a Secret Keeper. That's someone who's been nominated to remember the story —every generation has someone who is in charge of memorizing the curse *verbatim* from the past generation."

By the time I'd finished reading, all the hair on my body was standing on end.

"This is it," I whispered. "Do you know who the current Secret Keeper is?"

Dr. Peabody shook his head sadly. "No, I don't know who this person is. It's not listed anywhere."

I reread the curse. "This sounds just like the one the MacDonagh brothers told to me. Here, this is the part I was looking for: 'When they have walked the lonely halls of despair will I bestow upon them a peace I once held long ago and then, only for a moment,'" I recited the words and fell silent.

"What are you suggesting?" Dr. Peabody asked.

"Well, it seems obvious, doesn't it? That what she's saying is that only when the MacLaoch chief shares her pain, and I assume here that she means, feels pain equal to or greater than the one she felt, that only then will the clan be free of the curse. Or, in other words, once you walk in my shoes, I'll lift the curse—you can love freely as you would have done before me," I said and sat back.

"And?" Dr. Peabody asked.

"And what?"

"Well, my dear, we know that Rowan has seen the likes of her pain, so the question is, now what do you do?"

"Wait now," Deloris piped up. "I don't want to pry, but I gather ye both think that Rowan has seen the likes of her pain?" She pointed to the transcript of the curse.

Dr. Peabody and I looked at each other, then back to her, and said, "Yes."

"Oh, all right, then. So how come the chief seems still to be cursed?"

I had felt it earlier but now it was much stronger: the low hum in my belly. Since I had become aware of whom—not what—was the cause of the hum, I could not ignore it. Rowan was near.

"I don't know," I said. "It seems from this that the simple act of having seen the likes of Lady MacLaoch's pain would do the trick. The MacLaochs, however, are strong believers that the descendant of the Minory will break the curse."

Peabody nodded, spectacles swinging in his hand as he looked off into the distance, contemplating. "Yes. You are right the MacLaochs do believe the Minory will break the curse, and those who stick to the original concept of it realize that the Minory returning is the signal of the broken curse—mission completed, if you will."

"Oh, so you are saying that my simply being here has broken the curse, if the chief's pain hasn't already?"

"Yes, my dear, I do believe that. However, I am just one person, and if Deloris here believes it as well, that makes for only two people. I'm afraid that just because we believe it doesn't mean that the rest of the clan will. And there are a few who are dogged in their determination to become better acquainted with you because of it."

"Oh, brother," I said. "The eternal fan club."

"Hmm," Peabody said. "More or less."

This time it was my turn to think. I didn't have the deep, satisfying feeling that came after a long slog of research ending in the right answer. There was more.

"In the past few days, I've had a recurring dream about Lady MacLaoch and an ancient ring. In those dreams I'm wearing the ring and it belongs to me, but in reality it's sitting in the Castle Laoch antiques display."

The glasses dropped from Peabody's hand. "You mean *the* Lady MacLaoch ring?" he asked breathlessly.

"Yes."

"You've dreamed about it? Have you seen it in real life?"

"Yes and yes. Though I first dreamed about it before I saw it on display at the castle." It felt a bit odd admitting to having dreamed of something before having seen it, though I did realize I was talking to Dr. Peabody.

Peabody sat back and blinked rapidly. "I think . . . " he said and stopped—he seemed to be immersed in a very serious internal dialogue. "I think, Nicole, that . . . I believe, and this is just a theory—one I've just thought of, so I haven't addressed all the holes in it but . . . " he said and was silent again.

Deloris and I both leaned forward.

"I think," he repeated, "that Lady MacLaoch has begun a final work. Specifically, she means to have you fulfill what she was denied a millennium ago. I think the final piece, the key, is for you and Rowan to somehow unite. You and Rowan are to marry—that is what the ring is symbolizing."

Thirty-One

"Thank ye, Josh," Rowan said to his gillie, who had prepped the estate's old military-issue Mercedes G-Wagon, along with support vans, for the long, rough trek to the hunting grounds. "And the cabin, if we need it?"

"'Tis all prepped—spare rifles, munitions, food, and first-aid kit, should ye need it. Though if it turns out that you'll need a night up there, only one room on the lower level is made up—the upper rooms havenae been aired out—extra bedding in the storage room. Just like last time."

Rowan nodded and dismissed Josh, and then, to keep his mind busy, rechecked the vans and his vehicle's supplies. The weather was going to hold for the hunt; the roads wouldn't be too muddy, but he had the winch on the front just in case.

Rowan opened the rear door of the old military vehicle and pulled out his rifle case. He'd cleaned and checked the gun earlier in the week, but felt his hands perform, automatically, the check once more. He flipped the bolt handle and peered into the open chamber, then relatched and sighted the scope, making minor adjustments that he'd most likely undo later. Rowan's mind wandered to her again, the soft feel of her under him just last night, the pull she had on his gut, as though he were caught in her dragnet, her ridiculous beauty—he told himself he was a going to regret her for the rest of his life. He was a fool to have touched her. The zinging of his scar reminded him all too viscerally: Lady MacLaoch would punish him for Cole—it was his fate. By blood, she was the last, it seemed, descendant of Lady MacLaoch's betrothed, and that meant so many things. But of one thing he was certain—should Lady MacLaoch seek her final vengeance upon him, if Vick's blood hadn't been enough, to take Cole before his eyes would no doubt settle the score. The two of them reliving the last moments of that original couple was a dark thought that had settled in, and now he couldn't shake it.

"No," he said aloud to pull himself from the shadowy recesses of his mind. He would overcome this, he thought. "Rationalize it," he mumbled to himself as he looked down the barrel through the scope and into the woods bordering the parking area. "It's Glentree, not the sandbox—she'll be fine, she's not Vick. She'll be fine. Distance yourself, old boy, and you might be fine too."

Rowan took a deep breath, placing the rifle back in its case, when he heard the gravel crunch behind him.

"Aye, sir, sorry tae bother ye . . . "

Rowan looked over his shoulder as he snapped the case shut. One of the temporary castle groundsmen stood behind him. Rowan waved him forward, not knowing how long the man had been standing there, but it had been long enough for him to be looking warily at the chief.

"I've been told the railing on the southside terrace is loose—apparently one of the guests nearly took a plunge off it. I dinnae know if it's a real problem or if they were drunk off their arses, but I thought I'd tell ye, if ye want to get someone on it now," the man said. "I'm off tae see tae the tent set up by the archery field. I can do it after if ye would like." The man indeed had his arms full of ropes and wooden stakes.

Needing another distraction until they were ready to depart, Rowan said, "No. Thank ye, I'll take a look myself and see what's tae be done."

THE TERRACE, A NARROW PATHWAY ON THE CLIFF SIDE OF the castle, was rarely used in the present day. Historically, it had served as the site of the castle's first line of defense against the rare siege from that side of the property.

Rowan emerged from the dark breezeway and looked left and right down the narrow terrace. The groundskeeper hadn't specified where the problem was, but Rowan had assumed he would be able to see an obvious section rattled loose, since someone had nearly pitched himself off it. He saw none.

The weather was changing—his scar pinched, the sensitive tissue feeling the change in atmospheric pressure. Another storm was coming.

Rowan walked the length of the right-most section of the terrace, running his hand along the rough stone, feeling for any loose areas. He turned back to the left side—and found himself walking toward Kelly, who was leaning against the castle, a foot up on the stone in a pose that told Rowan he was there for something beyond taking in the scenery.

Leaning against the railing opposite Kelly, Rowan crossed his arms and regarded his spoiled cousin. "Aye. Ye have me alone. Very clever. What's it tha' ye want?"

Kelly regarded his older cousin, his eyebrows lifting in mock surprise. "I don't know what you're talking about, Rowan, I just heard that I could find ye out here."

"Really."

"Really," Kelly said, looking over his shoulder down the darkened passageway.

"Ye expecting someone, Kelly?"

"No, why?"

"Kelly, I don't have the time to stand here while ye figure out what it is ye want with me. When ye figure it out, come find me," Rowan said and made to leave.

"I don't think so," Kelly said, stepping in front of Rowan and putting a hand to his chest.

Rowan looked at his cousin's hand, then to his face. "Well now, ye do have something to say? Because if ye don't, cousin, I'd take your hand off—"

Out of the corner of his eye, Rowan caught movement as Eryka side-stepped out of the shadowy breezeway, a silver 9mm pointed at him. Rowan let a low growl of frustration escape him and looked back at his cousin, who was now wearing a smug look.

"Ye shouldnae have fired her, Rowan," he said, his voice rising, as if he'd been working on that thought for some time.

"What are ye doing, Kelly?" Rowan could feel the stinging poison of betrayal from his own kin sink its teeth in.

"Kelly, don't talk to him," Eryka cut in, her husky voice sounding delighted in the circumstances. "And Rowan, don't think you can talk your pretty little vay out of this."

"And what do ye mean by 'this'? What exactly is *this*?" Rowan took in the way Eryka held the gun, loose and with the safety on, unaccustomed to its weight.

Eryka's lips pulled back into a grin. "An intervention, Rowan dear. What does it look like?"

"An assault. But just what do ye think ye are intervening on?"

"You, of course. I didn't spend all these years working tirelessly for Clan MacLaoch just to be thrown out when a new piece of ass came to town."

"Working?" Rowan said, letting the last piece slide. "Eryka, don't lie tae yourself. Ye haven't worked a day in your life. Ye were fired for good reason, and a Walther PPK isnae helping your situation. Put it away. If ye're really interested in getting yer job back, we can discuss it," Rowan lied.

"Oh no, Rowan, we are much beyond that—I don't want to work here. These past few years have been hell, but I've slogged through them because I held out *hope* that you would come around and see me for what I am," Eryka said, jutting her chin out.

"And what exactly are ye?" Rowan asked buying time.

Eryka snarled, "Worthy of you. I could be your bloody wife, Rowan; I could have made you happy, could have raised our children here."

Rowan scoffed, "Stow it, Eryka. As soon as your feet touched Castle Laoch soil ye were sharing my uncle's bed, and when he died, leaving ye nothing, ye looked for new prey. So what do ye really want? Money?"

"No, Rowan," she said, suddenly calm. "I'll tell you the truth—"

"Eryka!" Kelly boomed. "Don't! Father said—"

"Shut up, Kelly! Your *daddy* isn't here, so I'm in charge," she spat at him and then turned her attention back to Rowan. "After we call the police to clean up your obvious suicide—"

Kelly sighed loudly.

"—Kelly and I will get married, and I'll have all I've wanted. Now, Rowan, be a good boy and stand back against that sketchy railing of yours." She waved him back with the gun.

Rowan didn't move.

Kelly said, "Best do it, cousin. She's serious."

"Back!" Eryka shouted over Kelly's words. "I'll shoot you right here, Rowan, I will, but blood on stone is so hard to get out. I don't want Kelly's and my children to ask us what the stain is."

Rowan ignored Eryka's ranting and looked at Kelly. "Why?"

Kelly looked startled, as if Rowan were a statue that had just spoken to him. "Why? Tosh it, Rowan, don't ask me why. Ye should know why, ye prick. Why?" he scoffed. "The chief position is mine. I was here when ye were flying around having the time of yer life! Ye. Ye just come in as I'm making my plans for my ceremony and take it all. That's all ye have ever done tae me, is take what's rightfully mine!" Kelly said, building steam. "And now!" he shouted, the veins in his neck and forehead bulging. Rowan simply waited for it. "Ye're boffing my chances tae break the MacLaoch curse!"

"What?" Rowan asked, not expecting that to come from his cousin's mouth.

"Cole," Kelly hissed. "She's mine."

Eryka cocked the hammer on the gun and flipped the safety off.

His cousin's announcement was distinctly similar to that of his cousin's father.

Reacting, Rowan stepped toward Eryka, swiping her gun to the side, and jabbed her chin with the knuckles of his other hand. The gun fired lodging the stray bullet into the railing. Eryka hit the wall behind her and slid to the ground just as Kelly leaped for the gun, but not faster than Rowan's foot could connect with his head. Rowan picked up the PPK, popped the magazine, dislodged the chambered round, and unsheathed the slide. He threw all three pieces over the railing.

He turned and made it nearly to the breezeway before Kelly, like a bull that sees the red flag in the arena, went mad. But Rowan had been counting on his cousin's predictable nature. As soon as Kelly landed on Rowan's back, Rowan used Kelly's momentum to flip him over his shoulder and lay him out on his back on the stone terrace. Rowan's foot came down on his neck and pressed.

"Where's your father?" Rowan asked, adjusting his wrenched sweater and retucking his undershirt.

Gurgling was all Kelly could manage as he clawed at Rowan's foot.

"I'll ask ye once more, then I'll apply enough pressure tae break your larynx and make ye mute for the rest of your life. That's no' a curse from Lady MacLaoch—tha' one will be personally from me," Rowan said calmly over him.

"Let's try again," Rowan said as Kelly tried to buck his foot and nearly succeeded. "Stupid fuck." Rowan cut down harder and watched as his cousin's eyes widened in surprise. "Yes, now ye know I was being nice. Now ye really can't breathe, can ye? Where's your father?" he asked again.

Kelly became instantly cooperative, his lips moving, trying to tell Rowan.

"What's tha'? I can't hear ye." Rowan let up just enough for air to pass over Kelly's voice box.

Kelly's lips moved but Rowan only caught the most important word: "Cole."

Rowan released his cousin and walked a few paces away to keep from putting his fist through Kelly's face. When the urge passed, he turned back to his cousin and found him struggling on all fours to stand.

Rowan squatted next to him. "Say it again," he said quietly.

Kelly sat back on his haunches, a hand on his throat. "He's gone tae get Cole."

Rowan nodded. "Where?"

Kelly shrugged his shoulders. "Don't know. Dinnae fucking care," he sneered at Rowan.

Rowan counted all the way to five, by fives, then broke his cousin's nose with his fist.

Thirty-Two

I stared at Dr. Peabody. He was serious about Rowan and me marrying to break the curse. "I don't even know him."

"Oh, on the contrary. If you are really the descendant of the Minory, then you've known him for hundreds of years." Peabody said it as if that were the most rational thing.

"No. I have just met Rowan James Douglas MacLaoch. Your clan may have known about the Minorys for centuries but I can safely tell you that my family never heard of the MacLaochs until I got here."

"Consciously, yes. But your blood is the same as the blood that flowed through the veins of your Nordic ancestor who took Lady MacLaoch to be his bride. That same blood flows through Rowan—he is a direct and the last, I should add, descendant of Lady MacLaoch. No one else can share the bond that is between the two direct descendants of the curse."

"Wait a sec. What about Kelly Gregoire?"

"Oh yes, Kelly," Peabody said disdainfully; apparently he and I were of the same mindset on the heir to the MacLaoch throne. "His bloodlines were traced back to a distant cousin of Lady MacLaoch—not her direct descendant, but a relative."

"OK, but how am I a direct descendant? I didn't think the Minory had children. I thought that I was related through another branch of the Minory family."

"Oh! I see. No, they both did."

I rolled my eyes. "And how do we know this?"

Peabody opened his mouth to respond and then thought better of just jumping in. "The long version or the short version?"

"Short, please."

"Lady MacLaoch, after being 'rescued' from the Minory, was forced to marry the man her father had gifted her to. They only had one child —she died after it was born. The Minory"—Peabody smiled—"you are not going to believe me, but I hope you'll understand that with this short version, I'm leaving out the extensive research that was done. Though if you ever get curious, it's all there." He pointed to the box on the counter behind him. "The Minory had two children before he met Lady MacLaoch. Whether he had one or two wives prior, it's uncertain, but it is extensively documented that the Minory was a widower. He was about to take his third."

I sat there, mouth agape, looking at Peabody then to Deloris. "Does this make sense to you?"

"Aye, well," she said, standing, "I've heard rumors to that extent. Though I don't need to believe in that tae be able to tell ye that ye and the chief were meant tae be together."

"What do you mean by that?" I asked as she made her way to the box on the counter and began sorting its contents.

Peabody leaned back in his chair to take in her words as well.

"I might be old and spend most of my time down here, but I'm no' blind. From the first moment ye were here, both ye and Rowan came in here complaining of butterflies in your stomachs and humming in your veins. Then ye meet and Rowan does something that he's never done before, an that's take ye as his date to the Gathering gala." Deloris put down the file she'd pulled out of the box. "He has never—and I've known him since he was a wee boy—taken a date to the opening gala. Oh aye, he's had more than one woman in his life before he was chief, but none that have mattered enough tae him." She reiterated what I'd heard from Wanda just days before.

Just then it felt like a freight train was moving through me, taking my breath with it. Rowan's voice sounded in my mind, *Cole, where are ye?* Stunned, I simply thought back, *The library.*

"I know it's a lot tae take in, Cole dear, but don't look so surprised. Ye must have known on some level that Rowan and ye are more than just acquaintances?" Deloris asked.

"What?"

"Are you OK, Cole?" Peabody asked.

"Yeah. I'm fine," I said. "I just had the strangest sensation that Rowan was asking where I was. It was really weir—"

Deloris looked to the room's doors just as they were yanked open. Rowan walked in.

"Deloris, Edwin." He nodded to them; they were both transfixed.

I had barely turned in my seat when Rowan grabbed my arm and pulled me up, out the double doors, and up the steps to the main entrance.

"Stop!" I said and, in one deft movement, twisted my arm free, surprising Rowan. "I need my things, just wait." I threw over my shoulder: "Then I expect an explanation."

Thirty-Three

I found myself getting into a boxy old Mercedes SUV, and I said a little prayer in the library parking lot as Rowan and I tore out of it and down the street. We came to a halt several miles down the road, across from the B&B.

Shutting off the engine, Rowan spared me a glance as I reached for the door handle. "Stay."

"No."

A long arm shot past me and yanked the door shut. "Please stay in the car. I'll be right back."

I turned to face him, only to find he was already out his door and jogging down the sidewalk. I watched as he slowed his approach to the B&B and placed a hand on the hood of a black car. He paused for just a moment there and then continued into Will and Carol's. I waited. He would have to come back and get my key from me. And I wouldn't be so nice about it either, I thought—I'd make him tell me what was happening before I'd fork it over.

I looked at my watch. It had been too long since Rowan left—he didn't need that much time to get to my room, find it locked, and come back for the key. And to make matters worse, it was harder and harder to not think that it was ridiculous that I had been told to stay in the car—and that I was! Reaching for the door handle, I saw Rowan emerge from the B&B with my black suitcase, fabric from hastily shoved clothes visibly fluttering as he approached. Had he just checked me out of Will and Carol's?

Rowan placed the bag in the back of the Mercedes and then got in himself, reaching silently for the ignition.

"Start explaining or I'll start screaming. Because this is kidnapping." I grabbed his hand to prevent him from turning the key. His knuckles where wet.

"Ugh!" I said, involuntarily pulling my hand away.

Rowan wasted no time with my distraction, whipping the vehicle from its spot and heading away from town.

I looked down. His hand wasn't just wet—it was wet with blood, as was mine, now. Several of his knuckles were raw and oozing, and if I knew anything about the MacLaoch chief, only some of that blood was his.

"There was an obstruction I had to get through to get your bag."

I swallowed bile down as I rubbed my palms clean on my jeans, without caring whether they stained. "You, you struck Will? Carol?"

"What? No, Cole—what do ye take me for?"

I looked incredulously at him. "Just last night you were a guy who stormed away after Kelly pointed out that you have violent nightmares from your time in the military. Now I'm sitting in some ex-military vehicle, speeding down the road away from town, after you broke into a bed-and-breakfast to steal my suitcase." I took a deep, stabilizing breath. "Right about now, I'm wondering if I should be lunging for that rifle case in the back, or if I'd have more luck just leaping out of the car."

A small and unreassuring smile curled at the corner of his lip. "Neither. Rifle's empty. You'd be better off hitting me in the head with the butt of it."

"I'll keep that in mind."

"Gregoire was in your room. If he was your guest, then I'm sorry for what I did tae him. No, actually, I'd no' be then either."

"What? What was he doing there?"

"Ye didn't invite him up then?" he asked snidely.

"How dare—no. To hell with you, Rowan—you know damn well

he was there uninvited. Answer my question. What was he doing there? Or did you bludgeon him to death before you asked?"

Rowan was quiet. Something most of my family had never learned: silence holds truth better than noise.

"Oh god." I put my head in my hands as Rowan took a left turn off the main road onto a rutted dirt road. "You didn't. Please tell me you didn't," I mumbled into my hands.

"No. Unfortunately, he's still alive, despite the fact that he broke into your room and was waiting for ye to return, and no' with a handful of flowers."

"You're so damn cryptic. What does that even mean?"

"He had a bloody sgian-dubh, Cole."

"A what? What was covered in blood?" I heard my voice rise a click on the volume control to match his.

Rowan waited a few beats, his jaw tightening and untightening. "A fucking short blade."

My stomach dropped and I felt the distinct urge to vomit. I rolled my window down and leaned my head against the frame, taking in deep quantities of mountain air as we flew through it. Concentrating on simply breathing, I blocked out all other thoughts; the rest would come soon enough.

The road wove back and forth through fields of heather, the soft-pink flowers of the stiff shrub exploding against the gray sky, climbing the low hills above Glentree and then up into the mountains. Cold fog shifted as we drove, lifting then thickening again over the road. Eventually a large stone lodge loomed out of the swirling white. Rowan brought the car to a stop in front of a red door that matched the heavy shutters closed tight over the windows.

"Where are we?" I asked quietly, rolling up my window.

"The MacLaoch hunting lodge. The Gathering's hunt, meant for tomorrow, has been canceled, and we're keeping guests at Castle Laoch."

Not that the answer really mattered to me—I didn't understand the bigger picture. Mind numb, I grabbed my things and headed after Rowan into the lodge.

"Rowan? What are *we* doing *here*, and shouldn't we call the police or something?"

"They've been contacted."

We kept hustling along the buffed dark wood floors, past massive stone fireplaces, leather furniture, animal-hide tapestries, and the mounted heads of hard-won kill. There was no mistaking the place for anything but a hunting lodge, and I wasn't sure if that comforted me or not. I wasn't yet sure which side I'd gotten myself onto—the hunter's or the prey's.

Rowan disappeared through a cellar door in the kitchen; I tried to follow, only to have him return and shut the door. I reached for the doorknob, and just let my hand rest there. I was still focused on my breathing.

"I've got the generator going," he said when he returned. "Lights will work now—should take some time before the radiators are warm. Ye should make a fire if ye are cold."

I followed him back to the entrance and watched as he unzipped a bag, confirmed its contents, then grabbed it and the rifle case and headed for the door.

"I'll come with you."

"No. I'll be right back. Stay here."

I was done paying attention to my breathing. I had regained enough energy to be angry. "Stay? I'm not a goddamn dog Rowan—if I need to stay, you need to tell me why, and not just strong-arm me."

Rowan whirled on me, his storm-blue eyes flashing lightning. "It's not safe for you to come."

"Why?"

"I'm making sure we have safeguards in place before it gets much darker outside."

"Well, it seems safer having someone with you—*safeguards* and all." I said in what I hoped was a rational tone.

This made Rowan's face twitch. "Ms. Baker," he said, all patience lost. "I'm going to booby trap the shit out of the hillside so tha' if anyone comes up here, their cover is blown. And I'll do better if I'll no' have tae worry about ye. So ye will do what I say and tha' is to stay."

By the time I got to the door, Rowan—and the car—were gone.

Despite the furnace's efforts, the lodge seemed to be growing colder as the day progressed. I'd calmed my initial agitation by giving myself a tour of the floors, so I set to making a fire in each of the fireplaces I'd seen. Supplies had been stacked neatly next to each stone behemoth.

And then I was done with that and agitated again, with everything. Going to my pack, I pulled out the only hair tie I had, a cashmere scarf. Even my hair had become an agitation.

I tied my hair back, then looked at and replaced book after book in the main living room—war, warcraft, political prowess, historical idealism; herbology, zoology, and gun cleaning. Finally, all I could do was sit and wait. Which I did, on the edge of a chair, closest to the door. This, of course, gave my thoughts center stage, and those were not calming or distracting.

What in the world had brought Gregoire to my room with a sword, and why wasn't Rowan more surprised about that? How had Rowan known where to find me? And the most irritating, heaviest thought of all: if Rowan truly knew I was in danger—if Gregoire had divulged some crazy plan to him last night—why wouldn't he have told me? Unless he was in on it, or didn't believe Gregoire would really do it.

Tires crunched on the gravel outside the lodge, followed by a door slam. I was so deep in terrifying thoughts that the noises nearly sent me out of my skin.

Rowan was unloading his gear in the front hallway and, like an escaping cat, I slipped through the shadows and out the door. As I went I pocketed the keys that had been carelessly tossed on top of one of the bags. I had my pack on my back and my suitcase in hand.

"Cole!" Rowan called from behind me.

I ignored him and worked quickly, tossing my things into the muddied vehicle. It looked like it had plunged through a bog and then been washed with a mudslide.

I got the driver's door open just as Rowan came up behind me and slapped a hand on it, closing it again.

"What are ye doing?"

With all my stored up adrenaline, I hollered at him, "I'm getting the hell off this mountain and away from anyone named MacLaoch—Gregoire, Kelly, or who-gives-a-damn! You all are insane and I'm getting on the next goddamn plane home!"

Rowan was wound tight, too, and just sneered, "A little too late for tha'."

"You can't just keep me here against my will, Rowan."

"If ye knew the whole story, ye wouldn't be here against your will," Rowan growled back at me.

"Which is exactly what I've been asking for this whole time! Go ahead! Enlighten me, Rowan—why the hell am I here?"

"Come back inside, Cole. Ye need to be sitting down when I tell ye all tha' happened." His eyes glinted coldly in answer to my challenge.

I buried my need deep so that it didn't betray me on my face. Instead, I gave a short nod and started walking toward the lodge. Rowan strode past me, his foul mood radiating, making him seem larger and darker than he actually was.

"This had better be good," I snipped at him as he passed, playing my part.

I watched until he reached the lodge door; then I pivoted and sprinted back to the Mercedes.

I wrenched open the door and slammed it shut behind me. In the driver's seat, everything was backward from an American car—the gear stick was on the left, as well as the parking brake, I slid the keys from my pocket and into the ignition, which thankfully, was still on the right. The door locks were manual and I elbowed the lock down just as Rowan hit the door and yanked. I cranked the motor to life.

Rowan wasted no time with words or demands. He slid over the vehicle's hood in one effortless move to get to the passenger door before I could. Instinctively, I reached to slam the lock down, knowing it was going to take me more than a second to find reverse, but missed—the interior was wider than I thought. I wrenched myself out of my seat to hit at the lock again but got nothing but air.

Rowan reached in and grabbed ahold of my wrist, pulling me from the driver's seat.

"Let go of me!" I said between clenched teeth and tried to yank my hand back.

Rowan's grip on my wrist was like an iron band. "No," he said, pulling me forcefully over the parking brake and passenger seat.

I clawed at the beaten leather seats and dashboard with my free hand but could hold on to nothing.

I changed tactics. Just as my feet hit the passenger seat, I pushed off for all I was worth into Rowan, sending us both into the heather-covered slope next to the driveway. Rowan hit the ground and I hit his belly, with my elbow. He had been ready for it, but not enough so—his grip on my wrist loosened and I wrenched free.

I made it to my knees before he plowed into me from behind, sending me face first back into the heather.

I let out a blood-curdling scream and elbowed him in the ribs. "Get off of me!" I shrieked into the shrubbery.

"Not until ye calm down," he said, as quietly as if we were playing chess.

I bucked and slammed my elbows back against him in response. Rowan felt like a ton of bricks on my back. He methodically grabbed each of my wrists, securing them under his power, pinning me bodily to the earth, and ultimately bringing me to a screeching halt.

I was trapped, downed, and helpless.

My breath came quick. A low and terrifying sound growled out of my throat, tearing the air in aggravated frustration.

"Cole . . . " Rowan's voice was warm on the side of my face, pleading. "Calm down and I'll let ye up."

"Go to hell." I slammed the back of my head against his face.

"Oh!" He rolled off me.

I scrambled up on all fours. The heather caught my shoes and grabbed at my sweater. I'd lost control over my arms and legs as they all fought, but not in sync, to propel me forward fast enough, unwieldy with a lethal dose of adrenaline roaring through my system.

I didn't get to the car.

Rowan came up like a tidal wave behind me. His arm grasped me about my middle, lifted me into the air, flipped me over, and slammed me down hard onto my back. I realized belatedly that earlier, he had been playing nice.

Despite the shrubbery breaking the blow, air flew out of my lungs and my head thumped the ground like a door knocker. It took me a moment to orient myself. Rowan came down upon me, his legs pinning mine, his hands over my wrists.

"I've already been shot at and otherwise threatened by my own kin, and I bloodied a man who was going tae do god knows what with ye. I'm all out of patience, so ye can either do what I say or I'll tie ye up until ye are calm enough to think straight."

The sight of his blood (from a split lip) and the sound of his rapid breathing (which I noted not without a little satisfaction), along with his confession of what had happened to him already that day, had a profound effect on me.

A single, uncontrolled tear rolled fat and hot down the side of my face.

"Cole . . ." Rowan whispered.

All I wanted to do was relax every muscle in my body so much that I would be swallowed up by the earth and wake up elsewhere, but I could not stop the hot liquid squeezing out my closed lids.

Then Rowan pleaded, "Stop. Oh Cole, no, no, don' cry, please?"

I felt a rough thumb wipe my cheek. His forearm still pressed my wrist captive.

I just shook my head. "I don't know what's up from down anymore, Rowan."

"Aye," he said then wiped my other cheek. "Fighting with me isnae going to help ye any."

I looked at him. "You might be right, but in this case you just told me more than you did during the entire car ride here."

"I'm sorry," he said quietly. "I've been focused on one thing, and tha' was to make sure ye were safe. I've no' given much thought to much else."

My head was coming back to normal but I was starting to lose feeling in my hands. "Safe from who? And Rowan? I can't feel my hands."

Rowan sighed. "It feels like I have to keep ye safe from everyone.

Listen, the drive back down is booby trapped. I'll drive ye back in if ye want. Just don't go tearing off without me; ye will get hurt when ye get to it—even in this thing," he said, nodding at his vehicle.

I nodded. "I think I'm just going to lie here for a while. My head is still ringing."

Rowan sat back on his haunches, and I slid my legs free. He touched his lip where it was split. "Aye, mine, too. I think your head is made of rock."

"Bakers are known for their hard heads." Adrenaline's aftereffects started to give me the shakes. "OK," I said, "I think I need to hear the whole story. Start from the beginning. What happened today?"

Rowan told me about finding Kelly at the terrace and Eryka nearly shooting him.

After my initial horror, I realized that Rowan's nonchalance was almost comical. "Took her gun. Wow, so she just gave it to you, huh?" I said, coming up on one elbow.

"Och no, but it didn't take much to get it from her. If ye have a gun, Cole, use it, then chat later—much more effective. Hesitating to use it means ye don't want to, which makes ye seem weak. And then ye are weak."

I held my breath for a moment and then said quietly, sobered, "Like the difference between Eryka and the man who shot you?" It was blunt and unladylike of me, but I hoped beyond hope that he would answer my question.

Rowan slowly sat forward, bracing his arms on his knees. "Aye, like tha'. I knew he was no' the hesitating kind." He looked back at me. More words were on the tip of his tongue, I could tell, yet his mind wrestled with whether or not to divulge them. He looked away again and made up his mind. "He had just dispatched my best friend and navigator not two seconds before, blowing his brains out as I watched." Rowan turned to look me in the eye, his pain visible and raw, as if he were in the desert right then, reliving the very moment.

My stomach dropped. This was the darkness of Rowan James Douglas MacLaoch.

"So ye could say I had an inkling on what he would do when the muzzle turned its black eye on me."

"How'd you not get shot in the head too?" I asked softly, knowing that he could close me out at any moment.

He snorted in mirth, a dark, deeply dark, sound. "A bit of luck," he said. "We were both on our knees." He hesitated over something again, and again decided to continue. "I had the advantage of going second. Vick took the first bullet, and my name was on the second, but I leapt up as he pulled the trigger and instead of death, he gave me a token to remember him by for the rest of my life." His hand seemed to drift reflexively to his side, where his scar was.

I couldn't stop the flood of questions, especially now that the secret seal had been broken. "How did you get out?"

"Get out?" he asked, looking over at me.

"You were in the Middle East, right? How'd you get out of the desert?" I said, coming up on one elbow.

"Aye, we were in the desert, but how did ye know that?"

I opened my mouth to tell him all about the dream he and I had shared, to let my wall down as well. Instead I said, "I just assumed, since you were RAF and saw combat."

"Aye," he said reluctantly, as if not believing what I said, even though it made perfect sense. "Your Americans airlifted us out."

"But how, with all those men shooting at you?"

Rowan took a deep, purging breath. "Aye, they barely did." Then, to my surprise, he began to retell the dark tale. "Going in, it was a single strike effort, in an' out ye could say, but a surface to air missile probably from a deaf and blind man—tha' would be my luck of it—shot the wing off us."

The fog about us thickened like shredded clouds falling down on us, misting our woolen sweaters and dewing the heather. The creatures of the mountain were silent, seemingly listening to Rowan retell his darkest moment, rapt and thoroughly disturbed.

"Vick was struck unconscious as we ejected, or from the blast from the missile. By the time the desert wind had dragged him to where I had landed, he was torn up. I carried him behind a rock as the desert rats surrounded us . . . Right after Vick was shot—" Rowan stopped speaking, and instead started rubbing his thumb on his forehead as if the simple act would erase the imagery that was burned there. "I dinnae remember much but I do remember tha' when the plane crashed, I thought tha' because of the type of errand they'd sent us on, we'd no' be getting immediate help. But the Americans in the area responded to the plane's crash beacon. They were the ones who rained down enough metal to send tha' small town back to the Stone Age and lift me and Vick's body out."

Rowan had gone pale and sat like a stone on the hillside, his lips alone moving, spilling his horror into the cold mountain air.

"The hardest thing I've ever done was to tell his parents tha' he died as a chance of luck, to stand there telling them tha' their youngest child, their only son, was dead. Had we no' been hit from the sky, had I crashed us somewhere else, had I leapt up sooner, had I just . . . done something else, he might still be here.

"The months after were a blur. The hospital in Germany, the news my uncle died, that plane ride back with the pain pills steadily coursing in my system, then inauguration to the chief's seat: I barely remember. Then the dreams started, realistic and demonic. I drank—excessively," he said honestly. "But I realized tha' made them worse. Then I started running and swimming in the ocean loch, and took up the laird of MacLaoch position with a ferocity tha' scared some folk. But it was the only remedy tae the dreams, to be too exhausted at night tha' I slept a dreamless sleep."

He had been picking at the pink heather, restlessly plucking the flowers and tossing them down the hillside, one by one. As if realizing the nervous habit, he stopped then and laced his fingers together.

"With the Gathering, something was happening," he said so quietly that his voice was like a whisper inside my head. "The dreams started back up again. I was there again, gripping my side and coming back up with my blood—Vick's hollow eyes looking up at me, saying if I hadn't buggered it all, he'd still be alive. Stopped sleeping for a while—it's easier just to avoid it. Then ye arrived here and when the visions of Vick would come to me, ye would walk up and take my hand, pulling me away with ye." Rowan continued, "So ye see Cole, I've been completely selfish with ye and all this business. That's why I didn't drive ye straight to the airport and put ye on the next plane home. For the life of me, I cannae not do it. I cannae bare to have ye go a moment sooner than ye must."

Rowan's words had been simple, and straightforward, and they had my insides rolling about, tying themselves into emotional knots.

"But ye know what did me in, Cole? Was just a little bit ago when ye asked me about the sandbox and the men who had surrounded us. No one told ye, did they?" he asked turning to face me. "No one told ye tha' it happened in the Middle East and tha' we had been surrounded."

"Ah . . . " I said, feeling the gunmetal gaze of the MacLaoch chief pin me under it. Rowan put a hand back next to my elbow and very slowly lowered himself next to me so that we were face-to-face.

"Tell me the truth," he whispered.

My insides became honey, slowly churning into a sweet intoxicating liquid, making my voice barely audible even to my own ears. "No, no one told me," I admitted, giving him what he wanted to hear—I'd have given him anything he wanted.

"Tell me," he said, looking at my mouth, then back to my eyes. "Where was it, Cole, tha' ye knew it from?"

I wet my lips and my wall came tumbling down. "You were in my dream," I said slowly. "You've been in many of my dreams since I first arrived in Glentree."

"Tell me."

And so I did.

"Rowan . . . " I whispered afterward. "In the dream last night . . . I could even smell your blood." I shook my head at my own disbelief. "You asked me to help you, and I tried to. I hope that I was able to take you from the darkest moment of your life and show you the beauty that still exists in this world." I smiled at the memory, and I could see he was following them exactly, as well as he had in my dream. "Peaches in South Carolina will make you weep for joy, especially the ones still warm from the day's sun, the ones that fall into the palm of your hand they're so ripe. And the juices . . . " I said, watching Rowan's face.

A smile pulled at the corner of Rowan's mouth as he looked down at me. "Aye, I didn't know peaches could bring me so much joy."

The way he said it, the way he lay on the ground next to me, up on one elbow, a smile playing upon his lips, told me volumes about what he really meant.

Slowly Rowan reached for me, hooking a finger through a belt loop on my jeans, and pulled me closer to him. "Do ye remember how the dream ended?" Rowan asked, his hand slowly tucking under my sweater, making sweet skin-to-skin contact.

My mind went fuzzy. "I—I'm not sure exactly. I just remember a few seconds after you . . . " I was unable to complete my thought.

"After I what, Cole?" he said as his hand glided over my belly, sending ripples of excitement through my midsection, cold air kissing the small, exposed area of my bare stomach.

"Oh my," I breathed. I put my hand over his, capturing it. "Maybe *you* should tell *me* what happened next."

I felt him move in, the heat of his skin warming the air between us, his lips a hair's breadth away from mine. "Maybe it's better that I show ye." Rowan shifted farther over me, his knee settling between my thighs.

"Oh god," I whispered, closing my eyes against the emotional onslaught.

Rowan's lips brushed against mine. "I like Rowan, but ye can call me anything ye want."

And right then I wanted nothing more than to live out my dream in the hot and humid peach orchard with the MacLaoch chief, despite my misgivings.

The cold night air electrified goose bumps along my skin, and I shivered. The little chill brought me to a more immediate point: the heather was stabbing me relentlessly in the back, and it was far from hot and humid out.

A smile tugged on Rowan's lips. "I felt that all the way through my sweater. Are ye cold," he asked, "or are ye really excit—"

"Cold," I said, cutting him off and looking back at him.

And yet I wasn't sure that I still wouldn't end up naked and frozen with him in the heather if I let him keep talking.

"OK," he said, breathing deeply over my lips, sounding regretful of what he was about to do. "I believe you. You did wake up after I suckled ye, didn't ye?" He kissed my neck lightly, breathed deeply.

"I-I did." I shuddered.

"Are ye sure ye don't want me to show ye what we did?" he asked, hopeful, and planted another soft kiss on my jaw, then my ear, warming them both with his breath.

I didn't trust my mouth any more, not with him that close—I simply nodded.

"OK," he said again. He gave me one last long look before he stood, helping me up as well. Dusting the debris of the heather from our clothes, we climbed out of the brush and hurried to the front door.

There, Rowan paused, one hand on the old wrought iron knob.

"Just for the record, Cole," he said, slowly and forcefully bringing me in against him, his pelvis pressed against mine, his hand at my lower back. "I'll have ye know tha' I made randy fucking love to ye until the sun came up, and now I want to know if it's the same in real life." He gave his words just a moment to sink in, and watched my face as the recognition played across my features. With a wicked grin, he yanked the door open and strode inside.

Thirty-Four

I took a moment more in the foggy damp outside to collect my thoughts that had just gone dark and sultry with the chief's honest words. They mingled with the heat of his hand from just moments before in the heather. A few seconds later I went in, unable to fully shake them. Rowan met me in the living room with a whisky in hand, the only visible effect of his true mood in the amount of whisky he had poured himself, it being twice the measure of mine.

"Let's see," he said, "Kelly and Eryka want to kill me, and Kelly to then marry ye. And then Eryka to kill ye, so she can marry into the family. Gregoire was waiting with a sword in his hands for ye in your room, after swearing at the gala the other night tha' ye were his to marry and complete the curse with. And you are now stuck with the cursed MacLaoch chief in his hunting lodge without cell-phone reception. I'll no' lie, I'm getting the better end of this, I'll tell ye tha'," he said and lifted his tumbler at me in cheers.

I gave a derisive snort and felt reality break through the lusty fog in my mind—placed there, no doubt, by his design. "Yes, that you are." I smiled, taking a sip of the warm liquid. "And all of it is because of a legend. You said you called the police, right?"

"I made sure tha' was done before I left. Thinking clearer now, I should have stayed instead of snatching ye and running. But I've no' been thinking clearly since I met ye."

I smiled; I knew exactly what that felt like. Before I could comment on that subject, my stomach rumbled loudly in protest at being ignored.

Rowan laughed, heartily, one that seemed to start from deep inside, quite unlike anything I'd ever heard from him.

I felt my head go light with his joy and said distractedly, "I'm not sure I can survive on a whisky-only diet."

"Och, not many can—tha' is, unless ye are a Scots, which in your case, ye are, just out of practice," he said, his smile still bright on his face. "Come now, no need to starve, with the hunt being canceled all tha' food needs to be eaten." He walked past me and into the kitchen.

Moments later we were back in the living room with bread, cheese, cold cuts, pâté, dried fruits, nuts and, of course, more whisky, spread on the wooden coffee table between us. I'd also set out the files I'd gotten from Deloris and Dr. Peabody before Rowan had yanked me out of the library.

Rowan sat in the leather chair across the table from me and I sank into the buttery leather couch. We washed bread and cheese down with the sweet whisky and I felt it blooming with heat on the way into my stomach. "About the curse . . . " I said, feeling it was now or never. "I think I need to tell you about Peabody's newest theory."

"Aye?" Rowan said, curiosity and a healthy dose of wariness coloring his tone.

"That the curse is over," I said plainly.

Rowan's brows rose in surprise. "Aye? And how did he come to that?"

I plucked the file from the table and slid a paper from it over to him.

Rowan read through the Secret Keeper's version swiftly and tossed it back onto the coffee table. "Aye, I've read that one countless times. Did Peabody find something new?"

"Well, you'll remember that he had measured your energy reading or whatever it is he does with the gadget he keeps talking about. He's come to the conclusion that you've seen the likes of Lady MacLaoch's pain. Since you were shot and with Vick's associated death, apparently, it makes a big impact on your force field or some such."

"I got that."

"So we both agreed that since the curse states—as you know—that once the chief feels the—"

"Aye, likes of her pain. I heard ye and I know tha', but Cole, I dinnae think tha' what I felt was enough for Lady MacLaoch. She had to stand by and watch as her betrothed got his head severed. I dinnae think she'll accept a bullet and a friend instead. More likely she's looking to have me watch ye be strapped down and killed as payment made in full."

I blinked. "I'm sorry. What did you just say?" I asked, then realized that this had been Rowan's personal fear for some time now.

"I know tha' it does not fit in with Peabody's or your theories, Cole, but ye have to understand tha' it is I who lives with the curse and has her blood beating through my veins. I'll gather I have more experience than either of ye on this subject," he said plainly, not answering my question —yet he didn't look to be purposefully dodging it either.

"Rowan," I said. "Why would she kill me? I'm the other half to this; I have the blood of her betrothed pumping through my veins," I said, using his words. "I doubt she'd want to kill me."

"And ye know this how?" he said, trying to make me realize I had no basis. But I did.

"Because she's shown me."

Rowan's whisky glass was at his lips when I said this; his hand stilled and then replaced the glass on the coffee table without his having taken a swallow.

"She . . ." he said and stopped. "How?"

"Two things, before I tell you." I held up a single finger. "One, do you remember the day I came to Castle Laoch and I asked you if the ring in the glass case was Lady MacLaoch's?"

"Aye . . ."

Two fingers raised, I said, "Second, the dream we shared." No need to ask him if he remembered, as I was now well aware that he remembered that dream vividly. "They both involved her. In the first dream, I was on the island that's named after her, looking back on shore. In that dream, the ring was on my finger. We walked down the beach, she and I —she was within me, as if we were one, though she left me as a man came toward us." I looked Rowan in the eye—he was not missing a word that left my mouth. "You have to understand that the whole time, she was joyous, jubilant with something—a homecoming. I thought it was because the man was coming home, only realizing afterward that I was the one returning—he'd been here all along." I plunged on, "In the second dream, it started there—happy, lovely feelings once again, only this time the man who had no face in the first dream was standing next to me."

"And tha' man was me," Rowan said softly.

"Yes. So now do you believe that Lady MacLaoch has lifted the curse?"

"Aye, I can believe ye," he said, his voice sounding hoarse, "but, what is it, Cole, tha' is left, because ye know as well as I tha' she's no' done."

"Yes. That's where Peabody's second theory comes in," I said, feeling my heart ratcheting up, not knowing how I was going to tell this chief, this laird of MacLaoch lands that he and I were to wed. My words struggled to form and, in my silence, my rational mind began to fight a loud and determined fight. I picked up my whisky and slogged it back, heedless of its sweet fiery heat. Placing it a little harder on the table than I'd intended—like a college drinker at the end of finals week —I stood and put some distance between us. The coffee table was no longer enough—I felt that his presence was all too, well, present for me to easily tell him my next piece. At the moment I would have preferred to have the conversation with him on the phone. Long distance.

"Ye are making me nervous," he said, lacing his fingers together and leaning back in the wide leather chair, looking anything but.

I rested my hands on my hips, trying for all I was worth for a similar look of nonchalance. "I'm not sure how to say this next piece without sounding completely ludicrous."

Rowan simply grunted, his eyes never leaving mine.

"Peabody assumed the same as we did—that even though the evidence points to Lady MacLaoch's curse coming to a close, there is something more that needs to happen. After I told him of my dreams, of seeing the ring and you in them, he came to the conclusion that the next piece involves you and me. Umm, closely." Feeling a bit of background was needed, I added, "Did you know that Iain Eliphlet, and I suppose me, as well, is a *direct* descendant of the Minory who was killed?"

"Aye," he said, "I asked Peabody to research tha' the day I met ye. Aye, I know tha' ye are the product of the legendary Minory's own loins, and that's what scared me—tha' ye were here to ensnare me and then die as I watched, helpless. I tell ye, tha' would be a fitting end for me for Lady MacLaoch—to crush the last bit of light from my soul," he said with vehemence.

I felt myself wince at his words.

"It might seem impossible but, Cole, when ye watch someone killed in front of ye once, the thought of it happening again is no' so outlandish as it may seem," he said in simple truthfulness.

"I'm starting to see that," I said, then realized distractedly that he had had Peabody, rather than the official MacLaoch historian, research my history. "But why did you have Peabody research it? Wouldn't Clive have already known the answer?"

"Clive," Rowan said, "is a very opinionated auld bugger and won't challenge research tha' has been done more than a century ago. When ye told me your story, I placed the pieces together tha' Iain Eliphlet dinnae die but rather left." He brought the subject back around to what I had been expertly avoiding: "From what ye described of your dreams, I can guess Dr. Peabody's second theory."

"Really?" I asked. "Because it took me by surprise."

"Lady MacLaoch wants fulfillment of the one act that she was denied all those years ago," he said.

"You are a quick study," I said, feeling my heart rate gently increase once again. "Yes, Peabody thinks that with her showing me the ring and then you in the dreams—well, the rest, I suppose, should have been obvious . . . " I let my words drift out into the air between us.

Rowan smiled, eyes glinting. "Not if ye weren't looking for it."

"And you were?" I asked, hearing my voice crack for the first time, my carefully controlled demeanor slipping.

"Aye. I was looking for it. Looking for another way, tha' I could be wrong and now ye—and Peabody—have given it to me," he said, sitting forward, resting his elbows on his knees. "Cole, do ye know what handfasting is?"

I felt recognition ring the air as he asked me this—while the words themselves were foreign to my ear, they were not to my body, nor to my soul.

It was as if the forces of nature understood his words as well. Thunder rolled in the distance, long and deep, the telltale sound of a rainstorm building outside the lodge walls.

"No, I don't know what that means," I said. "Should I?"

"Handfasting is ancient, Cole—it's no doubt what Lady MacLaoch and her Minory would have done if they'd lived," he said, and stood.

My heart tripped over itself as he slowly walked around the coffee table, coming for me, as he spoke. "It'll bind ye to me, and me to ye. We must be sure tha' is what Lady MacLaoch wants. Are ye sure this is it what she wants?" he asked; then, as he got closer, "Is it what ye want?"

Would I want to bind myself to him forever?

"How do I answer that?" I asked, feeling as though a freight train would be easier to face down than the laird of the MacLaochs and the heavy discussion between us.

Rowan came to stand in front of me. "If I know ye, Cole, as I feel I do, ye need to answer it with this"—he gently laid his fingertips just above my left breast, covering my heart—"then with this." His fingers trailed up to and along the side of my neck, caressed my ear before cupping the side of my head. His thumb brushed my temple. "Because this one is crying out for ye to be rational, yet love is anything but."

My heart caught in my throat as his eyes looked directly into me and saw everything. "They are in direct opposition in their opinions," I admitted.

Lightning flashed outside as the pitter-patter of fat water droplets pelted the side of the lodge.

"But what does your heart say?"

"That I would be a fool to walk away from you," I said. My insides went into pleasant knots and my breath became erratic. "God, what are you doing to me?"

"Nothing that ye aren't doing to me," he said, sliding his fingers into my hair and loosening my ponytail, pulling the cashmere scarf free and dragging it over my shoulder. "MacLaoch plaid," he said as he fingered the material. Its blood red was run through with rich blue and yellow stripes, the distinctive tartan of Clan MacLaoch.

Plaid between his fingers, his knuckles grazed the skin of my arm as he grasped my wrist and wrapped one end of the scarf around it. Thunder cracked vehemently, drowning out the crackle of the fire and rattling the windows. He wrapped the other end of the scarf around his own wrist; seemingly of its own accord, the fabric tightened us firmly together. I watched all this as a woman might watch a distant lightning storm, detached but in awe of the strangely beautiful power she was witnessing.

Thunder shook the shutters even harder, and the rain pouring down the chimneys made the fires snap and hiss.

Words, silky and smooth, warm and lilting like whisky spilled from his lips. The Gaelic he spoke wound about us, pulling me closer to him and him to me, strings silky and silver bound us together. He broke from the lilting words to translate in English: "I take ye, my fair woman, and I bind ye to me, tha' we now become no' a man nor a woman but one mind and one heart. Forever your blood will be my blood, my thoughts will be yours, and your breath the only air I will breathe until I die. From this moment on, ye are mine and I am yours. This vow I will seal with my body and the seed of my loins," he said as his free thumb brushed over my lips. "Tell me, Cole, forever your blood will be my blood . . . "

My mind jarred awake as I opened my mouth to speak, stalling the words in the back of my throat—demanding me to be rational, just as Rowan had said it would. But in my heart I knew that, should I look back on this moment as an old woman sitting on my front porch, I would not be happy telling the children gathered around that I had walked away from this man. My mind was telling me to do just that, but I knew in my heart that I could not, and it was in that moment that I realized this was love. I was caught up and entwined forever with the man to whom I was bound at the wrist, even before I spoke the words.

"Forever, Rowan James Douglas MacLaoch, will my blood be your blood."

His blue eyes flinted with emotion. I felt his strong fingers tighten around my forearm; his other hand cupped the side of my face as my free hand gripped the sweater at his waist.

His voice was thick as he continued, "My thoughts will be yours . . . "

"And my thoughts will be yours," I responded.

"Your breath the only air I will breathe until I die . . . "

"And your breath the only air I will breathe until I die."

"Until death, ye are mine and I am yours."

"Until death," I said, feeling the weight of my words as if they were a stone falling into the palm of my hand. "You are mine and I am yours."

Lightning and thunder smashed light and sound together as Rowan took a shuddering breath and leaned down to my lips, sealing our words together, tasting me. The last of his translation rang in my head: *And I am yours—this vow I will seal with my body and the seed of my loins.* Heat blasted through me as I relinquished control to the chief, as I promised I was his, my blood, my thoughts, my breath, his. And he, *mine.*

Rowan broke the kiss and stood back from me. In one movement, he pulled his sweater and shirt off over his head. The scarf fell loose and rippled to the floor just as Rowan tossed his clothing onto the couch.

His chest glistened with sweat and heat—it rose and fell with his heavy breaths, emotions no doubt gripping his insides as they were mine. The MacLaoch chief stood before me looking much like a man who chased, fought, and regularly thwarted the demons that hounded him. He was as sculpted as a warrior, broad shouldered and muscular, the flat plains of his chest and taut belly marked only by that of the circular scar of his bullet wound, the injured tissue shiny just above the waist of his black pants, just next to the long crevice his pelvic muscle made.

Stepping in against me once again, Rowan brushed his fingers down the sensitive skin on the back of my arm as he held me firmly against him. His fingers found mine, pulled them up, and placed them against his scar, pressing the tips of them into the hardened skin there.

"I want ye to feel it, to know that I'll always have it—tha' with it, I bring my demons, but with ye by my side, I feel tha' maybe"—he pressed a kiss against my neck before breathing me in—"tha'maybe with ye at my side I'll have more light than dark in my life."

Letting my cheek brush against the rough stubble on his, I sought out his lips. "I'll take all of you, Rowan, light and dark."

I heard him groan against my lips, a sound that rumbled deep in his chest, mimicking the storm outside. "Ye are the angel to my deviled side, love. God, I pray I can be gentle with ye."

My body yielded to him, his lips parted mine, and his tongue delved into my mouth, tasting me, and I tasted him in return. His tongue was still smoky and sweet from the whisky, and just as intoxicating.

His Gaelic words spilled against my lips. "This vow I will seal with my body and the seed of my loins," he repeated in English as his hand found the edge of my shirt and pulled it up over my head. One hand entangled in my hair and the other hovered at the curve of my lower back; he pressed me into him as if we could simply meld together then and there. Our mouths tasted and felt and repeated the vows we'd just made.

Rowan's fingers traced my spine to my bra—with a single hand, and extreme talent, he unclasped it. Rowan's mouth separated from mine and found the nape of my neck, and my hands splayed across his shoulder blades as my knees liquefied under his ministrations. His kiss seared the tender skin at the base of my neck, bit into my shoulder. Gently he slid one bra strap off my shoulder, the satin smooth in its descent, and oh so slow, sending anticipation rippling through me—and in turn, through Rowan.

He gathered me up into his arms and strode with me to the plush of the fireside's sheepskin rugs, where he laid me down and made quick work of my jeans and socks, and even quicker of his own.

Seeing his whole body for the first time, in that moment, my heart stopped. Rowan was like no other man I'd been with before—I realized later that was because Rowan was just that, a man. The others I'd been with had been still boys. His muscles lithe, held powerfully in check as he lowered himself slowly down onto me—and with an education of the woman's body I dared not think about—Rowan kissed my stomach.

Then the tender lips between my legs.

I gasped, my fingers threading into Rowan's hair and gripping as my legs spread wantonly.

"Oh god," I gasped as his tongue found what was hidden like a pearl. Euphoria ripped and cascaded, spread out and squeezed tight. I tried to catch my breath, but the air became elusive as pleasure rocked me. I felt my feet slip and slide—I found no traction as I squirmed within my own skin, an explosion threatening. "Rowan," I moaned, "please . . ."

I felt his mouth leave me, for just a moment, and then it was biting gently across my belly to my breasts. "Please what?" he asked as his mouth covered the taut darkness of my nipple.

"Oh!" I exclaimed. Erotic electricity flooded my breast and then plunged down my middle, filling the intimate need between my thighs.

Rowan's tongue played across my areola, teasing it even tighter, and my hands gripped his hair with equal measure.

"Ouch, love. Use your words," he said as his deep chuckle melded with another crack of thunder.

I looked into his eyes filled with wicked humor, glittering dark blue through the fringe of his black lashes. His lean, angular jaw for once was not set in some stage of tension; his lips were moist from his work.

I felt my own lips quirk at his power over me, his feeling of being completely in control—though pressed against my leg was hard evidence that his control was wavering. Spreading wider, I slid his hardened self deep within my slick confines.

Thunder slapped the lodge with such force objects rattled around us, and the fire spurted alive with vengeance, the individual flames wild with movement. The clap and rattle nearly drowned out the gasp and growl that tore out of Rowan's chest as he sunk into me. Pleasure rocked us both, stealing our breaths as we clung, unmoving, to each other, riding the aftershock of our long-awaited union. Arching him deeper within me, I felt him lay heavy upon me before he lifted himself again, to a single elbow, his other hand gripping my hip and stilling my thrust.

"My vow sealed with my body and seed of my loins," he said against my lips.

I took a shuddering breath. "And mine, oh god, and mine."

My head fell back as my arms gathered myself against the hardened steel of Rowan's body above me.

Rowan's intoxicating power rocketed through me, his rough breathing matching my own, as needy and rhythmic as our lovemaking. Pleasure slammed through me in unison with his thrusts, building pressure, making me moan and grip Rowan's back, pulling him deeper, needing to feel him even closer, for his blood to become one with mine, our thoughts and breaths to become a single entity.

I cried out as the first of the blissful culminations rocked through my body; my nails dragged against his skin as the tremors of the final earthquake began to shake me.

The molecules, the very air around us, fissioned, ripping through the space. The fire beside us shot up the chimney as if stoked by gasoline, and the thunderous storm sent a low, bellowing roar through the stone, knocking books from their shelves.

My belly clenched as I gripped Rowan and he, me; sweat dripped out under my breasts as we moved, sweat-slickened, together. The second storm cascaded through me, making me gasp out for air in relief, and then, like the lightning that lit the night sky, Rowan uttered an oath in release.

Energy hot and white tore through us, and my legs around Rowan pulled him even deeper as I rode the last waves of the orgasm to its finish. A voice much like mine screamed in ecstasy, echoing off the walls of the lodge, matching the energy and strength of the storm battering at the doors and windows. Rowan's voice responded a low rumble that tumbled us both until we collapsed in exhaustion on and within each other.

Thirty-Five

A some point in the night we'd moved to even more comfortable surroundings, and the next morning we lounged naked under the bedcovers in one of the sparsely furnished lodge bedrooms. Light streamed through the slats of the shutters, spilling ladder-like light upon the floor and illuminating small dust motes as they floated in the beams.

"Ye know, there is one thing tha' I'm curious about," Rowan said, his arm around me as I rested my head on his chest.

"Oh? Just one?" I asked, playfully biting him.

"Ouch!" he said, giving me a look of mock stern reprimand. "No, no. I have many, but for now, just one. I was remembering back to the night ye put down Eryka on the terrace at the gala. Which one of your brothers taught ye tha', and how big is he?"

"Why?"

"Aye, I'll have to make a phone call to your family, letting them know what has happened, I just want to know which of your brothers, or how many ye have, tha' will be coming for me. That's all."

"Oh, that's all, huh?" I said, coming up on an elbow and looking down at him. "Well, first. I'll be calling my parents, so you won't have to—"

Rowan made a noncommittal grunt, telling me that he'd probably call them anyway. "But how many brothers do ye have?" he asked, looking up at me.

"Just the one," I said. "What else are you thinking of?" I could see his mind had changed subjects and was now elsewhere.

"Mmmph." I felt his hand slide into my hair. "Ye, of course," he said. "What are ye thinking of?"

"Well, right this moment I'm imagining how nice it would be to have you cook me breakfast. But I know that won't happen, since the power seems to still be out."

"Aye. Maybe we should head into town. I need to be in touch with the police today, and I don't know when the phones will be back up."

I put my nose to his chest and breathed him in. "Can it wait a bit? We're perfectly safe up here, and I'm sure it'll be fine as long as you're in touch with them by this afternoon—it's still early yet. I was thinking, since you can't cook for me, that you could do something else for me . . . "

Rowan raised an eyebrow. "Och love, if it were just a matter of stolen property I would, but I dinnae want to take chances with this lot and ye. Honestly, I'm having a hard time thinking of much else."

I smiled. "Was that a challenge?"

Thirty-Six

It was some time later, after Rowan gave in and we "made randy fucking love" all morning, that we departed for town (after untrapping the hillside). Glentree focuses on restoring power to the most populous areas first. Without knowing when it would come back on that day—if that week, even, considering the remoteness of the cabin—we were forced down from the mountain so Rowan could make the necessary phone calls.

Even though Rowan didn't ask, I was sure the question would come up soon: how much longer could I stay? In any case, I felt that researching a permanent visa and submittal requirements seemed like a good starting place. We reluctantly parted at the library, Rowan only letting me go after Deloris said she'd seen hide nor hair of Eryka, Kelly, and Gregoire and I promised I'd call him when I was done so he could escort back to his place—our place—at Castle Laoch.

I was keenly aware that coming down from the mountain was like leaving another planet, one where only he and I existed. While I could do the research I'd intended at his offices, I was back in reality and not ready to display for all the world that we were together, opening ourselves to public comments, just yet. However, we did plan to take the first step later, back in the privacy of his apartment—calling my family and informing them of what had happened in just a few days. Despite Rowan's encouragement, I was still debating how much to tell them; I didn't want them to have a collective heart attack or, despite the inevitable, feed on this gossip until the day I died.

Deloris was relieved that everything had been OK after Rowan's and my unorthodox departure. I didn't tell her all the ugly details—she'd get them, no doubt, when the arrests of Gregoire, Kelly, and Eryka broke the news, as I was sure they would be arrested. After some time with her, absentmindedly, and admittedly punch-drunk with love, I left the library and meandered toward Will and Carol's on autopilot. I got all the way to the front door of the bed-and-breakfast before I realized that I had neglected to call Rowan. Feeling the need to capitalize on my presence at Will and Carol's—thank them after my hasty departure and settle any debts—I headed around back to the private patio where they sat in the early afternoons.

I got only halfway down the alley between the rows of old houses when something hard pressed into my lower back. Before I could turn, before I could yell, a pop of fizz sounded, my muscles contracted, and the world went black.

Thirty-Seven

R owan stood furious in his office at the administrative building, the phone digging into his ear under his own angry force, while he waited for the investigator to come back on the line. Eryka, Kelly, and Gregoire all had apparently airtight alibis and, with the phones and power being down, the police hadn't been able to contact him and had not taken them into custody. The investigator had just put him on hold to dispatch police to the threesome's respective homes and get more information on their last whereabouts.

A light rap on the doorframe drew his attention. Dr. Peabody waved in his light-hearted style. "Oh! You are on the phone. I'll just wait then," he said, reclining into the chair in front of Rowan's desk.

Rowan just shook his head at the professor, "Not now, Peabody."

"Oh, OK." Then he asked, "Is everything OK?"

"Aye—" Rowan said, and he felt the room pitch, then fizz with electricity.

Cole's voice came softly to him: *Rowan.*

He felt his knees give out from under him, and then the world went out.

Thirty-Eight

I dreamed of driving, bumping over and through potholes on a clogged freeway in the dead of night. Fear was in my rearview mirror, pushing me to keep my foot on the gas. The other cars seemed to automatically slide out of my way, letting me speed by unseen in the dark.

My mind recoiled when it realized that it was dark, suffocatingly dark, in my dream. Exhaust fumes filled my lungs and burned my nose, choking me.

I awoke in a rush of fear and panic to find that I was living part of my dream. I was in a cramped space, breathing exhaust, and listening to the undeniable sound of a car motor. I'd been folded into a trunk. My hands and feet were bound with packing tape, as was my mouth, which I realized when I screamed and heard only muffled silence.

The realization of all these things came slowly and at a rate of one understanding at a time, individual small explosions timed to build to a grand finale. My hands bound, feet inseparable, and mouth gagged, I felt a full-blown claustrophobia attack close its debilitating arms around me.

Only something else entirely happened. Something I had not counted on, another emotion filling the space and derailing the attack.

One that ran hot and fierce through my ancestry and my family, making us, and ultimately me, the hotheaded, stubborn species we were.

Anger swept through me, directed toward those who had zapped me, taped me, and stuffed me unceremoniously into the back of this automobile. In a moment of pure inspiration, I thought of all those ridiculous e-mail forwards that my mother regularly sent to me—one in particular, concerning what to do when kidnapped and trapped in the trunk of a car. The only thing I remembered was the recommendation to kick out a tail light.

Had the person who'd written that e-mail ever even seen a trunk, let alone been in one? There was barely enough room for me lying still, let alone me slamming my feet forward. But slam I did, and with vengeance.

The car stopped suddenly, rocking me backward. This was followed by the sounds of footsteps on gravel. I hunkered tight, like a coiled spring.

A key scraped inside the trunk lock and led to the unmistakable clunk of the latch giving way, letting the lid rise up.

As soon as I saw flesh, I kicked.

I put everything I had into that single move and was rewarded. My feet made solid contact with a narrow frame and sent it staggering backward.

Somewhere in me I'd known that Eryka had been the one who'd stuffed me into the trunk of this car. It was as if my body remembered the sound of her voice and the cruelty she had shown me.

I wasted no time wriggling from the trunk, falling heavily onto the ground, and squirming, then hopping, for the trees.

The road and trees, oaks and pines, felt strikingly familiar. If it was indeed the forest I recognized, then Eryka was more of a fool than I had thought, or she assumed I was, because Castle Laoch would be just over a low rise and across a small stream.

The roadside sloped sharply down into the forest, and I didn't hop far before I lost my balance and pitched forward. Saplings and small shrubs slapped and scratched me as I tumbled by. I heard a shot ring out, and then the bullet splintered a tree just past me. I'd fallen out of sight at just the right moment.

But that wasn't enough for my insides, which had gone liquid with fear at being shot at. My belly clenched, and I ripped the tape from my mouth with my bound hands just as I was sick on the forest floor. I didn't—couldn't—pause. Scrambling, I hopped and threw myself forward toward a large oak—its expanse would be more than wide and thick enough to protect me. A second shot whined past my ear and struck the oak's trunk, ricocheting pieces of bark into my face. I slumped lower.

Behind the tree, panting, back pressed against the rough bark, I acted on instinct. I bit and tore at the tape at my wrists. Blood dripped into my eye, and I wiped it away with my shoulder and went to work on the tape wrapped around my ankles.

I heard an animal-like scream, and my oak was peppered with bullets.

"I'll get you! You can try to run, but I'll get you!" Eryka shrieked, her voice echoing hollow and demented through the forest.

Oh my god, I thought and steeled my nerves against the instinct to curl myself into a ball and whimper.

My mind, through the chaos, became sharp. I acknowledged that this was indeed the back part of Castle Laoch. Eryka was mad for having pulled over here and especially for setting off a Fourth of July's worth of bullets—someone would no doubt hear it and call for help. Though not, I knew, before she kicked off her heels and came for me.

I swore. Then ran.

Thirty-Nine

Rowan jolted awake to Peabody shaking his shoulder. "Rowan! What just happened? I'll call a doctor."

"No." Rowan struggled to his feet and sat back heavily on the edge of his desk. Bracing himself there, he shook his head to clear the clanging—it sounded like his head was a bell tower at noon.

"Rowan . . ." Peabody said, concern in his voice. "Are you having a flashback?"

"Flashback?"

"From the war . . . "

Rowan's eye twitched. "Aye. No, I've not had . . . " he trailed off, then finished simply with, "No. It's not tha'."

"Have you eaten anything today? Here, let me fetch you lunch— that must be what it is."

It came back to Rowan in a rush: "Cole."

Peabody halted at the door and turned back, his eyes wide in recognition behind his spectacles. "You've shared an experience . . . and one that wasn't so good."

Rowan was frozen, trying to feel for Cole, to feel that reassuring vibration of her living and breathing on his lands, that she was alive and close.

Anguish crossed Rowan's face and he strode past Peabody and from the room, grasping a windbreaker from its wall hook on his way out.

Peabody had to jog to catch up to the chief. "Rowan! Please wait—what has happened? Has something happened?"

Peabody skidded to a halt as Rowan whirled on him, pain and fury crossing his features and reminding the professor of what he'd heard about panthers: they quietly go about their business, avoiding others as much as possible—but corner one, and it becomes as lethal as a well-placed knife.

"What do you think?" he hissed at the professor.

Peabody took a steadying breath and looked the panther in the eye. "I think that you are panicked because you cannot feel her."

The chief simply sneered, "Correct, professor."

"Then let me help," he said.

"How?"

Peabody dug keys from his pocket. "Let us go wherever it is more swiftly than by running."

Rowan snatched the keys from the professor and ran for the tiny Vauxhall rental.

"So, where are we going?" Peabody cried as he ran after Rowan.

"To Castle Laoch," Rowan threw over his shoulder.

Peabody was barely in the passenger seat before Rowan rocketed them out of the parking lot and onto the main road toward the castle.

The top speed and shocks of the Vauxhall were all tested as small dips in the road became speed ramps, shooting the tiny car airborne. Peabody closed his eyes until suddenly the car screeched to a stop, throwing him against his seatbelt. In the next moment, Rowan was out of the car, slamming the door behind him.

THE LADIES STAFFING THE FRONT DESK AT THE CASTLE HAD not seen Cole. She was not in his—their—personal quarters upstairs, where they were supposed to meet and call her parents. The ghostly face of Vick, a black hole in his forehead, flashed in Rowan's memory.

Rowan, standing in his flat, roared in frustration and panic. He picked up the nearest object and threw it with all his might. The desk lamp shattered loudly against the far stone wall.

He reached for another object and stilled.

Something stirred his blood. It wasn't panic, frustration, or even anger. It was the low tone of the woman he loved—the one that, a single moment before, he thought he'd lost forever. The hum reverberated through his being.

At the bottom of the stairs, he nearly bowled over the professor, again.

"You've found her?"

"Aye, and no. I just know that she's alive."

Right then the elderly front-desk ladies came running, hands flailing, toward them.

"Sir! Oh, my Lord!" the first one cursed in fear. "Sir!" She gripped the front of her blouse with one hand.

The other, a hand on her colleague's shoulder in support, said, "Gun shots, sir."

As if on cue, he heard the bustling below of more people rushing in and spreading the news.

"Where?"

The two women shook their heads. "Dinnae know . . . It's just that all the guests are saying that they heard them. Maybe in the forest behind—it was not too close."

"Get the police here," Rowan called over his shoulder, already almost at the doors. "Where is John?"

"He's out the back gathering in the guests."

"Aye, good," he said, and left them.

Forty

Running full out, I zigzagged around trees and saplings, my feet crunching dead leaves from the previous winter on the forest floor. Another shot rang out, and again it went wide. Without breaking my stride, I reached the river.

Running high with the spring and early-summer rains, the river was too dangerous for wading, even with a gun pointed at me. Large, moss-covered rocks formed a hopscotch bridge across the river, and I had to take my chances that Eryka would continue to be a terrible shot. I clambered up the first rock, hands and knees slipping, taking chunks of moss with them. Crouching, I inched to the edge and sprang to the next rock. My foot hit wrong and I went down, slamming my chest into the basalt. Another shot, closer than I'd expected.

Breathless, I looked back. Eryka came to a sliding halt and brought her pistol up, aimed steadily. I did the only thing I could—I slipped off the downstream side of the rock. Another shot rang out and, just as I pitched into the freezing water, I heard the bullet strike rock.

The water's chilly fingers saturated my sweater, jeans, and shoes instantly, and the current took me. I struggled to breathe and avoid boulders as the water slammed me under, and then spouted me back up. Eventually I realized that this was much faster than trying to outrun

Eryka, and I would soon be at Castle Laoch, where I could alert Rowan, and possibly set myself on fire. I figured—as I passed under a service bridge at the outer edges of the gardens, where the water noticeably slowed—that would be the only way I'd be warm enough to feel my appendages again.

I dog-paddled to the shore. Further downstream was the narrow bridge that crossed the river and led into the gardens and, beyond, to Castle Laoch—but the service road was immediately to my left.

Heavy and freezing with cold river water, I still moved with speed. The service road ended at the boathouse. I leapt over the curb and sloshed down onto the parking lot and tried the boathouse office door. Locked. I started pounding on the door before I saw the handwritten note hung on it: *Gone. Will be back in 10 minutes.*

I cursed the person who'd written it, gave the door a kick in distress, and ran for the pier.

Two tiny fishing boats bobbed in the water at the end of the pier. The water was low, several feet below the pier. I cautiously climbed down the wooden, makeshift ladder and toed myself into the first boat. The boat rocked fiercely when I sat and nearly capsized. Just as I leaned to pull the starter cord on the outboard motor, I heard tires squeal into the boathouse parking lot.

Grasping the cord, I tugged. Nothing.

I pulled it again, and nothing. I yanked and yanked and got nothing, not even a sputter. Looking around wildly, I figured that the other boat was close enough. At the edge of the one I was in, I leaned for the other, fingers stretching.

I heard a frustrated scream and the sound of a shoe kicking the door of the boathouse. "Open this door or else!" Eryka yelled, as though I had simply locked her out and would just as simply let her in.

Rapid gunfire was followed by the shattering of glass—she was going in through the boathouse window.

As quietly and as gracefully I could, I set one leg over into the other boat, then the other.

Eryka screamed. It was a simple and terrifying sound, one that reminded me of a wild animal screeching at the lost scent of its prey.

Only I was wrong.

Her frustrated screaming was not as terrifying as the soft "Oh" I heard her say next, followed by the knowing click-clack of her heels moving swiftly down the pier.

I shoved myself fully into the second boat and threw myself at the little outboard motor. Sending up a prayer, I grasped the handle of the starter cord and yanked with such ferocity that the motor barely chugged before it started richly, spewing a black cloud of exhaust out the back of the boat and over the water.

In the same instant that the motor kicked to life, announcing with certainty where I was, I switched to reverse. The motor strained and the boat went nowhere. My mind reeled—I was still attached to the pier.

I staggered forward and tried with bumbling fingers, shaking with adrenaline and fear, to undo the simple knot at the bow. My insides churned as Eryka's steps got closer. My right foot wobbled on something, and I instinctively looked down.

A fishing knife.

I didn't waste another second: I picked up the knife, swung with all my might at the taught rope, and severed it in half.

The motor idled the small boat backward while I made my way to the rear so I could twist the engine's throttle to full. Even with the engine flogged, the boat moved with strained effort through the water in reverse. Sitting on the rear plank, I brought my hand up, still gripping the fishing knife as if it were a perfect form of defense against a gun.

Eryka came into view. She shot wildly at me. Water spewed as each bullet hit the surface; wood fragments splintered and shattered into the air as some bullets hit my lifeboat.

Terrified, I pulled my legs up so that I was in a protective ball, my arm shielding my face as if it were bulletproof.

Suddenly the peppering stopped. I looked up to see Eryka steadying her gun, taking the careful aim of a last-attempt shot.

Shit, was my first thought as the seconds ticked by. It was followed by the hope that when her bullet hit me it would be a body shot, something I could recover from, the way Rowan had. The following second brought a sickening third thought: this was my end. I had come all this way, fallen in love with a man and he with me, only for us to be immediately torn apart forever.

I realized this was Rowan's fear. The legend of Lady MacLaoch rearing its ugly head once again, with me as the pawn to be torn from this world just to make Rowan suffer. This was the culmination of the curse—a twisted trick from Lady MacLaoch to have the ancient love be rekindled just so that it could die once more.

Paralyzed with indecision about what I could do, let alone what I should do in such a nightmarish situation as this, I saw Eryka's finger squeeze the trigger to engage the bullet—the trigger which gave the command to propel the bullet from the chamber and through the air and into me. I flinched as I heard the hammer hit with a click that echoed off the water.

In that fractured second it was as if I weren't sitting in a boat where violence had exploded all around me. My mind, instead, transported me somewhere else, a happier time. A place where I was calm and able to notice details, like the briny smell of the water and the feeling that, despite my sodden clothing, I was warm, hot with exertion. As this peace settled into me, I had the thought, *Here I go—now I die.*

Incessant clicking, the sound of an empty cartridge being checked and checked again, snapped me back to the present.

Relief flooded through me as I watched Eryka turn into a small, raging inferno on the dock. She just kept pulling the trigger, as if the gun would suddenly refill with bullets and start shooting. I turned my attention to my boat as Eryka ran back to her car. I didn't want to be anywhere near her after she had reloaded.

Forty-One

In the open water, I followed the coastline toward Glentree harbor. Eventually the harbor came into sight and I could see other vessels, fishing boats in Glentree Bay, in the near distance. I was almost safe. At least now someone would hear me scream.

The motor suddenly coughed, then sputtered, and then continued, as if nothing happened. Looking warily at it, I realized that if I ran out of gas, I had no oars.

I shook off the fear that tried to wrestle me down, gave the outboard motor a pat—good dog—and prayed for a miracle, big or small.

The motor roared for a few yards more, then sputtered again and, like before, came back to life. Only its second life was short-lived, and I soon found myself in the deafening silence of the wide, flat ocean loch, drifting ever so slowing toward Glentree.

I tugged the starter cord, and it sputtered again.

The sound it made—the chugging that precedes the roar of a motor brought to life—made me go wild with hope, and I yanked and yanked on the cord, willing with all I had. I kept at it. I could feel my hand become raw and my shoulder ache with the effort. Tears blinded my eyes, making the world go bleary.

I didn't stop, not even when the motor made no sound and it had become just me and the whooshing spring pull of the cord.

"Aye! Ye will get more blood from a turnip, ye will, lassie!" called a craggy, well-humored voice from behind me.

Shocked, not realizing how long I'd been at it, I turned to find Angus and Bernie MacDonagh slowing up beside me. Relief flooded through me at the sight of their faces.

"Oh, ye a'richt?" Bernie asked taking in my full appearance, as they idled to a stop next to me. "Ms. Baker it is, aye?"

I simply pointed at the motor. "No gas."

Angus and Bernie exchanged a look. "Well now. We were just heading to Castle Laoch to get refueled ourselves. It's too far tae go with a tow on our tank of gas, so we'll head to the fishin' post o'r there," Angus said, pointing to a small isle behind me, speaking calmly and slowly as if he were talking to a madwoman. "Best ye come on board wit' us. Your skiff looks to have taken a wee bit of a beating."

Bernie and Angus helped me into their boat and wrapped me in a wool blanket that did wonders to keep the wind off me. We set out at a slow pace toward our destination, quietly digesting what was happening until Bernie broke the silence.

"Ye ha' the look of someone who's tangled with a mountain cat," he said softly. His tenderness reminded me suddenly of my grandfather, and that was enough to break me.

I wept, loudly and soundly, about everything. Sobs wracked my body until my eyes ran dry. I sucked in a shaky breath and let it out slowly, easing the pressure in my chest.

"Dinnae worry, lass, Bernie has that effect on all women," Angus said behind me.

I smiled at both of them and dried my eyes. "Sorry, and thanks for stopping," I said. "I wasn't sure what to do next."

"Och! It's nothing," Bernie said, getting uncomfortable. "'Tis just, lass, isnae there more than that?" he asked, and then added, "When we saw ye the other day, ye seemed happy and jovial about the possibilities that ye could be from this place. Have ye found trouble or has trouble found ye?"

"It's a long story," I said.

"Och! Now those are that best kind! We ha' a long while before we get ye filled back up an' on yer way."

I looked at Bernie. He just stared back at me as though he did indeed have all day, then leaned forward and placed an old hand on the top of my head. His thumb touched a gash at my temple. I'd forgotten that I must have looked like a twister had had its way with me.

"Maybe it'll be easier if ye start with how ye got this," he said softly, his voice low and gruff with age.

I too felt the gash and remembered the wood fragments ricocheting off the oak. I must have said as much because Angus spoke next.

"And who was it that was shooting at ye?" he said calmly, as if he asked people that question every day.

"Oh," I said, trying for nonchalance and thinking I really needed to contact the authorities and tell this story to them. "A woman named Eryka."

"Och! Now she's a one!" he said. "Jealous, aye, and wanting that seat beside the MacLaoch chief for a long time. Before Rowan, even. What does she want with ye?"

"My blood, apparently."

Angus was more shrewd. "The chief fancies ye, doesn't he?" he asked.

"Yes," I said, deciding to try nonchalance, too. "He and I have hand-fastened, or whatever you call it, so yes, I think he fancies me."

Silence.

It was Angus and Bernie's turn for quiet reaction.

"Hand-tied?" Bernie asked. "The MacLaoch chief? Rowan?"

I just nodded.

Then from behind me, as recognition struck him, Angus said, "Oh."

"Aye." Bernie nodded. He looked at his brother, then to me with new reverence. "Ye are then."

"Yes, we are hand-tied. Why are you looking at me like that?" I asked.

"Aye, ye have bound yourselves together. Ye are wedded, that is," Bernie said absently, still staring at me. "So ye are the descendant then? Yer ancestor was the Minory of the legend?"

"Oh, wedded," I said using the word as if I'd just heard it. "Yes, it turns out that I am the descendant."

Bernie looked around me at his brother again, then at the low mound of island we were approaching.

My stomach dropped. "Is that—" I didn't want to finish.

"Aye. It is the Isle of Lady MacLaoch," they both said as they brought the small boat up to a makeshift pier in the shallow rocky inlet.

Long fingers of pasture and heather tickled the black, smooth rocks of the beach, allowing them to take over and then gently slope into the clear, cold water. I could see a small but sturdy-looking stone building with a slate roof just beyond the pier.

I followed Bernie out of the boat to shore and waited as they secured my boat, went into the little building, and came out with a gas can. Silently we all did our jobs; mine was observing. The clouds were starting to form an odd pattern. Had I been on the South Carolina coast, I would have said that a hurricane was coming. The fluffy, low ceiling over the island began to form harder, longer, swirling shapes that curled about a center point. It was as if someone above were stirring the white mass with a finger.

"Aye," Bernie said, lumbering back from returning the gas can to the shed. "That is taken care of." He looked over as his brother came to stand next to him; then both of them looked at me with the same watery blue eyes. Could I be more uncomfortable? I could be.

"We have something tae tell ye. Back when we were kids we were told the story of the Lady MacLaoch, as was every wee bairn, but Angus and I were told more," Bernie said. "Ye see, every generation in our family has had one, and being as we are twins, we both were told. We were the Secret Keepers for our generation. Unfortunately our grand-children have laughed it off, too engrossed in the Internet and their tele-phones tae believe in something more real than they'll ever know.

"But anyway, with ye here, that tells us the curse is broken, which means there is much for us to do, and it's no coincidence that we've come tae be standing here on this island. It just is another sign that the last is soon tae come," Bernie finished.

"Now, Cole, do ye have one of those telephones? I think Rowan needs tae come now," Angus asked.

I looked down at my half-dry clothes, then back to them askance. "No," I said simply, not wanting to have to explain that even if I did, a soaked electronic device would not be so very useful.

Just then we all heard it, a motor being shut off. We hadn't noticed the gradual hum until it was suddenly silent.

I looked past the stone building and down the beach to where it curved around the end of the island. Both Bernie and Angus strained their eyes on the horizon, looking for the boat. The island wasn't very big and there was a possibility that whoever it was had simply landed on the back side of the island's low hill—a fisherman, maybe, or a tourist.

Only the rush of goose bumps on my damp skin said that it was best if we fled, and fled right then.

Forty-Two

Down in the lower hallway, Rowan yanked open the sticking door that opened onto the outer terrace and found John ushering groups of people toward him.

"Aye, everyone please go inside and stay there till we come tae tell ye all's OK," John said as he herded guests past Rowan and into the castle.

Rowan closed the door on them and turned to John. "Where'd ye hear them?" he asked.

"Back in the forest but, sir," John called as Rowan made to turn and head that way, "I've just heard two more shots down by the boathouse."

"What do you mean? Just now?" Rowan said, closing the distance between them, his heart pounding, ready for action. "Where's Simon? He's supposed to be down there."

"I know," John said and took a step back from his chief. "But I've just seen him—he's inside wi' the rest of them. There's no one down there who's supposed to be down there, and discharging a gun, no less."

"Aye—"

Rowan's words were cut off by the rapid fire of a pistol.

John's eyes went wide as he looked at his chief. "There," was all he said. He stood rooted in place.

"John, get ye inside, and lock that entrance." When the man didn't move, Rowan added, "Now would be a good time, John."

That was all the patience Rowan could afford—heart hammering, he took off sprinting for the boathouse.

The gardens were a blur—low brick walls and boxy shrubbery that he and Cole had walked through just days before. He launched himself over them and was nearly out of the gardens when the sounds of a car reached his ears.

He felt his feet shift south before the thought of changing direction had registered in his mind. The car was a late-model Peugeot—his uncle had owned one and, while it was small and maneuverable, it was dog-slow up hills.

At the river Rowan's pace didn't falter as he leaped onto the first hopscotch-bridge boulder's back and kept moving. His mind registered the deep gouges in the moss and the shattered gouge that had been carved in one rock.

Anger fueled him. He had to be faster.

The Peugeot's motor sounded its struggle as Rowan made his way through and around trees, saplings grasping his sweater, pulling for attention.

Adrenaline made him lose feeling in everything, mind and body, returning him to the machine he'd once been. Focused on the target, Rowan ran after the rusty black Peugeot, now in his sight.

Through the trees he chased it, leaping over the last few stumps and then out onto the service road. He closed the distance between the blond behind the wheel and himself. Digging deep, he came up along-side her door. His prey, unaware of his presence, held the gear shift in one hand and a cell phone in the other, steering with her knee as she yelled to the person on the other line. She did all this without wearing her seatbelt.

Perfect.

Rowan grasped the moving car's door handle and yanked it open. He reached in, pulling a startled, shrieking Eryka brutally from the car and onto the pavement in front of him. Leaping over her as she tumbled to the side, he caught up to the moving car again. He jumped in and shut it down, placed it in park, and pocketed the keys. Rowan turned back toward the woman whose single purpose was to kill him and everything he loved in the world.

Face scratched, her blouse hanging off her, and having lost a shoe, Eryka started to laugh—wild and maniacal laughter—as she hobbled to a relatively upright position and waited for him to come to her.

"Oh, Rowan, if you wanted to have your way with me, all you had to do was call. You didn't need to pull me passionately from my car, love."

Rowan strode to her and cracked his fist across her jaw. The blow threw Eryka backward to the pavement. Even though it was Eryka, Rowan felt the guilt all the way to his bones for striking a woman. That was something he thought he'd never do, until he met her.

He turned back to the car and popped the trunk. His insides squirmed at what he saw inside it. Tape, rope, boxes of bullets, and two extra-large garbage bags. Rowan took deep breaths until the desire to feel Eryka's neck snap in his hands passed. Counting to ten, he moved to look into the car—seeing the muzzle of a 9mm made him lose count at five.

Turning to the groaning woman on the ground behind him, Rowan leaned back against the car and folded his arms to try to contain himself.

"Where'd ye get the second gun, Eryka?"

"Piss off," she said, sitting up and feeling the side of her jaw. She smiled wolfishly at him. "Actually, Rowan, I'll tell you, if you tell me something."

Rowan eyed her. "Ye are saying that you'll no' tell me who sold ye the gun unless I tell ye something?" he said more calmly than he felt.

"That's right, Rowan. You have to give something up before you can get what you want," she said, intoning much into her words.

"An' what might that be, Eryka?"

"You have to promise to let me go after I tell you."

"Mmmph." Rowan turned and opened the trunk.

"I mean it, Rowan—I'll not tell you a thing if you do not let me go," Eryka said, strain obvious in her husky voice.

"Aye. I believe ye." He turned back to her, the tape and the rope in his hands, his intent obvious.

Eryka screamed and, in a movement that seemed to defy the tightness of her jeans, leaped to her feet, hands poised claw-like, and attacked Rowan. She ripped at his face with her fingernails, leaving long red scratches.

Rowan snarled, shifted the goods in his hands, and grasped Eryka by the neck. He threw her against the back of the car and bound her wrists together, keeping her pinned with his elbow on her spine.

"I'm going to fucking kill you!" she screeched.

Wrenching her off the trunk, Rowan forced her into the backseat, only taping her mouth when she changed her murderous tirade into plain screaming.

Rowan reversed the Peugeot back down the service road to the boathouse and parked at the entrance to the parking lot.

Getting out, he saw that it was obvious Eryka had been on a rampage with her pistol. The boathouse window was shattered. Several indentations in the steel door said that she had tried putting a couple bullets through it, too. He crunched over the broken glass to look into the boathouse. He wasn't sure what he would find when he peered inside, and was relieved to see that Cole's lifeless body wasn't there. Where the hell was she?

Voices behind him announced the cautious arrival of Simon, the overseer of the boathouse, and Professor Peabody. Rowan counted the shells on the ground. Just a couple—one through the glass and two at the door. But the shots he'd heard earlier were rapid-fire, the unloading of what seemed like an entire magazine. Where had that been?

He looked out and down the pier, where a littering of brassy tubes angrily reflected the day's fading light. Heart pounding at what he would find, he reminded himself that he still felt the low hum of Cole, that she was all right. Alive. He corrected himself: there were a lot of forms of alive. He jogged the rest of the way, to the end of the pier, and looked over the edge for a floating body. The only thing floating was a boat; the other boat was gone, and the realization of who had it had his knees buckling in relief. Rowan doubled over, breathing deeply, hands braced against his knees.

Through the rush of blood in his head, Rowan heard the running feet of the men behind him and their shouts.

Peabody's was the most insistent. "Rowan! What has happened? What have you found?"

"Nothing, and she's not here. It's OK. Tha' boat's gone and she's in it," he said, relief obvious in his voice.

Wits quickly returning, he turned to Simon. "Have the authorities arrived yet?"

"Aye. They're taking accounts from everyone—that is why we came down was tae get ye; they're asking after ye," said Simon.

Suddenly Peabody looked puzzled. "Is that screaming?"

"Aye," Rowan said, nodding toward the car. "I've got Eryka trussed up in the back. She had tape, rope, and rubbish bags in the back of her car—no doubt used on Cole, or intended to be used on her." He turned to Simon again. "Tell the authorities tha' Eryka is here, and that she shot up the boathouse with the gun in the front seat."

"What in the world . . . " Peabody said, looking up at the sky.

The sky had blackened considerably in the few moments that they had stood talking.

"Dinnae know," Rowan said softly.

The storm's center perched over an island in the distance.

As if on cue, the wind picked up, pushing at their backs and then coming back around and whipping at them sideways. The sky growled; seconds later, sheet lightning lit up the sky below the swirling cloud mass.

"You," Rowan said to Peabody. "We've no time to waste; ye come with me."

Rowan checked the remaining boat's gas tank and, finding it empty, filled it. He loaded Peabody, then himself, into the boat and set course for the island. Rowan called to the stricken Peabody, "I hope your family is no' expecting ye anytime soon."

He shook his head and righted his glasses. "Nope, they're safe at the castle."

"Good, now tell me what ye found," Rowan said, keeping his eye on the horizon.

"Well," Peabody said, "I asked around, thinking that your abrupt departure with Cole yesterday was worthy of looking into. My apologies if that is a breach of your personal rights, but I'm most curious as to what is going on. You see, I heard that Gregoire had words with you the other night, and the older folks here are saying that he was claiming himself to be the rightful heir to the chief's position, which meant Cole was rightfully his. I'll not bore you with the obvious facts on why that is completely untrue, but it made me dig a little further into this real-life drama. I discovered that Kelly, after the incident on the terrace, said many things about your person and made oaths of vengeance against you.

"When we were all mingling in the main banquet earlier, I made a quick search about the room and saw that neither Gregoire nor his son were present. That tells me that the gun shots were possibly from those two . . . " Peabody's voice drifted before becoming shrill. "Oh. Oh. Oh!" he said, fright and excitement taking over him, both at once. "Rowan! She's there! She must be there!" He pointed to the island they were heading toward.

"I know."

"No, Rowan, this is completely exciting and horribly terrifying—the clouds, the storm, it all means that there is some sort of energy collision that is happening at the island right now."

"Aye," Rowan said, but he was only partially listening, thinking instead about the best way to get to the island undetected, and who would be there.

"Don't you see, Rowan?" Peabody continued. "Gregoire and Kelly must be there, and they are upsetting some sort of balance."

"What?" Rowan said, looking to the professor; he had his full attention now.

"Yes! Gregoire said to you the other night that he wanted Cole for himself. To handfast himself to her. This would cause dramatic rifts in energy because he isn't descended from Lady MacLaoch herself—only you are." Peabody thought on it for a bit and then went white and whispered, "Unless . . . "

Rowan looked at the professor, his insides twisting, but he had to ask, had to know what else. "What? What else would cause tha'?"

Peabody just shook his head and said, "Hurry."

Forty-Three

We felt his presence before we knew he was behind us. Following the brothers' lead, I looked up the hill toward the man who was ambling down to us in a white dress shirt, full kilt, and tartan socks, a long walking stick in hand. And I wanted to throw up again.

Gregoire waved at us as he picked his way carefully down the hill, walking as if hurt. I prayed he would trip in his fancy dress shoes and save us all the trouble.

Turning to the brothers, I caught the movement of something ducking just behind the stone building. Alarm bells went off in my mind. "Get to the boats," I said, putting my arm out to herd them in that direction.

"What is it, lass? It's just Gregoire—ye will have no need tae be afraid of him. Besides, we are with ye," Bernie said, taking my outstretched hand and patting it in what I can only assume was meant to be a reassuring gesture.

"You'd be surprised what that man is capable of," I said matter-of-factly. "Please, we can discuss this on the way back—please just trust me and get into the boats. We need to go."

"Oy, man," Angus called, greeting Gregoire. "How are ye? Ye are looking smart for a leisurely stroll, aren't ye?"

"Good afternoon, gentlemen and lady," Gregoire said, curtseying, jesting that we were the royal court and he our subject. I noticed a strawberry bruise on his temple, as if someone had clobbered him with his royal chief fist. "The weather has turned, but nothing a nip won't take care of, and as long as it does not rain, my wedding day will be marvelous."

Bernie and Angus exchanged a look, and I groaned.

"Well," Bernie said, seeing that things were becoming strange even for him, "we were just leaving, so we'll let you tae yer stroll in peace."

"No, no, gentlemen, I'm afraid you'll need to leave your charge with me. She and I have a date with history, do we not, dear?" he said and winked elaborately, nearly upsetting himself. He was indeed three sheets to the wind, if not closer to ten or twelve.

"I think not. Let's go," I said, confident that I would be successful that time in rounding the brothers into the boats.

"Ha ha!" Gregoire laughed, yet the sound was completely devoid of happiness. He pulled an old revolver from his sporran.

"I'm so done with guns," I said.

Bernie and Angus put their hands up in a placating manner. "Now, Mac, we're not going to cause trouble, so just let us go, aye?"

I watched as Gregoire processed the words. He was slow, excessively drunk.

"Nope," he said, popping the *p*. Something behind us seemed to distract him just then—his eyes widened in shock, then squinted in anger, and he yelped, "Not yet, ye fool!"

Something hard struck something else hard, with a sickening *thunk*, behind me. I turned and staggered backward as Kelly dealt a blow with a wooden paddle to Bernie, Angus already crumpling to the ground, blood oozing from his head.

"Oh . . . " I said, not fast enough to catch Bernie as my knees went weak and I fought the rise of bile in my throat. Bernie and Angus, I was sure, could not have survived such brutal blows.

Kelly's face had changed—he was truly grotesque. A putrid purple and yellowy-blue bruise covered the left side of his face, and his nose angled strangely. The colors stood in such stark contrast to his pale skin and red hair that I had a hard time looking away. He tossed the paddle down and yelled at his father, his voice constricted through his broken nose, "What'd ye mean she's to be your wife?"

I sent up a prayer for the old fishermen but could not wait to see the outcome of their argument. I didn't care that Gregoire had a gun—he wouldn't shoot me if he wanted to marry me alive. I bolted for the boats.

"Get her!"

I pushed myself as fast as I could go, but I was a whole foot shorter than my aggressors. Sometimes it's athletics and sometimes it's simple physics, but longer legs will cover more ground than shorter ones.

It felt like I had been struck by a Mack truck, I was hit with such force. The blow knocked me clean off my feet and into the water. I barely caught my breath before my head went under. A hand caught a fistful of my hair and held me there.

Rocks slipped under my hands when I tried to push back; the only ones that seemed rooted in place were the ones painfully cutting into my forehead. Legs planted on either side of me, Kelly held me under until my last bit of air bubbled out my nose and up to the surface. Then he held me under longer. I grabbed rocks and tried to smash his feet with them, only I was moving slower and slower, and then I stopped.

Violently my head was yanked up. Cresting the surface, I gasped and coughed, sucking in air and water droplets, careless of the painful pinching in my oxygen-depleted lungs.

Getting a second lungful of air, I mimicked my first action out of the womb and screamed my head off.

My scream was accompanied by the thundering of the clouds, shaking me to the very bone.

Kelly lost his grip on me. "Get the hell off me, old man!" I heard him holler at his father.

I made my way to my feet, keeping an eye on Gregoire, who was whaling on his son with his walking staff—the gun tucked away, no doubt, in the fur satchel on his belt.

"She's tae be my wife! But no' if ye kill her!"

"Wife?" Kelly asked and swatted the staff away. "Ye daft? Ye are already married tae mum."

A wicked smile crossed Gregoire's face, making me wonder if he was really all that drunk. "Oh yes, ye are right, son, I misspoke. She is tae be yer wife—ye shouldn't kill her, or ye'll have the curse forever on ye and our family. Ye don't want that now, do ye?"

Kelly looked at me, his bludgeoned face a bloated pout.

I began to shiver, the cold of the water having taken up residence in my core and adrenaline making my body shake. My muscles had been deprived of oxygen too long, effectively making me a human jellyfish. But I kept flopping forward, trying to get away.

Kelly picked me up under one arm and dragged me over to his father. "Pick up yer bloody feet!" he snarled at me.

"I can't," I said faintly.

"The hell ye can't! Don't talk back to me!" He wrenched me higher, grasping both my shoulders and shaking me until it felt like my head was going to snap off and roll down to the water's edge.

I heard Gregoire chuckle through it all, a tight, low sound. "Come now, Kelly, don't damage your bride-to-be."

Kelly stopped and glared at me through a puffy eye.

I gave him an equal, though less bloated and more bedraggled, look back, and wished for just a moment that looks could indeed kill.

Kelly threw me at his father's feet as another blast of thunder and blinding lightning burst the sky wide open.

"Hurry!" Kelly said. "I wannae get out of 'ere."

"All in good time, my boy," Gregoire said and leaned over me. He pulled from his bag a long strip of plaid that was not MacLaoch plaid, and grabbed one of my wrists; as soon as the cloth touched my skin, hell broke loose.

Thunder rolled continuously while electricity arched and webbed through the spiraling clouds. Sleet in white sheets slammed down from the heavens.

I found I had the strength again to do simple things, like stand, which I did.

"Ho-no ye don't!" Gregoire cried out, grabbing for my arm.

Kelly had an arm over his tender face in protection from the sleet. He was not trying to help his father.

After successfully standing, I felt that I could run. So I did that, too.

"Stop!" I heard Gregoire scream and then, seconds later, the distinctive pop of a gun, its sound miniaturized by the climactic weather beating around us.

I ran until I was halfway up the hill. For every two crawling steps forward, I slipped one back on the slick ground. Wind lifted me up one moment and whipped around to slam me down against my backside in another.

I kept looking back—I couldn't trust my sense of hearing, with the thunder, to know how close my pursuers were. Kelly had wrestled the gun away from his father and was slamming it against the old man's head.

I hoped they'd stay busy with each other. When Kelly was happy, he was a pervert extraordinaire; now that he was angry, something much darker, filthier, and vile moved in the depths of him. With renewed effort I pushed for the top of the hill—their boat would be on the other side.

I made it to the ridgeline before I was grasped from behind.

I lost my balance, and Kelly and I hit the ground in a tangle of arms and legs. Twisting and hitting, each of us wrestled for the upper hand. I came rolling onto my back, and in an instant Kelly was straddling me. Hands still free, we kept at each other; he tried to capture my wrists as I swatted at him. Panic was widespread within and around me, as if the wildness that I felt inside was being mirrored in my surroundings.

"Leave. Me. Alone!" I hollered through my exertion to both avoid him and try to free myself from under him.

"No! You're mine! I'll have ye if I want ye!"

I wasn't fast enough to see his change in tactics until it was too late. His wide hand smacked across my face, slamming my opposite cheek into the grassy rocks.

"Give me your hands, ye bitch!" he hollered.

Stars danced in my vision and I gasped at the pain that spiked in my skull. "Fuck—" I said, getting cut off as he smacked the other cheek.

It felt like my head was going to rip off under the force of the strike.

Moments passed as my brain slogged a torrent of expletives and ringing of commands. In those precious moments, I missed Kelly's tirade of yelling.

I finally heard him say, "I said to watch me!"

I looked up at him. He'd gone wild, crazy wild. His face contorted in anger as it screamed at me to watch. I still didn't understand, until I realized his hands were at my button fly, the demand for my hands completely forgotten.

I felt my jeans pop open as he ripped at them and the cold, snapping wind made direct contact with the skin of my belly. Kelly wanted me to watch him as he forced me to have sex with him, and that wasn't what I had planned for the afternoon.

A shock of cold rage poured in and filled me. Lady MacLaoch must have felt something very much like this in her final moments—rage, the kind of spitting-mad rage that consumes you from head to toe. The hot and moving feeling that anger creates when something has crossed a primal threshold, an attempted trespass that violates the very essence of you.

I grabbed his occupied hands and the second we made eye contact, I said, "I told Rowan that if you ever touched me again I'd break your balls with my knee and your face with my fist, and I keep my promises." I slammed my knee into his crotch, making the connection the way a hammer does with a nail. Kelly coughed out his breath, pitching forward—as he fell, his face came close, and I kept the second part of my promise. My fist connected with the swollen tissue of his already bruised face and grindingly crunched his nose.

Kelly screamed, clutching his face as he staggered and slipped backward down the hill. I knew I had only a few moments, but I had to button my pants—the need to have that in place consumed me. My fingers shook, but I got each button secured. At the last button, I looked up—to see Kelly, a rock in his hand and intent written clearly upon his face.

Before my mind could tell me to roll out of the way or kick at his legs, or tell me anything at all, something unexpected happened.

The howl of a battle cry rose up from behind me—something in the sound made the hair on my entire body rise. The air quieted, sleet slowed its fall—it felt like the peach orchard before a tornado hits.

I watched as Rowan crested the hill behind me and descended upon his cousin. His elbow cracked across his cousin's jaw just before he tucked his head, tackling Kelly like an all-star defensive end.

The sky opened up once again, rioting, feeding on our energy.

Sparing just one glance toward Rowan and Kelly before making my escape, I shuddered at what I saw. Rowan had become a dark shadow of the loving man I'd gotten to know; this was the take-no-prisoners, listen-to-no-pleas, kill-all-them-sons-of-bitches Rowan MacLaoch. It seemed that each one of his demons had come to the surface, and each one wanted to exhaust itself in battle with Kelly. To pummel his kin with practiced restraint until Kelly's blood ran into the soil of the island as a sacrifice to Lady MacLaoch herself.

Employing a mixture of crawling and scrabbling, I made my way to the fishing shed before I breathed again. Only then did I remember Angus and Bernie. I looked to the place they'd fallen, prepared to see the bodies of my beloved fishermen. They were no longer there. Not on the shore, not in the churning water, not in the boats.

I looked back up the hill, toward Rowan and Kelly and, in the distance to the side of them, a different movement caught my eye. Lightning arched and disappeared in a roar of thunder. It was the MacDonagh brothers.

I watched as they made their way, hunched against the sleet and wind, to a low, flat-topped boulder. A brother on each side, they ripped at the grass covering its surface and then placed their hands upon it.

Realization dawned: as Secret Keepers, they were the final link in the curse breaking, and this was why they needed Rowan. As I watched them, the air above the rock became misty. A solitary fog began to form over the flat-topped boulder.

Kelly's short scream pierced the air, pulling my attention.

Rowan had turned away from his cousin's crumpled body on the ground, and he was walking toward me. I tried to smile at him but the happiness faltered on my face, and I pushed off the shed to help close the distance between us.

In that moment I saw the crumpled body move, and I remembered the gun I had forgotten all about.

My horror must have shown on my face because Rowan pivoted, stones flying out from under his boots.

Kelly hadn't bothered to stand—using his knee as a brace, he held his father's revolver steady and took aim.

"No!" I screamed as I surged forward, my body instinctively rushing to protect all that I loved, and as I did so, Rowan did the same.

Rowan and I were like human freight trains rushing toward Kelly, each hell-bent on the single purpose to protect the other, moved by an instinctual and ancient bond.

The air felt like it had changed to liquid. Electricity built around us, and the hairs on my scalp began to tingle—somewhere in the back of my mind I recognized what was happening. I felt something white-hot spike through my middle, stopping me cold, and Rowan seemed to experience the same. Thunder clapped overhead. It felt like we'd been shot, but in the next instant I understood.

As the thunder pounded the air so hard our bones shook, light erupted from the circling clouds overhead and spiked to the ground, attracted to the metal revolver in Kelly's hands. Before the force of the spike shoved us backward, I watched as Kelly's arm went stiff with the electricity—then his entire body blew backward.

But not before the gun went off.

Forty-Four

Rowan had had many years to think about how he would have gladly given his life to take the bullet for Vick; he was not going to miss the opportunity to save me if he could. The instant the bullet left its chamber, it was destined to hit one of us. Kelly had made sure of that.

And it did.

Facing down a bullet is a little like facing down a ghost, because you never see it, you only feel it.

I felt it as it tore into Rowan's shoulder and embedded itself there, flesh, muscle, bone. I was close enough to break Rowan's fall, and we slumped as one to the round rocks of the shore.

"Rowan, Rowan, Rowan," I said in a panicked chant. I watched his face morph from a look of determined intent into one of realization; he'd succeeded in taking the hit.

"Uggh," he said, and his face pinched tight in pain, his free hand automatically going to his shoulder.

Rowan had shed his sweater at some point, and I made quick work of tearing open his gray shirt and compressing the wound. It was luck or just pure physics that we were so far away and that Kelly had used his father's revolver, which was not as powerful as the modern one that Eryka had used on me earlier.

Rowan let loose a string of expletives as he took over applying the pressure, rolled to his good shoulder, and stood.

I just watched in awe as he faced back toward Kelly, on guard even under all that pain. But Kelly was not going to be hurting us again for a while—he lay splayed on the hillside, taken down by the lightning.

And yet, something more was happening.

Moving like a serpent along the ground, rolling white fog whispered and billowed, drawing my attention to it. The hair on my arms and my back stood up as it approached.

Standing next to Rowan, I followed its tail to the Secret Keepers' stone.

"What in bloody he—" was all I heard Rowan say.

Her voice came the way a memory would, as if I had heard this conversation once before and was replaying it back in my mind. She was the woman in my dreams—this was Lady MacLaoch.

My child, she said. The fog folded onto itself. Its edges became more distinct, until it was a woman—the woman who walked with me in the dream—who stood before us. I felt rather than saw her smile.

Rowan cursed again; he knew who the woman was.

It is over. Never will I walk this earth again, but I will go in peace. What I set out to do before I died has been done. You, Rowan, my child, will never feel the pain we have shared ever again. This I promise.

Lady MacLaoch came to my side and smiled falteringly at me. *It is good to see you once more, Minory.* She spoke in a language as ancient as she, yet I understood. *Know that you and my kin have been destined to be together since the day your father of fathers set eyes upon me and I upon him. You will bring each other joy from today until your deaths, many long and healthy years from now.*

The fog faltered, then dissipated as if burned off by the sun, taking Lady MacLaoch with it. With her departure the island continued to riot, and I wondered what a spirit like her leaving would do to the energy around us.

Forty-Five

Rowan had fallen to the ground and I cradled his head in my arm, my free hand applying pressure to his shoulder. The wind picked up again and didn't stop gathering. My hair whipped around Rowan and me, wild; the wind whistled over the land, sucking sleet, leaves, twigs, droplets of ocean spray, and both of us backward.

"What in the hell is happening?" I hollered into the air.

Rowan was losing consciousness, and the boats sloshed in the waves that began crashing on shore. As if in response to my question, Peabody came tearing over the hillside, wild-eyed and scared.

"Energy expulsion!" he cried, coming to a skittering halt in front of us. Distracted for a fraction of an instant by all the blood on Rowan, he asked, "What happened? Never mind—we have to go! It's an energy expulsion!" He moved in to help me move Rowan. "Go! Into the shack!"

"The brothers!" I yelled when we reached the fishing shack.

"No! They must finish!" Peabody hollered back.

I just shook my head at Peabody and moved to get them. Yet I didn't get out of reach of Rowan. "No," was all he said, gripping my wrist.

Just as his hand touched me, the air exploded. The force of it yanked me up off the ground. Rowan never lost his grip, his face going crazy with pain.

I fought against the rush of air, trying to get even a single foothold. I was like Dorothy refusing to be sent to Oz.

Then suddenly all went calm.

"Get! In!" screamed Peabody from the shelter's doorway, and Rowan and I did.

We watched through the windows as balls of lightning snapped and crackled along the ground and then lifted up over the heads of the white-knuckled MacDonagh brothers and into the eye of the storm.

Silence and snapping were all we heard, and I sent a prayer out to the brothers. As the silence crept on, I began to wonder if that was indeed the end of storm. I was just about to say as much when the ground began to shake.

I heard a grunt and felt Rowan put a hand on my head, pushing me to the floor, his body covering mine. His labored breathing sounded. "Peabody . . . What is this . . . "

Peabody's voice shook. I had been scared before, but I was now in a space beyond that—a place where some incredible force was in my face and scaring me to my soul.

"I-it is the absence of energy . . . We are going to equilibrium, scientifically speaking."

"What the bloody hell does that mean, Edwin . . . " Rowan said.

"Black hole," I said. "That's what he means."

"What?" Rowan hissed in the dark.

"N-not necessarily, there is an element I'm aware of that has an effect—the chanting and that rock—I'm not sure what that does . . . "

Air whistled under the door; metal objects rattled on their shelves and glass hit the floor, shattering. Our ears popped as the door began to creak under the strain.

Suddenly the air shivered—I felt the vibration—and was followed by a series of rapid bangs and piercing snaps. We were pelted with shards of wood and glass; the air itself seemed to implode and, for an instant, I couldn't breathe.

Even under Rowan and through my closed lids, I could see a burst of light illuminate the world like the midday sun. In the snap of a finger, it was gone.

Forty-Six

Later, I would remember the medical smell of the ER and the way the short, no-nonsense bobbed haircut of the nurse moved as she wrenched my hand from Rowan's. I don't remember the words I said to her but I remember her ignoring them and taking him from me.

I waited in the stark, white room outside the ER, not feeling or seeing the MacLaoch clan members gathering. I tuned out the words that prayed for his life. I clung to the words of Lady MacLaoch as I would a ship in the midst of a storming sea.

It seemed that summer, fall, winter, and spring all passed by before a man in green surgical scrubs came out and asked for both Cole and Nicole. Pulled from my fog, I waded through the people who crowded the ER waiting room; I moved through old and young. They all looked at me in wonder.

The surgeon was not a smiling man. My mind tortured me with thoughts that he'd in fact not smile when telling someone that her loved one had died.

"I'm sorry . . . " were the only words I heard him say. I closed my ears against his words, against the sobs from the crowd, and collapsed into a chair.

I felt the surgeon kneel in front of me. "Ma'am? Are you Nicole? Do you know where Cole is? Is Cole here, too?"

I swiped at the tears that were streaming down my face. "I am Nicole. Rowan calls me Cole." *Called* me, my mind corrected, and I fell deeper into my personal darkness.

"Oh." He looked at me strangely. "Then I take back my apologies. I assumed it was two people, and we can only have one person in to see him at a time."

Confusion must have crossed my features because he added, "He's asking—no, demanding—that he see you." He stood. "Come with me, please."

In a haze I left the murmuring waiting room with the surgeon. He explained that Rowan was an extremely lucky man—the bullet entered and lodged itself in the meaty tissue of his shoulder, only coming to a stop when it hit his shoulder blade; any lower and his heart would have been punctured and he would no doubt have died swiftly. The surgeon was direct and vivid in his details of Rowan's wound and all the possibilities of how it could have gone horribly wrong.

He left me at the door to the recovery room, saying that he'd give us some time. The investigators were most unpleasant about having to wait, yet the doctor would not deny a man to see his wife.

The word *wife* settled low and pleasant in me, the thrill of it like a free pass to an exclusive club. Speak it, and people instantly know how important you are to the one called *husband*.

Rowan lay still—it was obvious he'd been given a sedative—but his eyes tracked me as I crossed the small room to his side. The only sound was his breathing and the low whirr, interrupted by rhythmic beeps, of his monitoring equipment. The beep slowly increased in tempo as a rugged smile spread over his face.

"Hi," I whispered as I took his hand. "How are you feeling?"

The smile never faltered, his eyes took me in, grazing along my face to my mouth, down to our clasped hands and back up to my eyes. Emotion shone in his own dark-blue irises. "I love ye."

My steel gave way—I slumped under the weight of his words, the weight of the entire day, and I wept. I very gently lay down next to him, my arm around his midsection, and kissed his stubbled cheek and then his lips.

Softly I whispered, "I love you too."

Forty-Seven

T he investigators made us pay for making them wait.

Peabody was delayed returning home several times by their questioning and re-questioning, but he was finally cleared.

The MacDonagh brothers stayed in the ICU for some time. The rumor that they were indeed the Secret Keepers of the MacLaoch curse was hotly debated. Eventually the hard-headed old men made a recovery and claimed to remember nothing of the fateful day on the Isle of Lady MacLaoch.

Old Gregoire was treated and released from the hospital, but was subsequently arrested for intent to use a deadly weapon and attempted murder. Eryka admitted to everything that she was accused of, but only after she had fled back to Iceland. Her extradition was in progress.

The one who felt the heavy hand of justice the most was Kelly. His brain, we learned, would never return to full function again. The last I heard, he was recovering into an incredibly chipper and happy person who had the mental maturity of a three-year-old. His mother moved him closer to her in Glasgow, into a long-term care facility where he was reportedly doing quite well, for a toddler.

Forty-Eight

I stood in the kitchen of our apartment at Castle Laoch, coffee mug in one hand, flipping through a photo album on the counter with the other. The living room was filled with the boxes my mother had sent, and I was unpacking. Mother was happy to have me finally settled but was breathing fire that I had found my husband so far away. She had had the movers ship everything from my apartment, including the office wastepaper basket, still full, as well as some stuff she'd been trying to get rid of from her house. I was just happy that she hadn't sent the entire contents of the refrigerator.

I was trying to get my things sorted quickly, as cataloging of the wilderness area and managing research students needed the majority of my time. I was also coordinating with my family the plans for our wedding at the castle the next year. Rowan seemed blissful that it was taking place in Scotland but was also conveniently absent when wedding details needed to be sorted out with my mother.

I didn't have to be too particular with my unpacking—Rowan's apartment in the upper part of the castle was soon to be used exclusively as his office; we were moving into a refurbished crofter's cottage by the sea. The renovations of which were nearly done.

Sipping my coffee while I paged through the album, a lone photograph caught my eye. Pulling it out from the plastic sheeting, I realized it was old, very old. The man in the sepia image was standing next to a woman who held a toddler on her lap. They all looked severely unhappy, the way most people look in old photographs, as if they were convinced the camera was stealing their souls.

I heard Rowan come in behind me, the flap of the kitchen door sounding just before he leaned against my back and took the mug of coffee from me.

"What's tha', love?" he asked before taking a sip.

"I don't know. Relatives?" I leaned back against his warm body.

"Mmmm," he said into the mug. "Flip it over and see what it says— maybe their names are on the back. Tha' man looks some like ye."

Flipping the photograph over, I read the names, then read them again. Only when Rowan started chuckling did it really sink in what I was seeing. It was doubly confirmed when he started laughing outright.

It said, in shaky cursive, *Iain Eliphlet Minory*.

Minory with an *o*.

Glossary of Scottish Terms

Bairn: Child

Bawbag: Useless person

Gillie: Hunting or fishing guide; or a male attendant or personal servant to a Highland chief

Quaich: Scottish drinking cup of the seventeenth and eighteenth centuries having a shallow bowl with two flat handles

Sgian dubh: Small, single-edged knife

Acknowledgments

No person is an island, and it takes a village to raise a child. Both sentiments are completely appropriate for describing the community effort that it took to raise this book from an idea to what you have in your hands now. And it starts with you, dear reader. I've dedicated this book to you because without you, I'd not be an author. Thank you for taking a chance on me and my first book. I also want to thank my editing team at Indigo Editing & Publications—Kristin and Susan, you guys rock! This book was rough when you first received it, thank you for your hard work and story tweaks to get it to where it is today. I also want to thank the community of people that surrounded me in the writing of this: Anne de Ridder, Adam Stonewall, Chris Lytsell, and Jennifer Newton. Adam, I'd be remiss if I didn't thank you for your awesome idea of incorporating a larger portion of the curse in the story—the benefits, I think all would agree, are stupendous. To my peer review group, Annie Small, Ayn Generes, Joelle Allen, and Heather Vaughn-Lee: all of you brought enthusiasm and loving critique that buoyed me and *The Legend of Lady MacLaoch*'s characters to new and even greater heights. To my father-in-law, retired US Air Force Master Sergeant, Mike Mannthey and my uncle Ray Duvall for patiently explaining about fighter jets, and that when a pilot and copilot eject from an airplane, they don't land together but rather, miles apart. To my friends who made me wild with jealously when they visited Scotland and then those who introduced me to the fabulous Highland Still House in Oregon City and its co-owner Mick. It's because of you all that I went to Skye, fell hard for Scotch whisky, watched the RAF do training maneuvers, met the bartender who was the inspiration for Rowan MacLaoch and the wonderful couple Bill and Charlotte of Ben

Tianavaig B&B. A special thanks goes to my family for their support and encouragement. And finally, because he is the most important one to thank—the one who has stood by me day and night, the one who has encouraged me from the first inkling of an idea, the one who held his hand out to me in support when things got tough, the one who taught me what love is and what it can become—thank you to my husband. You are my best friend—thank you.

Author Bio

Becky Banks is a bestselling and award-winning indie author from an old Hawai'i family, who currently lives in Portland, Oregon, with her husband and two children. Becky likes to craft dark romances that stem from her past and require love to see her characters through. When she's not crafting love stories, she's packing lunches for her little ones and breaking up *Minecraft* fights.

Visit Becky Banks online at beckybanksbooks.com and follow her on social media for updates on new releases and more.

facebook.com/beckybanksbooks

instagram.com/authorbeckybanks

amazon.com/author/beckybanks

goodreads.com/beckybanks

bookbub.com/profile/becky-banks

The Legend of the Viking

Enjoy this preview of book 2 in the Clan MacLaoch curse series, The Legend of the Viking, out now in ebook and paperback!

Prologue
Outer Hebrides, Scotland
The Year of Our Lord 1210

Quiet fell in the stone hall as the old woman made her way back down the long table, an engraved bone cup in her hand. This time she would not be turned away. The rushes scattered on the floor muted her steps and absorbed the echoes and murmurs of those gathered there.

"Grandson," she called, her craggy voice carrying over the heads of the raiders seated there. As she continued under the gaze of cruel men, she closed her eyes and moved toward her grandson and with an ability she should not possess, around those in her way. She tightened her fist about the engraved cup she'd been given by a guard loyal to her. "Hear me, Grandson. Do not dismiss my warnings. For now, I have seen it thrice." She held the cup for him as though to indicate the tea dregs within it.

"Silence," he commanded her.

"You must know," Her voice carried to him clear as crystal in the humid and smoke-tinged air. "You must hear me, Grandson."

The room shifted as they looked to her then back to their self-proclaimed king.

"Once the boughs of love are gently rocked—"

"I said—"

"Rocked by her embrace," she shouted over him. There was gasping and a small cry of outrage. "You will want of nothing else; it is foretold, in the feral times of man, that another will come to stand between you and that which you love most. If it should come to pass, if his vengeance against you should succeed, your spirit will forever walk this land. This will be the truth until your retribution breaks the bounds of nature and settles the balance. Blood will be spilt; hearts will be shattered; and vengeance once started will not be stopped—"

The Viking's fist slammed down with a bang. "Enough!"

Earthenware cups and the boar's carcass jumped as wine spilt and another cry of alarm was heard. The old woman stopped and opened her eyes then. He smiled distastefully at the seer the village folk called Völva.

"His vengeance? Yes, you have said it again and again. So, tell me, Grandmother, what is the name of my enemy? I will slay him now." He bellowed a laugh that shook the foundation.

The old woman hissed out in disgust, "Grandson, 'tis not a man you will know until you have crossed him. Only when the blade he wields touches your skin will you comprehend my meaning. Yet, it is not too late; you can stop him now. Stop your lust for things you cannot have."

His gaze cooled dangerously giving her a warning he seldom gave to others, "What you speak of is treason. Will you condemn one of your people to a traitor's fate?"

"I did not say that the sword would be held by your kin—"

"That is right—you said nothing other than 'a man'!" He shouted then smiled at his people. "An ordinary man, whom I have yet to meet, will someday strike at me in anger." He bellowed another laugh. His wolf-like smile still in place, he said, "Grandmother, you speak of every man who wishes to sit upon this seat." He gestured to his intricately carved throne-backed chair.

The old woman nodded and worked the rest of the distance down the long wooden table to him. She trailed one hand on the backs of the chairs for balance as the crowd murmured and laughed with their chief. She made her way to his seat and smiled, placing the cup down; she held her hand out to him.

"Then, peace, Grandson."

"What is this? You wish to read more into my future? Perhaps get a name to that I can use?"

She continued with her placating smile, her hand outstretched. "Let us be at peace."

"Peace!" He laughed and made to shake her hand, placing his palm in hers. She grasped it then spat into it.

The Viking tried to pull his hand back, but her grip was unusually strong. She traced the lines of his palm with her thumbs as her murmured words washed over him.

Trying to pull his hand back, he hissed, "You are a pitiful old woman. Nothing but a bogeyman to scare children into obedience. I will make sure you pay for this." To his guards, he barked, "Remove her!" then shoved her back with his other hand.

She stumbled but, catching herself, stood upright as if possessed. Her filthy wrap slipped from her shoulders. Light dimmed in the room.

Her eyes, having gone cold as snow clouds, looked sharply down at her grandson, the most feared man of the Outer Hebrides. "Remember this warning"—the stone walls shook—"for it will be your last: Seek the unobtainable, and you will be blinded by love. She will outlive you and, in your absence, will suffer a fate worse than death. And your spirit, unable to succumb to the call to Valhalla, will roam these lands for eternity."

Light snapped back as she folded down into the old woman she was. She picked up her heavily worn blanket and wrapped it tightly about her shoulders. A firm hand with a gold-clasped wrist gripped her shoulder.

Ormr Minorisson, Viking chief and self-proclaimed king of the

Outer Hebrides stood then, towering over her. "Those words will be your last to me." He gestured to his men. "Take her to the church of the misty cliffs." Then, to her: "You will stay there from now until your last breath."

CHAPTER 1
Castle Laoch, Glentree, Skye, Scotland
Present Day

Rowan sat in the circle of light cast by his lamp. He glared at the bright screen of his laptop, keying in numbers here and there.

As a child, Rowan had watched his uncle work the ledgers, a large leather-bound book with lines that reminded him of rows of barley sprouting new and crisp in the spring's rich soil. As soon as he took the helm of the MacLaoch estate, he transitioned the whole lot to computers, saving the knuckle of his right middle finger from the permanent ink stain his uncle had always worn. That ink stain was a tattooed reminder of how tied the clan was to the coffers. How tied the castle was to the coffers. How he was now tied to the coffers.

The cell where the Gathering monies was bloomed a big round zero, a black hole in the spreadsheet. The annual net revenue line had a seven-figure number. Seven figures below zero.

Rowan pinched the bridge of his nose. The clan was fucked with a capital F. Not "attempt to sell the Rembrandt in the upper hallway and hope the posh want to pay millions" fucked, but enduringly fucked, because next year, he'd have to do the same, and the year after, ad nauseum, until there was nothing left in the castle save for the stone itself. Add ten years in arrears on bank payments to the devil, and now the Reaper was calling to collect his dues.

Clan members had run for their lives last summer as thunder and lightning and bullets rang out and took their Gathering registration fees with them. No one bid on the million-pound silent auction items, and the hunt up at the lodge—a ten-thousand-pound-per-night experience

—never happened. Instead, his cousin tried to kill him, and his uncle attempted to murder his newfound love.

Rowan's mind skipped at the bittersweet thought of Cole.

Cole was asleep in the cottage. That cliffside bothy, a building that was easier to live in and heat than an entire castle. Cole was his ray of hope in all of this bleakness, like the rare Glentree summer sun when it kissed his cheeks. He took a pleasant sojourn away from the defeat in front of him and reminded himself of Cole's sunset-colored curls reflecting the copper heat of that same sun and the fire she stoked in him. He wished she was there now. He desperately needed to do what he loved, to clutch a fistful of that fire and breathe her in as her arms wound around his waist, squeezing him tight. She was the only creature on earth who made him feel soothed, comforted, and completely at peace simply by being near him.

He knew that to pay respect to all she was to him he needed to officially make her his wife. It felt wrong to not have done it already, but as he looked back to the ledgers, he couldn't shake the feeling that to legally tie her to him was akin to tying her to an anchor and throwing both of them into the loch.

Then there was the bother of the ceremonies, vetting, and rites to follow, though the clan was occupied at the moment with raking him over the coals for the way the Gathering ended and the squabbling about whether to chop his uncle Gregoire's branch from the clan. It seemed selfish to ask them to rejoice in his love when everything was going so wrong.

He leaned back in his great-grandfather's Chesterfield desk chair—a three-thousand-pound appraised value—with a creak and blew out a breath. The phone call that had precipitated him sitting there for eight hours straight with the ledgers came back to him. If everything proceeded as the bankman threatened, there might be no castle for them to live in much less a clan chief for her to marry after his people hanged him at the old oak in Glentree's town square.

Rowan felt the pinch of his ulcer and reached for the pills he hid in the upper desk drawer. He dropped two powder-yellow pills into his palm and tossed them back then picked up his tumbler and washed them down with whisky.

CHAPTER 2

Phone to my ear, I stood behind Rowan's old oak desk up in his office in the castle's fairy tower. It was a lovely place to be and made me feel closer to Rowan now that he spent most nights away from home.

"Uh-huh," I said distractedly into the handset. I was at cord length on my tiptoes trying to see out leaded-glass windows, over treetops, down to the loch below. The late-afternoon sun was obscured behind the thick clouds making the sky a hundred thousand shades of gray. I got a view of the black, rocky beach of Loch Laoch, but too little. I needed to be able to view at least fifty yards worth of that beach to ensure I didn't miss that afternoon's phenomenon.

An excited anticipatory energy filled my body, like hearing the sound of an ice cream truck headed down the street. I was going to have to end my call. Just thinking I might miss it made my heart skip a beat and steal my breath.

I touched the rubber band at my wrist debating on snapping it for some focus. It was on my wrist in an attempt to reign in my temper, after a year ago I punched a woman at the Gathering gala. Now, I simply wore it as a physical reminder to remain present since I hadn't been angry in months.

I shifted my weight to my other foot. The potential student intern I was on the phone with was excited to get a call back and was regaling me of a story about her and her granddaddy de-braining a particularly aggressive Highland bull. Her granddaddy was our local large animal veterinarian, and she an undergrad in zoology.

"Adara—"

"But tha's when we gave him a quick snip and—"

"Adara, thank you, yes, thank you—"

"Oh no, I've talked too much? Grandda' warned me of talking too much if I were to get a call, and now, here I've done it. I've talked too much, haven't I?"

I stretched again, another vein attempt to see more of the beach. It was the exact same place where Rowan had tossed me into the ice-cold water, gala dress and all, last year.

"Adara," I finally interrupted, "I was calling to say that you've got the position. I'm sorry, I'm in a bit of a rush, so I'll email you the details tonight—"

Her ear-splitting scream had me yanking the handset away from my ear.

"Oh, my grandda' will be so happy! We're MacLaochs, ye know, and to study a site that hasnae been touched in..." Her Scots got thicker as her voice broke into a sob.

"Adara, honey, I'm so happy for you. That's wonderful to hear he'll be proud of you"—another peak out the window and a look at my watch—"but I really have to go. I'll email you." And with an apology to her—and my mother for my poor manners—I hung up. Quickly, I made a Post-it reminder, then began gathering my things. I picked up my to-call folder of folks, then the miscellaneous résumés I had on the desk. Swiftly, I shoved them into the open folder and reached for my pack behind me on the desk chair. In my haste, the folder yawned, and the papers slipped out. They scattered like a blizzard over the Persian rug.

"Shit!" I shouted and went to my knees in the mess. Another look at my watch. Another curse. I only had a minute left.

Noticing that sheets had scattered across the room and under furniture, I cursed again and left them there. I scrambled to my feet, slipping on the papers, and was down the tightly winding staircase and out into the upper hallway in short order. The sun made an afternoon debut right then and hit the western flank of the castle, sending long blazing beams of light over the parquet floors and down the main staircase. I was midway down the staircase myself, the sun warming my back, when Marion called to me.

She stood at the front administrative counter, her silver hair tucked back behind an ear and her cardigan was pale pink in celebration of spring.

Her blue eyes went wide with hope when she saw me. "Excellent timing, my lady! It's teatime. Join us in the sunroom—"

"Nope! Nope, nope, nope," I said with each step I flew down.

I ran past her and around the lower staircase then through the main hall to the rear of the castle.

She called from behind me, "Where are ye always headed at this hour?!"

"Nowhere!" I called back. It was my special secret, and I was telling absolutely no one.

Off the back steps I jumped, my rubber boots slapping my calves as I did so, and crossed over the closely cropped, aptly named bowling green. The scents of crushed grass and foliage tickled my nose as I stole a glance down to the loch. It was still obscured, this time by the stone balcony, and down those steps I jumped too, with another boot slap, then started up the rear gravel trail toward the whitewashed stone cottage.

My heart raced as I sprinted.

Was I about to miss it?

The trail split, forking toward the research field or the cottage that Rowan and I shared. I was going to neither place. I hung a sharp left toward the cliff's edge in the distance. My boots slipped as I exited the gravel path, making my arms whirligig to catch my balance. I slowed my pace as I got close—minding my step and the rocky edge between me and the tidal pools fifty feet below, I chanced a look up as the loch, all of it, came into view.

I was giddy with excitement and clasped my hands together. I hadn't missed it after all. The entire swath of the black-rock beach, melting into the curve of Lake Laoch, was visible from here, making it the spot for my wildlife viewing. The spot where Rowan and I had our first real lip lock was small in the distance but clearly visible.

I turned my wrist, looking at the time, and smiled—soon. It would happen soon.

My insides pleasantly churned as I waited for my ice cream truck of a moment to arrive. The onshore breeze brought with it the tang of seawater and twang of birdsong as they flit and flew, darting over the exposed tidal pools. A few more minutes passed before heat spiked in my veins, and he strode into view.

The MacLaoch clan chief wore a form-hugging dark-blue button-down. I'd buttoned him into it just that morning, stealing a kiss off his distracted lips with every round mother-of-pearl shell I thrust into its matching hole. His black slacks fit his athletic, lean hips and legs like the pants had been stitched around him, showing off the high and tight ass that I smacked with erotic glee each time I was within arm's reach. His sport coat, I frowned, was gone. It would not flap like a flightless bird as he wrenched it off today. I conducted myself as I did any of my wildlife biology observations. I deduced: The laird was furious again today and would partake in his afternoon ritual. It wasn't unlike sitting riverside, concealed downwind, from a grizzly as he fetched spawning salmon from the stream. It wasn't wise to approach the bear but instead just enjoy from afar the display of prowess.

Things with the Gathering the year prior had not ended well. In fact, it was still going. The clan wanted answers and were holding Rowan responsible seemingly for the cursed weather. They were split into two camps: some said Kelly and his father should be stripped of their clan rites, and others said to turn a blind eye. Each day Rowan "consulted" in his laird and chief roles, and he needed an outlet to vent.

It just so happened to be a beautiful outlet to watch, a capable man solving his problems.

A stone's throw from the water's edge now, Rowan stopped and toed his shoes off while working the buttons of his crisp collared shirt, giving me mini flashes of warm skin. I sighed, ready for this angry caterpillar to shed its cocoon and thrust himself into the cold loch water and emerge after a mile of open-water swimming, the beautiful powerful butterfly he was. Finally, he sloughed off his shirt, and even from my distance away, I could see his shoulders were taught. The muscles of his upper back and arms firmed as he gestured angrily, stabbing pointedly into the air as if in argument with the people and their noise he had had to consume that day.

My fingertips itched to touch his bunched muscles, to dig into them and massage them loose. I kept my thoughts quiet lest they call to him and break this gorgeous routine.

With a flick of his fingers at his belt buckle, his pants loosened. His mouth opened, and after a second's delay, his roar reached me. His warrior physique was primed for a fight. It appeared today had been extra hard. I noticed now that his black hair looked tossed and roughed up from his impatient hands running through it. Button and zipper undone, his pants and underwear were shoved down to rocks and kicked aside along with his socks.

I sucked in a deep breath and held the erotic joy from erupting out of me in a full-throated moan. Instead, I smiled and steepled my fingers, pressing them against my lips.

There he was.

Standing naked as the day he was born, Chief Rowan MacLaoch was the image of the Celtic warrior stripping bare to unleash his ferocity without anything to hamper his movements. His heated skin was a sharp color contrast with the obsidian-colored rocks and the dark hair that ran from his navel to his cock—which still impressed despite the cold.

His thighs and buttocks flexed their musculature as he navigated the rocky ground. The water, even though he'd been prepared for it, stole his breath, making him suck through clenched teeth. I could hear that intake of breath like a memory in my ear. His body warm and on top of mine, that sharp inhale with his eyes closed as if the pleasure of entering me were a surprise. I shivered at what he must be feeling and also fantasized being down there with him, knowing that together we could keep the chill at bay.

He took four quick breaths before becoming a water-based mammal. Into an incoming wave he dove, plunging himself into the depths of the loch. In awe, I watched as he expertly carved a path through the punishingly cold water. His bent arms kept time with the pace of a Highland jig, or a fist fight in a pub brawl. His fingertips were at times pointed, slicing the water out of his way, and for millisecond breaks caressed the water. While he would go a short and easy distance, if by boat, it was the evening wind making small chop on the water that made it Iron Man worthy. Each time he breathed, he had to do it through his teeth so as not to inhale wind-whipped water droplets off the chop. It would take all his focus to swim the round-trip mile.

If him sliding into the water was gold, him stepping out was diamonds. As he entered the shallow waters, his naked form became visible; it was a greenish hue under these waters, like a moving jade sculpture. I inhaled and bit my lip, waiting for it. Sensual excitement warmed my skin. It was one thing to ogle a man with whom you had no experience; it was another to watch a man with whom you did, knowing how that pelvis moved against yours and the petal softness of those lips on the skin of your breasts.

There in the shallows, he stopped moving, and like a monolith emerging from the water, he stood, the loch sparkling off him, running down his sharp edges. He wiped water out of his eyes, such a simple move, but it showed off the round his biceps. The V of his pelvic muscles was drawn deep, accentuating the lines of his abdominals. Each of his exhales was punctuated with water droplets that had run down his nose and off his upper lip. He pushed his way through the water with heavy steps, each one revealing more and more of his sculpted magnificence. I whimpered. I knew the weight of that body when it was on top of mine. I followed the tight midline of his stomach to his navel then the dark path of hair down to his relaxed manhood. Despite the chill of the air, he was warm, hot even, and he hung longer and thicker than the average male would, having just stepped out of forty-degree water.

When Rowan reached his discarded clothes, his expression changed. Despite the distance, I knew his was a happy look—it was the one he gave over shoulders when his eye caught mine across a crowded room. Suddenly, I shivered. My skin now felt as cold as Rowan's as our connection ignited, letting me feel the ocean water on his skin. His slow-blooming smile dimpled just one cheek. A hum moved across my skin before his face turned up toward me. Today, I had been discovered.

This second book in the Clan MacLaoch curse series, *The Legend of the Viking*, is out now in ebook and paperback. Turn the page to read about Becky Banks's other contemporary novels, or visit her online at beckybanksbooks.com.

CLAN MACLAOCH CURSE SERIES

The Legend of Lady MacLaoch. *Book 1 of the Clan MacLaoch Curse Series.*

Centuries ago a vengeful curse buried itself deep into the history of the MacLaoch clan and became a legendary tale told by all those not cursed by its words.

In present-day Scotland, the laird and chief of the MacLaoch clan is an ex-Royal Air Force fighter pilot who has been past the gates of hell and returned a changed man. Rowan MacLaoch does battle with wartime memories and a family curse that threaten to consume him—unaware that his life and that of the history of the clan will be changed forever by the arrival of an American woman.

Cole Baker, a feisty recent graduate of a master's program, stumbles upon the ancient curse while researching her bloodlines. Moved by the history of the MacLaoch clan and the mystery of its chief, she digs into the legend that had been anything but quiet for centuries.

On their quest for answers, Cole and Rowan travel to places they have never before been and become witnesses to things they have never before fathomed.

The legend—one started with blood—will end with more shed as its creator finally exacts her justice.

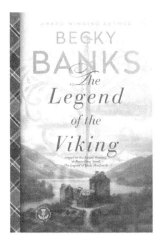

Book 2 of the Clan MacLaoch curse series, The Legend of the Viking.

In this second book of the Clan MacLaoch Curse series, we see our favorite characters, Rowan and Cole, return in their most passionate selves yet. Coming off the loss of the Gathering and the thought-to-be-extinguished MacLaoch curse, Rowan finally has a chance at his happily ever after. That is, until everything that he loves is put at risk, sparking events, that once set in motion, will not be stopped—except by love.

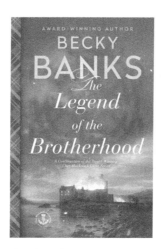

Coming soon. Book 3 of the Clan MacLaoch curse series, The Legend of the Brotherhood.

In this third book of the clan MacLaoch curse series, Cole's two worlds collide when her brother TJ stops by Castle Laoch for a surprise visit. His presence upsets more than the status quo at Castle Laoch; Rowan struggles to find a solution to the bankruptcy proceedings, which are starting to look like the end for the MacLaoch clan. Cole and Rowan - fresh off the battle on the cairn knoll - are bonded even more profoundly as they move to save the castle from bankruptcy and a villainous bankman set on a generation's old revenge. While Cole and Rowan's love is secure for eternity, the struggle for the ancestral MacLaoch home hangs in the balance. Can Rowan's determination, the Baker kids' ingenuity, and residual Viking power from Ormr Minorisson save the castle and clan from ruin?

ROMANTIC SUSPENSE TITLES

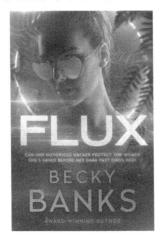

Flux. *Can one notorious hacker protect the women she's saved before her dark past finds her?*

Vega Flux, a notorious hacker whose single mission in life is to protect the weak from online trolls, crashes up against an impenetrable powerhouse of a man who wants nothing more than to slip the dark shroud off her persona and protect her from her torments.

In this smoldering high-stakes game of defense and one-upmanship, Vega takes a bet she knows she shouldn't and starts the largest hack she's ever attempted, against the only worthy opponent she's ever known, tech billionaire and ex-NFL tight end, Hoyt Kaho'okalakupua. Master of his domain, Hoyt, welcomes the chance to flex his power in a true challenge. With the stakes dangerously high, and his heart on the line, he enters a game with a woman he wants it all from. There's only one fatal flaw: Hoyt and Vega are following different instructions to the same game. He's a law-abiding billionaire, and the world Vega lives in breaks every rule.

Dark passions ignite in this fast-paced thrill ride from award-winning indie author and Maui girl, Becky Healani Banks. As the torments of Vega's past breach her defenses, she reaches for the one man who is uniquely capable of providing the shelter she seeks. And in that process, she touches a power she's never known, real-life love.

Forged. *First loves, dark pasts, and fast cars collide in this high-octane thrill ride.*

Managing editor of a Manhattan fashion rag, Eva Rodgers, couldn't believe she would ever step back into her old life, but the day her father called with his diagnosis, she had little choice. Returning home, and to the past she left behind, Eva signs up as editor-in-chief of the struggling Portland magazine, *Rose City Review*. There in the drizzling Portland metro Eva still holds firm to the New York city values that defined her time there: compromise on nothing. When her European auto, one luxury she missed in the walking and hired car world of Manhattan, needs fixing, she doesn't compromise. Even when the best European auto mechanic her assistant finds turns out to be an ex with a vendetta, Eva doesn't flinch.

Nathaniel Vellanova can't believe what the fuck just showed up at his garage. He'd gotten his life together, buried his dark past, and definitely put Eva Rogers in his rearview mirror. Right?

But fuck him if she wasn't standing right there in the pouring rain needing his help. He'd do it—help her out—just this once then forget all about her. Again.

In this dark and suspenseful story of broken first loves, readers will ride the smoldering heat of high-octane fast cars, glitzy club fashion, and tainted love and ask themselves, are first loves the only love?

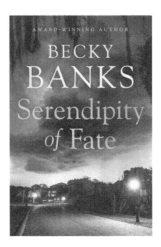

Serendipity of Fate. *Enemies to lovers romance. One war, one blood promise, and the love to save it all.*

It has been two years since Cason McPherson watched his best friend, Ryan Sparling, die in his arms. Now, with a blood promise tied to his heart, shrapnel in his hip, and a war behind him, he's focused on building a useful civilian life in his hometown of New Orleans. Living with Ryan's mother, a widow and retired nurse, he gives back the protection and care his best friend wanted. Only Ryan's sister, a woman whose well-worn picture got him through the darkest parts of the war, does not see it that way.

Savannah Sparling has spent the last five years building her career and life to the exacting expectations needed to achieve partner at Knight Interiors. And nothing could derail them except for the one person from her past who returned home a changed man. Cason McPherson and her brother Ryan had been her entire world once, but now she no longer recognizes him with his caustic attitude and effort to turn every conversation into a verbal sparring match. When a potential client, one large enough to secure her place as partner, requests her as lead designer, Savannah sets a plan for her final career move and Cason's eviction.

In a series of unstoppable events, Savannah's carefully laid plans backfire, and an unfathomable truth is revealed. In the aftermath, Cason and Savannah find that the only people strong enough to save them from themselves are each other. But will either one of them accept the help—and the love—that is offered?

FUTURE SERIES

Coming soon.

Set one-hundred years into a dystopian future, this socio-political romantic thriller takes place in the sprawling catacombs of The Peoples Republic of Portland. In a world that has been punished by the misdeeds of mankind, one writer sets out to answer one simple question: What would happen if everyone had hope again? Absorbed onto a misfit team of ex-war machine operators, junior journalist Wendy Wilson, moves quickly to adapt or die while trying to save the city she loves and maybe, just maybe, change the hearts and minds of even the most blood-thirsty among them.

Be sure to visit beckybanksbooks.com and sign up for the author newsletter. Newsletter recipients are the first to get book release news and giveaway alerts.

Made in United States
Cleveland, OH
07 February 2025

14155740R00156